Joanna Trollope has written ten highly-acclaimed contemporary novels: *The Choir*, *A Village Affair*, *A Passionate Man*, *The Rector's Wife*, *The Men and the Girls*, *A Spanish Lover*, *The Best of Friends*, *Next of Kin*, *Other People's Children* and *Marrying the Mistress*. *Other People's Children* has recently been shown on BBC television as a major drama serial. Under the name of Caroline Harvey she writes romantic historical novels. She has also written a study of women in the British Empire, *Britannia's Daughters*.

Joanna Trollope was born in Gloucestershire, where she still lives. She was appointed OBE in the 1996 Queen's Birthday Honours List for services to literature.

A Passionate Man

Joanna Trollope

BLACK SWAN

A PASSIONATE MAN
A BLACK SWAN BOOK : 0 552 99442 1

Originally published in Great Britain by
Bloomsbury Publishing Ltd

PRINTING HISTORY
Bloomsbury edition published 1990
Black Swan edition published 1991

23 25 27 29 30 28 26 24 22

This book is set in 11/12pt Melior by
County Typesetters, Margate, Kent.

Black Swan Books are published by Transworld Publishers,
61–63 Uxbridge Road, London W5 5SA,
a division of The Random House Group Ltd,
in Australia by Random House Australia (Pty) Ltd,
20 Alfred Street, Milsons Point, Sydney, NSW 2061, Australia,
in New Zealand by Random House New Zealand Ltd,
18 Poland Road, Glenfield, Auckland 10, New Zealand
and in South Africa by Random House (Pty) Ltd,
Endulini, 5a Jubilee Road, Parktown 2193, South Africa.

Printed and bound in Great Britain by
Cox & Wyman Ltd, Reading, Berkshire.

For Tobit

Chapter One

Old Mrs Mossop always put her teeth in for the doctor. She did not accord this honour to the vicar because the vicar was too much in earnest, and physically unprepossessing with it. But the doctor had sex appeal and to that Mrs Mossop responded, never mind being over eighty and in the process of dying slowly from a secondary cancer. So when the doctor's mud-splashed car pulled up outside her cottage – she was always on watch from her chair by the window – she would fish about in the tumbler on her windowsill where her teeth swam, and slot them into place.

This little ritual was never lost upon the doctor.

'All the better to eat me with, I see.'

Granny Mossop gave a high laugh.

'Spit you out again sharpish!'

Archie Logan smiled. He was very fond of Granny Mossop and he found her fierce gallantry in the face of her slow inexorable dying extremely moving. The room in which she sat smelled like a mouse's nest, crammed in every corner with cuckoo-clock furniture and ornaments and crocheted mats. Over the fusty muddle the great grey face of the television set presided calmly. Granny Mossop only turned it on to watch boxing and football and disasters on the news. She didn't mind blood, she told Dr Logan. Her father had been a gamekeeper. She'd grown up with blood.

He put his bag down on a fat armchair full of knitted cushions and rummaged in it. He had to toss questions nonchalantly at her or she would say, 'That'd be telling,' and they would get nowhere.

'Holding on to what you eat?' he said, his back to her.

'More or less. Don't fancy much.'

'I hope your daughter's looking after you.'

Granny Mossop snorted.

'Indian muck'n rubbish. I won't touch it.'

He bent over her to begin his examination. She was as small as a sparrow. While he was occupied, she peered into his thick hair and observed a scattering of grey hairs.

'You forty yet?'

'No,' Dr Logan said equably, listening to her heart.

'I didn' have a grey hair till I were fifty-three.'

'Ah. But you are made of sterner stuff than me. Back pain?'

She hated confessing, so she said nothing.

'Back pain,' he said, stating it.

He straightened up to write something down, dwarfing the little room and the littler woman.

'I'm going to give you something to slow the machinery up a bit.' He had said 'bowels' to her once and her response was so strong that now he resorted to euphemism.

She tossed her head.

'That all you can do for me?'

He surveyed her with affection.

'I could always shoot you.'

She loved that. She flung her head back with delight.

'You'd miss! You'd miss!'

'If you lose any more weight, you'll probably be right.'

She ducked her head suddenly and spat her teeth out into her cupped hand. It was his signal to go. When she'd had enough, she made it very plain and, in Archie Logan's view, her dignity and independence came even before the pace of her dying. Her teeth fell with a splash into the tumbler.

'I'll give the prescription to Sharon. She can pick it up with the next Indian take-away.' He shut his case

8

and looked over towards her. 'I'll be in again on Friday.'

She snorted again faintly. He let himself out, stooping through the low doorway that led directly into the cottage's front garden where the lank remnants of a runner-bean row flapped above an empty rabbit hutch. Over the fence in the next-door garden, Granny Mossop's grandchildren's impudent modern washing blew on a yellow nylon line. Her daughter Sharon had taken out the little cottage windows of her front room and replaced them with a single bleak sheet of plate glass, so that the room behind gaped exposed and defenceless to the public view. Archie Logan could see a half-adult boy in jeans and black leather jacket slumped in a chair in front of the television. How long, Archie wondered, slamming the cottage gate with vehemence, how long since that boy had been in to see his grandmother?

He looked up at the October sky. The sun was just beginning to go down behind some dramatic streaks of grape-coloured cloud and, for no reason that he could think of, Archie Logan was suddenly and poignantly reminded of a holiday he and Liza had had years before, an autumn holiday in Tuscany, when they had been caught in a thunderstorm at Bagni di Lucca, all among the rocks and the river and the chestnut trees. They had been drenched, soaked to the skin, and, while stumbling back to their car, had been accosted by a courteous man with an umbrella who had taken them back to his immense and battered Edwardian villa and given them baths and malt whisky. Archie could see Liza now, wrapped in her host's mothy old camel-hair dressing gown, sitting on a club fender with her bare feet held up off the marble floor, sticking her tongue down into her whisky glass. 'The Tuscan winter rains,' their host had said in his beautiful English, 'can be long and terrible.'

The thought of Liza made Archie think he would go

home before evening surgery. Liza would be at home because Wednesday was her whole day off from Bradley Hall School, where she taught part time. And Mikey would be back from school and he would see Imogen before she was put to bed. And there might be a letter from Thomas, a letter to heal the wound of his first letter from boarding school.

'I don't see why I have to be here,' Thomas had written. 'It's awful. I liked going to school in Winchester and then coming home for bed. I don't like going to bed here. It's when I cry.'

Archie got into his car and banged the door shut with unnecessary violence. He drove off at great speed, and old Mrs Mossop, who had been waiting for his farewell wave – although she planned to ignore it – drooped a little in her solitary chair.

Liza Logan, her red curls tied up in a Black Watch tartan ribbon, was sitting at the kitchen table hearing her second son's reading practice. Across the table Imogen, who was three, drew uneven suns and stars on the cover of a current parish magazine with a black wax crayon. In the utility room off the kitchen, Sally, a local farmer's daughter who looked after Imogen while Liza was teaching, and did a lot else besides, was pulling out of the tumble dryer an avalanche of socks crackling with static. A liver and white spaniel, sprawled on a blanket in a corner, was the only creature to rise politely when Archie entered and wag its feathered tail in greeting.

'It's Daddy,' Imogen said to her mother helpfully.

Liza raised her face for Archie's kiss.

'So it is.'

Archie kissed her mouth. He always kissed her mouth, however casual the kiss. It had been her mouth with its faintly swollen bee-stung lower lip that had first drawn him like a magnet, across a room at a party, to peer at her with desire and fascination. The party had been to celebrate Liza's engagement to someone else and Archie had been taken along by a mutual friend who disliked walking into parties alone. The morning after the party, Archie had begun to lay siege to Liza and within ten days he had captured her from Hugo Grant-Jones and, instead of a sapphire surrounded by very bright new diamonds, Liza was wearing a battered old half-hoop of garnets that had belonged to Archie's dead mother.

'Five stones,' Archie said, sliding the ring on to her finger. 'For five words: Will you be my wife. Will you?'

'Oh yes,' Liza said, and then without meaning to, 'yes *please*.'

It had been like 'Young Lochinvar'. Fosters, Fenwicks and Musgraves, in the form of Liza's outraged family and friends, unleashed a torrent of disapproval and pressure and objection. Archie put Liza into his car and drove her to Argyllshire where his father had a house on the shore of Loch Fyne, a house without a telephone, and kept Liza there for two rapturous weeks. Then he brought her back south, and married her.

'When I come home,' he said to her now, his mouth still almost on hers, 'why don't you get up and wag your tail?'

'Oh, I do. In my mind. You see, Mikey had just got to this perfectly riveting bit about what a kestrel gives its young for breakfast, and not even the entrance of—'

'Mice,' Mikey said suddenly. 'Kestrels eat mice. They like bloody things.'

'Tho,' said Imogen who had a lisp, 'do I.'

Archie went round to look at her drawing.

'Black stars. How very sophisticated.'

Imogen looked at him pityingly.

'The yellow ith broken.'

'Of course. I've just been to see Granny Mossop. No: a word of her condition will I breathe to higher authority or it will be hospitalization for her at the

11

double and she will die of a broken heart before her liver does it. Her fucking, bloody daughter—'

'Archie—'

'Sorry. Her selfish and heartless daughter brings her garbage from the Star of Agra take-away which her poor old guts can't even begin to cope with. Can you imagine?'

'I'll make her a milk pud.'

'You're an angel. But she won't thank you.'

Liza raised her face to him.

'But you will.'

He bent again.

'Oh, I will—'

'Fucking,' said Imogen conversationally to Mikey.

'Shhh,' he said delightedly.

Sally came out of the utility room with a plastic laundry basket heaped with folded clothes under one arm. Mikey plucked at her as she passed.

'Did you hear what Daddy said?'

Sally, whose home-life vocabulary was comfortably thick with obscenities, said she had.

Archie said, 'Sorry, Sal.'

'It's all the same to me,' Sally said, picking Imogen up deftly with her free arm. 'What you say about Sharon Vinney.'

Imogen put her arms around Sally's neck.

'I thaid fucking.'

'I heard you,' Sally said without interest. 'And if I hear you say it again, I'll smack your bottom. Come on, bath time.'

'*Not* hair wash—'

'Imo,' Archie said, 'won't you blow me a kiss?'

But the nightmare of probable hair wash had gripped Imogen's mind and she could not hear him. When the door had closed behind them both, Imogen could be heard still pleading urgently as she was carried up the stairs.

'Even if Sally wasn't a tower of strength,' Liza said,

'I'd employ her simply to wash Imogen's hair. Archie, your father rang.'

He gave her, at once, his complete attention. As she often remarked to friends, and to her sister Clare who was the only one of her family she ever really saw, she had never known a father and son as close as Archie and Andrew Logan. At first, she had loved it because she had felt taken into a powerful, impregnable male citadel as a precious captive. They had both brooded over her with exciting possessiveness. She had been transformed from being just the third daughter of a Haslemere accountant into someone particular and valuable. But of course, in time, she had grown used to that transformation and now the bond between father and son seemed to her rather more exclusive than inclusive, and to have about it an air of male self-sufficiency which, try as she might, she could not help resenting. She sometimes thought that if Archie had not retained his power to stir her so, she would not have minded his adoration of his father so much.

'What did he want? Isn't he coming on Sunday?'

'Oh, he's coming. But he wants to bring someone.'

'Of course,' Archie said comfortably. 'Maurice Crawford. It's about the new series—'

'No,' Liza said, shutting up Mikey's reading book, and rising. 'It's a woman.'

'A woman! Good God.'

Liza began collecting up the mugs and plates on the table.

'She is called Marina de Breton. He sounded quite excited.'

'Marina de Breton—'

'Yes.'

'What a deeply affected name.'

'She can't help that. She's the widow of a Louisiana cotton king or something.'

'American!'

'No,' Liza said. 'Greek. Or Italian.' She put the mugs

13

on the draining board and came over to Archie. 'Darling. Don't look so thunderous.'

'I'm not—'

'You look,' Mikey said encouragingly, 'just simply bloody livid.'

'Dad doesn't *have* women.'

'You don't know he has this one. He only wants to bring her to lunch, for goodness' sake.'

'You said he sounded excited—'

'Archie,' Liza said exasperatedly, 'don't make so much of so little.'

He would do this, cling obstinately and exaggeratedly to a mere shadow of an idea and make a whole imaginary mountain of it in no time, and it was one of the things about him that drove her mad. Others were his untidiness and the impulsiveness that throbbed in him as steadily and regularly as a second heartbeat. Perhaps he'd inherited all these disordered qualities from his Welsh mother, because Sir Andrew Logan certainly hadn't passed them on.

'You're being a fool,' Liza said to Archie. Mikey was watching them both with troubled interest. 'Your father says may he bring one harmless woman to lunch and you behave as if she was a – a—' She broke off, at a loss for an analogy.

'A wicked witch,' Mikey said, and then added, because his suggestion had fallen into a complete silence, 'I expect.'

Archie shrugged.

'Sorry.'

'Anyway,' Liza said, 'even if she is someone special, you ought to be pleased. For him, I mean.'

Archie looked at the clock above the cooker.

'Lord. It's ten to six. Liza, I've a few calls to make after surgery so half-past eight, maybe—'

'Maybe.'

He took her arm and pulled her to him so that he could kiss her, and while he was doing it, it occurred to Liza that if Sir Andrew really did feel something particular for this de Breton person then she could have Archie back all to herself. Thinking this, she responded to his kiss with enthusiasm.

'Wonder bird,' he said to her and, stooping to kiss Mikey as he passed, went whistling out to his car.

In the waiting room of the local health centre, a couple of dozen people sat about on green-painted chairs among the rubber plants and the low tables for magazines which were exactly the right height for toddlers to create mayhem on. It was a new health centre, with swooping roofs like a Swiss chalet, and immense windows to the floor which, at night, patients avoided sitting next to. Cork notice boards afforded plenty of space for exhortations about obesity, alcohol abuse, Aids and drug addiction, and, behind sliding panels of pine and glass, the receptionists and pharmacist sat like bank clerks.

When Archie came through, at a run, there was an affectionate murmuring. Dr Logan was always late, always, but then he was never too busy to see you and always had a smile and he was wonderful with children and the old people. The health visitors and district nurses were keenly conscious that the place had a different atmosphere on Dr Logan's days off, less energetic, less, well, less fun, really. He came in for a good deal of tolerant, maternal cluckings, except from the pharmacist who was clever and sharp and divorced and who cherished for him much stronger feelings than those of amused affection, and therefore kept herself aloof from him and was rigorously courteous when they spoke. When Archie and his rush of apology had disappeared through the double doors at the far end of the waiting room, the senior nurse on duty went off after him with quiet officiousness, to check that the slats of his venetian blind were discreetly pulled vertical and that the examining couch was suitably shrouded in a clean, disposable paper sheet.

'There we are, Doctor. Everything all right?'

He was hastily riffling through the buff packs of patients' notes on his desk.

'Yes,' he said absently. 'Thank you.'

'I've put out a clean roll of towel by the basin. And fresh soap. And I moved the disposable gloves nearer the bin. Seemed more logical.'

'Don't move things,' Archie pleaded. He looked up at her. She was a suburban little woman who was determined to reform the muddle and mess of this country practice into something altogether more trim.

'I only thought—'

'I know.' He flapped some notes at her. 'Not your fault. But I can only work in chaos. Ask my wife.'

Nurse Dillon allowed herself a little smile to show that she was not in the least disappointed that she had failed to please him. He had mud on his shoes, she noted. She looked at it penetratingly for a second and then went away to summon the first patient.

Archie liked taking surgeries. Long ago, long before Liza, he had had a raven-haired girlfriend who had demanded to know if he was going to be a doctor because he liked bodies. Yes, he said, he did like bodies, and, after a pause, he had added that he particularly liked women's bodies. This had given the raven-haired girlfriend the perfect opening for a great deal of predictable abuse which he came to see was an attempt to make him admit that he liked her body better than any other. He did, for a week or two – or perhaps it was really her lustrous waterfall of black hair that was so weirdly erotic – but then he became repelled by the rapacity of her character and her body ceased to interest him. But the bodies of the sick were another matter, a matter of extraordinary interest: how and why this delicate, complex and individual human machine should develop strains and faults, and how

16

those, in turn, were dependent upon the fuel of personality. He wasn't like his father, who preferred the seclusion of laboratory and operating theatre, and he grew impatient with manuals and books. What he liked was the listening and the touching, the sense of exploration and sometimes discovery that made even the prospect of old Fred Durfield, hobbling in now in a perfect gale of grievance against the arthritis that was gradually doubling him up like a series of human paper clips, an absorbing one.

'You're no use,' Fred said. 'Them damn tablets i'n't no use. I'm goin' to die as crippled as my father before me.'

He thumped a transparent brown plastic bottle down on Archie's desk. It was almost full.

'How many of these have you taken, Fred?'

'No more'n a couple. Didn't do no good.'

Archie began to explain patiently the mechanics of a course of medicine, knowing that Fred would neither listen to nor heed him. Fred's mother, seventy years before, had fed him her own rural fatalism along with his childhood porridge, a fatalism that ran in a black stream through so many of Archie's villager patients. He wasn't sure, however, that he did not prefer it to the helpless rag-doll surrender to ill health and state medicine of another section of his patients, an almost greedy abandonment of self-sufficiency to an endless cycle of pills and self-neglect. A permanent state of not being quite well became as natural and necessary to them as breathing. Children, on the other hand, could only be what they were, well or ill, and among the middle- and upper-class patients there prevailed an ostensible impatience with ill health, a desire to be seen to make light of anything the matter.

Diana Jago, who occupied the best house in Archie's village, and who now sailed in after Fred Durfield, began by kissing Archie as if they were at a cocktail party and went on to say with throwaway

17

nonchalance, 'Too boring, but it's my wretched foot, that poisoned thing, simply won't go away,' and then rushed straight on to ask about Archie's children.

Put Diana Jago in hospital, he thought, examining her big and handsome foot, and she'd be demanding at once to know why, in this day and age, the food was still so disgusting.

'Do you know, I don't think it's poisoned. I think it's gout.'

'Archie. Don't be *idiotic*. Gout—'

'Could be. Long-term side effect of the diuretic you take.'

'But I'm a woman. And I never drink port.'

'I'm afraid neither have anything to do with it.'

'Archie,' Diana Jago said firmly, settling her domed velvet hairband more securely on her sleek corn-coloured head, 'do not be an ass. How do I go home and tell Simon I have *gout*? He will simply crack up. I'll never hear the end of it.'

But she was enchanted at the ludicrousness of the possibility. Archie could hear her at meets – she looked mouth-watering on horseback, particularly in the severe sartorial glamour required for hunting – calling penetratingly across to her friends, 'You haven't heard, too utterly laughable, but I have gout, I tell you, no, I'm not making it up – it's total agony, I can tell you – but, yes, *gout*—'

He prescribed her Naprosyn, was kissed again, promised to bring Liza to supper soon and exchanged her breezy, attractive presence for a small boy who had fallen off a shed roof.

'What on earth were you doing up there?'

But the boy, who had been hiding from his step-father and who knew that further trouble awaited him for doing to his arm whatever he had done, merely looked at the floor and said, 'Nothing.'

Only when he came out of the surgery did Archie think

again about his father. Their bond was both strong and of long standing, because the Welsh girl whom Andrew Logan had found when on a walking holiday in Betws-y-Coed and had persuaded to come to Glasgow with him, and to marry him there, had been killed in a car smash on the A80 going out to Garnkirk to look at a dining-room table – golden mahogany, the advertisement had said, not red, and about 1820 – advertised for sale in the *Glasgow Herald*. Archie had been a baby, in a carrycot in the back of the car, from which he had been plucked by a policeman, with no more than bruises. His mother had died at once, from the impact of crashing into a van which had stopped in front of her without warning. She had broken her neck.

She had been married to Andrew Logan for three years, and, if he had ever opened his heart to anyone, she was the only possible person. He took her body back to her family in the Vale of Conway, and endured with difficulty the emotional Celtic fervour of her burial service. Then he resigned from his job at the Glasgow Royal Infirmary, sold his flat in Park Terrace, and brought his baby son south to London and a narrow Georgian house in Islington, convenient for public transport to the Middlesex Hospital. Once settled, he gave himself over to his boy and to his work on the secondary circulation of the heart.

Odd, Archie thought now, turning the car out of the health centre car-park and into the dark lanes of the Hampshire countryside, odd to think that his father's work on the heart had made him an international figure while leaving, quite literally, his own heart untouched. Sir Andrew had lived now for almost forty years without a woman. Archie's childhood had featured a number of housekeepers of whom only one, a strong-minded widow with a passion for Pre-Raphaelite painting, could he recall with either affection or distinction. She had taken him once, by train, to

19

the city gallery in Birmingham to show him the wealth of her enthusiasm, and he had adored the paintings with a kind of adolescent lust, and been badly thrown by his father's disapproval of the whole expedition.

'Great painting,' Andrew Logan had said to his son, 'really great painting, is without self-indulgence.'

He thought that, Archie came to learn, about life, too. Great lives, however visionary, must be underpinned by diligence and self-denial. Extravagance of feeling or behaviour would only dissipate those precious energies that were there precisely to enable a man to make his life of value. It was often hard for Archie, in whom a powerful sensual appetite had been planted along with a measure of wayward emotional and mental powers which he sometimes suspected owed their being to the more eloquent and excitable air of the Vale of Conway. Archie had ardour; his father, as far as he could possibly perceive, had not. His father had instead balance and judgement and, in addition, honour and a most effective compassion, a compassion that achieved results for its objects.

But no woman. My lifetime almost, Archie thought, flicking up his headlight beam so that distant objects, trees and bushes, seemed suddenly to leap out at him. And his father was so sweet to Liza, had been so from the beginning, from that first meeting at the Savoy Grill, where he always liked to eat, where they kept him a secluded table and where he was looked after by a waiter of great experience who owned a cigar cutter once given to him by Winston Churchill. They had sat Liza between them and persuaded her to eat the first oysters of her life and, at the end of dinner, Andrew Logan had picked up Liza's little hand, and kissed it and said, 'I'm a grim old stick, but you'll find me very steadfast.' She had adored it. Adored him. He had made a point, from the beginning, of including her in every way in his love for Archie. Indeed, he spoiled her. He seemed to like it. When Liza sometimes got

20

angry now and declared furiously that grown men, real *mature* men, grew out of this nursery dependence on their fathers, she never accused Andrew of favouring Archie, because, even in a temper, she knew it wasn't true.

And when the bizarre chance happened, and it was discovered that all the inhibitions Andrew Logan had about people simply fell away before the television cameras, Liza was quite as proud as Archie. That first series of *Meeting Medicine*, when half the nation, it seemed, stayed in on Tuesday nights to watch those quirky, humorous, fascinating explanations of their bodies to themselves, had had them both rejoicing, quite spontaneously.

Very occasionally, as his father's fame grew and he was photographed in groups that invariably included lovely women, Archie would say to Liza, 'D'you think he has a secret girlfriend?'

And Liza usually said, 'God, I hope not. I'd be so jealous.'

But now, faced with the possibility that he had indeed found a woman, Liza didn't seem to mind. You should be pleased, she'd said, pleased for your father.

'Well,' Archie said out loud, turning the car into a curved drive in front of a solid stone house thickly moustached in pyracantha, 'I'm not pleased. Not pleased at all.'

From an upper window a curtain moved and the anxious figure of the patient's wife peered down into the drive.

'In fact,' Archie said to his car as he slammed the door behind him, 'I'm bloody miserable. So there.'

Chapter Two

The doctor's house was not a pretty building. It was a
Victorian brick villa of great solidity, with double bay
windows in front whose sashes rose and fell with
reliable and weighty efficiency. The house was set on
the edge of the village of Stoke Stratton in a wide,
shallow trout-stream valley sloping down through the
gentle chalky hills to Winchester. Stoke Stratton, a
miscellaneous village architecturally, straggled along a
minor road parallel to the Stoke river, with path-like
lanes running down from it to the water's edge. Other
lanes wandered away from the road and the river
towards the northern lip of the valley, and on one of
these less desirable lanes – the best houses were of
course close to the river – Beeches House was set on a
gentle bank.

In front of the house a rough lawn dotted with the
paraphernalia of children's amusements – a climbing
frame, a sandpit, a swing suspended from an immense
cherry tree that flowered profusely and pinkly in
spring – stretched down to the lane and was separated
from it by a post-and-rail fence, patchy with brilliant
moulds. Behind the house, and beside it, was a
semicircle of beech trees, through which could be
glimpsed the fields of plough and pasture rising to the
modest skyline. The right-hand sweep of trees also
served to screen their only neighbour, a cream stucco
bungalow set in a regimented garden, inhabited by a
middle-aged couple who lived in terror of being asked
to be involved in anything. It was really on account of
the beeches that Liza and Archie had bought the
house.

Inside, the house had a sturdy, pleasant and practical feel that Archie told Liza was inescapably
bourgeois. It was, of course, but it was to Liza a very
much more acceptable variety of bourgeois than the
refined sort – fringed lampshades and Dralon up-
holstery – that had permeated the house in Haslemere.
Her mother disliked colour, indeed she was alarmed by
visual strength of any kind, and Liza's childhood had
taken place against a dim background of muted pinks
and blues and little lamps and midget ornaments. After
that, Beeches House seemed to her to have an exciting
and masculine strength, and its position, in open
country on two sides, to be properly uncompromising.
She had only driven Archie down the residential road
where she had grown up – her parents felt they were
making some kind of moral stand by refusing to
welcome him to The Lilacs – and he had said that he
had no idea that families lived in such places, not
really lived. And Liza, adoring him, reduced to rubble
when he kissed her, said he was right: they couldn't.

They were married five years before they bought
Beeches House. Before that, Archie was working as a
junior hospital doctor in London and they lived in the
basement of Andrew's house in Islington. Then he sold
it, to move into a mansion flat near Victoria Station
which he said reminded him of Glasgow, and Archie,
who had by now decided that general practice was
where his inclination lay, found a job with a rural
practice in Hampshire, and Beeches House. They
brought Thomas to it as a baby, and from it Liza went
twice to the maternity unit in Winchester, to give birth
to Mikey and then to Imogen. For family holidays, they
packed the children into the car and drove up to
Argyllshire, to the little house Sir Andrew had bought
when he left Glasgow, on the shoreline of Loch Fyne
going down into Inveraray. The view from the house
was directly across the water to a romantic castle-like
mansion designed by Sir Robert Lorimer and backed

by a famous pinetum and rearing purplish hills. Liza could never drive there without remembering the sheer glory of her first arrival, literally carried off by Archie and then wooed by him with unblinking intensity, both in bed and out, until, feeling herself to be his treasure, she knew herself also to be his slave.

Beeches House was the first house of her own that Liza had ever decorated. Her taste, strive as she might against it, tended perilously towards the tidy, so that after eight years Beeches House inside had an unresolved air as Liza's matching curtains and cushions and penchant for crisp cottons strove to hold at bay Archie's relentless acquisition of anything that caught his eye, the more peculiar the better. Birds of prey in glass cases, ancient fowling pieces, a Victorian sledge, threadbare rugs, immense jardinières, huge reproductions of Turner sunsets and Rossetti women, a fifties pinball machine adorned with cone-breasted girls in pedal-pushers, a rug made from a polar bear, old polo sticks and fishing rods, jugs and jars and antique medicine bottles, rioted triumphantly across Liza's stripped and waxed floors and leaned drunkenly against her clean pale walls. Although irritated by the mess they made, she admired them, because they represented a wholeheartedness she was afraid that she did not possess (briefly, when she first met Archie, she had hoped otherwise), but she did not know what to do with them beyond dust and polish and neatly glue back bits of broken moulding. So she left them mostly where they were – trying not to adjust the angles to something more conventional – and thus Diana Jago, coming to supper for the first time, met a suit of armour in the sitting room and a stuffed badger in the downstairs lavatory, and went shouting off to tell her friends that the new doctor couple were an absolute find.

It was Diana Jago who had organized Liza's job at Bradley Hall School. Liza had read French and Spanish at the University of East Anglia, and had then been to a teacher training college outside Cambridge – it was, indeed, at a party in Cambridge that she had met her first fiancé, Hugo Grant-Jones, who had had all the impeccable credentials of a family house in Sussex, a low golf handicap and a fledgling career in a big City accepting house, that had so endeared him to Liza's parents. When Liza and Archie were first married she taught for a dispiriting year in a North London comprehensive school – she concluded she was literally too small to make any impression on thirty fourteen year olds whose every energy was channelled into defeating her – and then got herself a post in the modern languages department of a London girls' day school, where she was extremely happy. She taught until Thomas was born, and then the move came, and two more babies, and it was only when Imogen was almost two that Liza began to feel that she needed to claw back some part of herself and her life that was not devoted to the sustaining of Archie and the children. She also thought she would like some money of her own. Archie was as open as the day about money and perfectly prepared to give her anything she asked for, provided he had it, but oddly, this very generosity put a constraint upon her capacity to ask for much. She found herself accounting to him painstakingly for expenditure, explanations that were perfectly incomprehensible to him because he both trusted her and was not much interested in the first place.

So when Diana Jago came in one day unannounced, as she liked to do, leaving a magnificent bay gelding tethered to Liza's garage wall – 'No, no, don't fuss, he's fine, it'll give him time to repent over quite appalling behaviour yesterday, *and* in public' – and asked, as she always did, if there was anything she could pick up for Liza in Winchester, Liza said, 'Well, yes, actually. A job.'

'Mrs Dr Logan dear, what do you mean? The checkout at Sainsbury's?'

'No,' Liza said, heating milk for coffee. 'A teaching job. I am a qualified teacher and I want to go back to it.'

'And what,' Diana said, 'does our revered physician have to say to that?'

'All for it.'

'I'd no idea. That you taught, I mean. I thought you were simply an all-singing, all-dancing housewife. Brilliant cook. You should hear the carry-on from Simon when we've been to dinner here. I just say to him, come *on*, darling, the nags don't complain so why should you? What do you teach?'

'French mostly, but Spanish if I'm asked.'

'Olè,' said Diana Jago.

Two days later, she rang Liza to say she'd been shopping for a job as requested and she'd got one.

'You don't mean it!'

'Interview all ready and palpitating for you. Bradley Hall. I've known the Hampoles since I was a child and, although they are madder than hatters, it's not a bad school. At least the children are told how to hold their knives properly and get walloped if they call the lavatory the toilet. June Hampole's waiting for you to ring her.'

'Oh,' Liza said. 'Oh, I'm so grateful—'

'Well, don't be. After one term there, you will probably be cursing my name for even thinking of it. Our two went before they boarded and it didn't seem to do them any harm. Must fly. I've got an appointment in London to have my fangs seen to. Curses, curses.'

Bradley Hall School was housed in an immense eighteenth-century barrack in decayed parkland some seven or eight miles from Winchester. The Hampole family were Catholic, either extremely devout or flamboyantly lapsed, and Bradley Hall had been their home for over a hundred years. It was built in a hollow square around a central courtyard, where a powerfully virile stone Pan rose out of a dry and crumbling fountain basin, and possessed a ballroom, a shattered orangery, a chapel and, in the grounds, an eerie domed ice-house roofed in grass.

It was June Hampole who, twenty-five years before, had decided to start a preparatory school – for both sexes – in the house, in order to enable her and her only unmarried brother to go on living at Bradley Hall. She was rewarded for this enterprise by discovering that she liked children very much indeed and also found them interesting. Her brother Dan was intermittently quite useful over the financial business of the school, but only intermittently, since bad behaviour of an exotic and eighteenth-century kind took up most of his energies. The one thing she could be grateful for was that his unorthodox ideas for pleasure did not include little boys.

Liza, arriving for her interview with Imogen sitting solidly on her hip, was shown into a most desirable room, a small, west-facing panelled room through whose immense floor-length windows the teatime sun was pouring uninhibitedly. The room was in chaos. Books, papers, folders and files were stacked haphazardly on pieces of furniture whose elegance and quality were quite unmistakable. Dirty cups and glasses stood about among plants in pots crying out for water and, in front of the lovely fireplace, two great basset hounds slumbered ponderously. When June Hampole came in, her appearance had exactly the same air of patrician disorder as her room, and in her greying curly hair two flowers of winter jasmine had caught themselves up, like yellow stars.

Liza had liked her at once. June had taken Imogen from her – 'What a stout little party' – and settled down for the interview with Imogen on her knee, to whom she gave some marvellous sliding old ivory toy for amusement. She seemed only anxious that Liza should be happy working at Bradley Hall.

'Order, you see, just doesn't seem to come to me naturally. I really do intend to employ you for French, but suppose Mrs West were ill, I might have to shunt you on to Common Entrance English sometimes. Would Latin terrify you? Or mathematics?'

'Yes,' said Liza. 'Particularly maths. I learned long before it was taught as a kind of logical exercise.'

'So fascinating,' June Hampole said, spreading out one of Imogen's fat hands, 'modern maths. What will you do with this little person if you come here?'

'I'll find someone—'

'Sally Carter,' June said. 'That's who you need! And she must get away from home a bit. Her father manages our farm and he uses Sally as slave labour. Shall I speak to her?'

'This is extraordinary,' Liza said. 'No sooner do I express a wish for a job than I am surrounded by people arranging it all for me.'

'We are *avid* for you,' June Hampole said. She reached for a tarnished silver box and took out of it a piece of shortbread, which she gave to Imogen. The basset hounds, scenting food from the depths of sleep, roused themselves and lumbered over to fix Imogen with lugubrious glares of envy and loathing. Imogen ate her biscuit unperturbed.

It was fixed that Liza should teach French to the three top forms – aged roughly ten to twelve – on two mornings and two afternoons of each week. In her absence at home, Sally Carter looked after Imogen – who rapidly became devoted to her because she was perfectly prepared to sing and play the same baby rhymes and games in endless repetition – and cleaned bits of the house. Liza was shy at first of suggesting she might clean lavatories or the kitchen floor, but Sally said the only thing in the house she'd rather die than do was touch anything fragile or precious, like Liza's Bohemian glass pitchers which stood on the drawing-room mantelpiece. After a few weeks, Sally said she'd come half of Liza's day off, too, and keep the ironing up together, and Liza perceived that the job was a refuge to her as much as anything, and was pleased to agree.

Bradley Hall School was not arduous employment. The classes, never over twenty in number, were composed of children whose upbringing had encouraged discipline of behaviour and outspokenness of mind. None of them were outstandingly clever and the intense parental ambition which Liza remembered from her London teaching days was almost wholly absent. A decent competence was expected, sufficient to get the boys into the right preparatory school before the right public school, and the girls into senior schools which could be trusted not to be exaggeratedly intellectual.

'Daddy says,' one ten year old said cheerfully to Liza, surveying a French pronoun exercise almost obliterated in red ink, 'that there's really no hope for me because I'm as utterly thick as him.'

Outside the classroom – Liza taught in a great white drawing room, floored in parquet and furnished entirely with scabrous desks and chairs – the school's eccentricity was manifest. Morning assemblies took place in the chapel before an altar and reredos crowned by a macabre and agonized crucifix brought back from Spain by a nineteenth-century Hampole. The figure on the crucifix, in order to defuse its possible nightmarish effects on the smaller children, was known in the school as Albert. Several pupils went on to their next schools with the conviction that Jesus and Albert were inextricable and interchangeable.

Lunch was eaten at the relatively watertight end of the orangery. June Hampole would have liked the food to be vegetarian, but, faced with relentlessly carnivorous parents, most of whom shot and fished with regularity and competence, she compromised by providing

29

the children with mounds of organically grown vegetables to accompany their sausages and stews. The atmosphere at meals was that of an enormous, excitable family, the younger children being offhandedly helped by the older – 'For heaven's sake, Matthew, open your stupid mouth' – and the staff member at each table keeping up a proper flow of conversation – 'Now what is it that makes you think a dog has a conscience?' Breaks were taken in various areas of the park, and running about screaming was encouraged in order to ensure the tranquillity of the ensuing afternoon: 'Come on, Melissa, haven't heard a really good bellow out of you all week!' Uniform consisted of stout pairs of blue or red drill dungarees worn over home clothes – a great impediment, the junior class teachers discovered, to getting to the lavatory on time – and a blue parka with a quilted lining which was worn indoors as well as out during the winter owing to the volatile temperament of the school boiler. Liza's classes, sitting blowing on their fingers in the glacial drawing room, resembled a Peking assembly line on a winter morning.

The staff room, which Liza grew to relish, had been the gun room of Bradley Hall. Square and darkly panelled with wooden pegged gun racks still in place around the walls, it boasted a cavernous fireplace and a gathering of elderly and welcoming armchairs. On a trestle table under one window stood an electric kettle on a tin tray, and an array of coffee jars and biscuit tins and heavy white mugs, once the property of the local British Legion hut. The room was never dusted or tidied up and you could always rely on finding someone in it to talk to.

Bradley Hall School depended on part-timers. Men and women of all ages who had had, at some point in their lives, some mild brush with teaching, pedalled or drove to Bradley Hall several times a week to teach everything from Greek to the French horn. 'None of

30

them are exactly mad,' Liza said to Archie, 'but most of them are pretty odd.' There were three teaching constants: Mrs West, who taught English formidably well along outmoded and grammatical lines; Commander Haythorne, who ran the so-called science department with fierce practicality ('First thing I do is teach a girl how to change a plug'); and Blaise O'Hanlon. Blaise O'Hanlon was June Hampole's nephew. His Hampole mother had married an Irishman of formidable charm and waywardness, and, when their only son had emerged unsteadily from Trinity College, Dublin, had decided that, if he were not to embark upon the same improvident and wearisome path as his father, he needed a little English stiffening. So she sent him to his aunt June at Bradley Hall, to teach history from a violently Irish standpoint and to supervise soccer, cricket, the school choir and the boiler.

Blaise O'Hanlon told Liza during the second week of her employment that she would save his life.

'You're lovely,' he said to her, making mugs of coffee for them both in the staff room. 'I have fantasies about you at night already.' He splashed boiling water from the kettle approximately at its targets. 'It's your mouth. How am I supposed to keep myself off your mouth?'

Liza had laughed. Blaise O'Hanlon was twenty-two. She was thirty-four and quite in control. She took her coffee mug and went to talk to Commander Haythorne. Blaise followed her.

'You'll never,' he said to Commander Haythorne, 'you'll never be keeping this woman from me.'

He hadn't stopped. In the four terms Liza had been at Bradley Hall, Blaise O'Hanlon had never ceased to tell her that she was all he wanted or needed. She had been, by turns, flattered and exasperated. He never tried to touch her and he never spoke to her amorously in front of the children. In the end, she began to feel it was simply a stupid, childish, sexless game, yet if one of her half-days went by without seeing him, she noticed. She would not let herself think she minded, but she noticed. She told Archie, occasionally, things Blaise had said or done, and he laughed. He did not laugh complacently, but with the unselfconsciousness of a man who, being faitful to his wife because he wants to be, assumes the same voluntary fidelity in her.

Sometimes, driving to school along lanes whose seasonal changes were very vivid to Liza – brought up, as she had been, to think of 'outside' consisting only of a controlled garden – the pleasure of her life struck her forcibly. She liked the shape of it, the small and manageable degree of independence she now had; she liked her country life and in it, her new authority as teacher of the children of so many people who were not only Archie's patients – 'Good Lord, you Logans, you simply *run* our lives, do you realize?' – but guests at the same parties, members of the same local committees, users of the same shops and services. Catching sight of herself in the driving mirror, she thought she even looked better because of it: less puppy plumpness, more interesting.

The only cloud was Thomas. Liza was afraid that Thomas was the last kind of child who should have been sent away to school. She had been in two minds about it all along and she still was. It was Sir Andrew who had suggested he board to prepare him better for public school, and it was Sir Andrew who was paying. All discussions about it were deeply unsatisfactory, largely because Archie, whose paternal instincts were wholly against the project, was equally at the mercy of filial instincts which made him incapable of overriding his father. They found a school in the New Forest, a jolly-looking place with Labradors in the headmaster's study, and plenty of family photographs and balding teddy bears in the dormitories.

Thomas, white-faced, said he liked it. He went to stay for a night to do some entrance tests and came home saying he liked it. He boasted about it at his day school in Winchester, starting most sentences with 'When I go to Pinemount . . .' and then occasionally, in the last holidays before he departed, had terrible weeping rages for no reason, and twice, to his unutterable chagrin, wet his bed.

Archie said to him when they were alone cleaning the .22 rifle Archie kept for shooting rabbits, 'Look, you don't have to go to Pinemount, you know. Nobody's forcing you. Grandpa thought you might like the chance, but a chance is all it is.'

'I want to,' Thomas said.

'Sure?'

'Yes.'

'There'd be no shame in changing your mind. We'd say at school that we'd changed ours, not you yours.'

'I don't want to change my mind.'

Liza and Archie took him down to Pinemount together. It looked reassuringly old-fashioned and friendly. Thomas walked away from them holding his old blue stuffed rabbit at arm's length as if he didn't like to be too closely associated with either it or them. There was tea for new boys and their parents which was, Archie said later, the most purgatorial social experience invented by man, and after it, they left Thomas and a few others in the care of an amiable man called George Barnes, who said, for the boys' benefit, that the sooner they could get rid of the parents and get down to business the better.

Liza cried most of the way home and, just the Winchester side of Romsey, Archie had to stop the car because he was crying, too, and couldn't see. He wanted to say to Liza that he felt he had somehow failed both her and Thomas, but he did not say it because she would then have had the added burden of feeling she must comfort him.

After a bit, she blew her nose with resolution and said, 'Thomas would think we were pathetic.'

'He's probably not even thinking about us any more—'

'No.'

'It couldn't possibly be a happier sort of school.'

'Oh no.'

'Liza—?'

'Yes.'

'One musn't confuse one's own misery with someone else's imagined misery.'

She said nothing. Archie started the car.

'Except,' he said, 'it's imagining his possible misery that creates one's own.'

Thomas was not allowed to write home for ten days. There were all kinds of sound, humane, teacherly reasons for this. When his first letter came, it was in atrocious babyish writing and contained all the resentful unhappiness they had hoped to cheat fate of, by imagining the worst beforehand.

'Why can Mikey and Imogen be at home,' Thomas wrote, entirely forgetting his own choice and resolve, 'and not me?'

At the bottom of the sheet, he had drawn a picture of himself and the blue rabbit and underneath he had written 'We are sad'. Liza took the letter to June Hampole, who read it with the serious attention she gave anything to do with children.

'He can't bear to blame himself for having got his expectations wrong so he *has* to blame you. But it will pass. I promise. Reality will block out his expectations and he will accept that. Poor Liza,' said June Hampole, putting an arm round her shoulders. 'The little fiends are so brilliant at putting the boot in.'

Privately, Liza thought she might put her own boot in. Just a small boot. She would produce Thomas's letter at lunch on Sunday, and show it to her father-in-law, in front of Marina de Breton. It was not so much that she wanted to make Sir Andrew unhappy, as to elicit from either him or Archie – and preferably

Archie – an admission that Archie's bond to his family came before that to his father.

In the car, going to school, she practised saying, 'Archie wouldn't have agreed to Thomas's going away if the suggestion hadn't been yours.'

She thought she could say this very smilingly, in front of a stranger. She felt suddenly happy and certain, driving between the hawthorn hedges with half-bare trees marching across the fields beyond them, against a translucent sky streaked dove-grey and pale-blue. Perhaps she could begin to move things as she wanted, perhaps her power – which she would never abuse, she was certain of that – was just beginning to spread fledgling wings. Perhaps the time was quietly coming when she would not be the dependent one, the cherished childlike one, and would move from the outer circle of their life, where she presently wheeled gently with the children, into the steering, driving heart of it.

She drove into the old stableyard of Bradley Hall, and parked her car beside the wire-wheeled Alvis that Dan Hampole drove to Winchester station *en route* for London and his arcane pleasures. A double file of small boys in football boots was jiggling up and down outside a doorway, and, in front of them, Blaise O'Hanlon, his untidy Irish glamour accentuated by a frayed tweed jacket of dashing cut and an immense, dirty yellow muffler, was talking and tossing a soccer ball from hand to hand. As Liza pulled up, he sent a boy to open her car door for her.

' "L'absence est à l'amour," ' said Blaise to her as she passed him, ' "ce qu'est au feu le vent; il éteint le petit, il allume le grand." Please identify the quotation.'

But she went by him, laughing. There was no need to obey.

Chapter Three

Archie, on duty on Saturday night, and called out to violent stomach pains just before midnight, and to a stroke which had smitten someone's houseguest just before dawn, slept until ten o'clock on Sunday morning. It then seemed fair to Liza to send Mikey up with a mug of tea and Imogen behind him with as much Sunday newsprint as she could manage. Archie pulled them into bed with him, but Imogen said she must take off her shoes, and struggled out again.

'Just thocks,' she said reprovingly to Mikey, climbing back in. Her hair, which grew in the same soft curls as her mother's, had been tied high on the back of her head with a ribbon woven with edelweiss. She wore a Shetland jersey under a triangular pinafore of green corduroy and she smelled of baby soap and Marmite. Archie put his face into the duckling nape of her neck and breathed in deeply.

'Nah-nah-nah-nah-nah,' said Imogen, holding a newspaper upside down and pretending to read it. 'Nah-nah-nah.'

'What's Mummy doing?' Archie said between slow kisses.

'You thcratch,' Imogen said, leaning forward. She twisted round and pushed his unshaven face away. He caught her fingers in his mouth.

'Doing lunch,' Mikey said. He offered Archie a photograph of an immense black American boxer. 'Would he beat you up?'

'Only if you were very annoying.'

'Now,' said Imogen, 'my finger'th wet.'

'Lick mine then,' Mikey said kindly.

36

'Bite,' Archie said, snapping his teeth. 'Bite, bite, *bite*. What have you been doing to those fingers?'

Mikey held up a hand piebald with purple stains.

'The felt-tip leaked. I was doing a picture for Grandpa.'

'What of?'

'A kestrel. With a mouse.'

'The mouse hath blood,' Imogen said with satisfaction.

'Grandpa is bringing a friend, you know.'

'Mummy thaid—'

'It's a lady,' Mikey said, running his purple finger round Mike Tyson's great gloved fist. 'She's called Mrs de Breton. Imogen drew her some flowers.'

'Did you, darling? What sort of flowers?'

'Black,' said Imogen.

Archie drank his tea.

'What is Mummy making for lunch?'

'She cut the bone out of the meat,' Mikey said. 'With a big knife. And then she put a whole lot of junk in.'

'What sort of junk?'

'Apricots and those little yellow nut things—'

'And rithe,' said Imogen. 'Black rithe.'

'Black rice?'

'She said it was wild,' Mikey said, lying back on the pillows. 'Looked pretty tame to me.'

Archie lay back beside him.

'Michael Logan, you have filthy ears.'

Mikey wriggled sideways so that his face was almost touching his father's.

'Clare's coming to lunch, too. She rang up and said she'd got the bad blues so Mummy said come to lunch.'

Imogen stood up unsteadily in bed, releasing a rush of cold air across Archie, and began to jump.

'Don't,' said Archie.

Imogen fell over.

'Just one'th—'

'No.'

He caught her and held her against his chest.

'No,' she said, her voice rising in protest. 'No, no, no—'

The door opened and Liza came in wearing a plastic apron which said across the front 'A Good Mother Makes a Happy Home'. She held out a jar of honey.

'I can't get the top off.'

Mikey seized the jar.

'Why d'you want honey?'

'To smear on the lamb.'

Imogen began to scramble out of bed.

'I do it—'

Archie took the jar away from Mikey and unscrewed the top.

'I gather Clare's coming.'

'Yes,' Liza said, stopping herself just before she said sorry. 'She sounded miserable.'

Archie swung his legs out of bed and stood up.

'Sometimes I think I'm getting compassion fatigue over Clare.'

'She *is* unhappy—'

'She loves being unhappy.'

'Archie,' Liza said. 'If, as we are, you are lucky enough to be happy, it really is the least you can do to include people in your life who are unhappy.'

Archie bent and kissed her.

'What a priggish little popsicle you are.'

'You only say that because you know I'm right.'

'Now then,' Mikey said, rolling himself up in the duvet, 'no argy-bargy.'

Liza put her hand on the door.

'It's a quarter to eleven. Your father is coming at twelve and the fire isn't lit and I don't know which wine.'

'Why are you cross?'

'I'm not cross. I'm just cooking Sunday lunch for seven and a rice pudding for Granny Mossop, having

38

been up since a quarter to eight and done the children and the dog.'

Archie pulled on a blue towelling robe.

'Well, I'm cross.'

Mikey, encased in wadding like a human Swiss roll, sat up.

'Why?'

'Because,' Archie said, 'I don't want Mrs de Breton to come to lunch.'

'*Archie,*' Liza said.

'Why not?' Mikey said.

'Because.'

'How can you be so *stupid* in front of the children?'

'Easily,' Archie said, and went off to the bathroom.

When Sir Andrew's city-clean Rover stopped in the drive, it was the children and the spaniel who ran out to greet him. He opened the driver's door and Mikey and Imogen scrambled up to kiss him while the spaniel bounced barking on the gravel.

Marina de Breton, who had scarcely seen the English countryside before and who was charmed by the rolling slopes of the Hampshire hills, said, 'Well, Andrew, this *is* a welcome and no mistake.'

Mikey looked at her. She seemed to him very golden. From his perch on the doorsill of the car, he surveyed her gravely across his grandfather.

'Marina,' Sir Andrew said. 'This is Imogen. And this is Mikey. And you two, this is Mrs de Breton.'

'Yeth,' said Imogen.

'Hello,' Marina said, smiling. 'I am very pleased to meet you.'

She had an American voice, like television. When she said 'very', she sounded just like television. Mikey gaped. Even her clothes were golden.

'Could you please let us out? Mikey, go round and open Mrs de Breton's door. Come on, Imogen. Hop off.'

39

Mikey trotted round the Rover bonnet and opened the passenger door. Marina de Breton rose out of the car like a swan.

'Thank you,' she said.

Her soft suede sleeve lightly brushed Mikey's face. He wished he had not written 'For Grandpa' on the kestrel picture, so that he might have given it to Mrs de Breton. To his amazement, she took his hand. At six, he hated to have his hand held, but now he led Marina de Breton towards the house.

'Mummy,' he said, feeling a sudden and uncharacteristic obligation to be hostly, 'has put wild rice inside the lamb.'

'My,' said Marina de Breton, '*wild* rice. That's Indian rice. Indians harvest that rice in boats. It's very rare.'

'Red Indians?'

'Of course,' Marina said. 'What other Indians would they be that poled their boats along the lakeshore looking for wild rice?'

What, indeed. Leading her carefully up the steps to the front door, Mikey fell deep into first love. In the hall, his parents were waiting.

'This,' Mikey said, 'is my mother and my father.'

Marina held out her free hand.

'Who I am charmed to meet.'

Liza took Marina's hand in both hers in a futile attempt to convey that, if it hadn't been for Archie, she too would have rushed out eagerly to greet her. Archie, amiable, equable, affectionate Archie, had abruptly thrown a fit of childish perversity and refused to leave the house when the Rover slid up the lane. And Liza, rather than risk a row at the moment of Sir Andrew's arrival which would then poison the air with furious and exaggerated insults, chose, against her better judgement, to stay with Archie. She made this decision on the second of observing, quite suddenly, real misery beneath Archie's defiance. He had glanced at her only for a moment, but that glance was full of unhappiness.

So she said, 'Truly, I don't know what you are afraid of,' and then she had stayed beside him in the hall for some minutes, and they neither of them spoke, and Liza felt very foolish. So, to make up for all this complexity, she greeted Marina de Breton with warmth.

Archie took her hand with unexceptionable courtesy, and then, as was his wont, put his arm round his father's shoulders and kissed him. Liza had never got used to this. She despised the terrified physical inhibition of her own family, yet was startled every time to see those scorned barriers broken down. And to kiss Sir Andrew, so spare, so Scots, so buttoned up in many ways, seemed a double audacity. But he responded to Archie. He always had.

His father looked, Archie thought in bewilderment, extremely well. He wore a suit of Prince of Wales check, and a yellow waistcoat, and his lean, upright figure seemed to have an uncommon elasticity. When he stooped to pick up Imogen, and swing her into his arms – usually he waited until he was sitting down before he lifted her on to his knee – Archie wondered if this youthful display of grandfatherly playfulness was for the benefit of Marina de Breton.

Marina said she would adore some sherry if she could have some ice in it. Archie said she could have anything she wanted in it. She looked straight at him, smiling.

'Like a nice little chili,' she said.

'Imogen,' Liza said quickly, 'leave Grandpa's moustache alone.'

'Grandpa doesn't mind,' Sir Andrew said through Imogen's investigating fingers.

'Tickly,' Imogen said.

'Too right,' said Marina de Breton.

Liza made a hasty sweeping gesture with one arm.

'Do please sit down—'

41

'I think,' Marina said, settling gracefully into a low chair, in supple folds of caramel suede, 'that this is a charming room. Mikey, who is that character in the corner?'

Mikey looked towards the suit of armour

'That's Sir Bedevere.'

'I found him,' Archie said, coming in with a tray of glasses, 'in a mystic lake.'

'Complete with mystic sword?'

'No,' Liza said, chattering. 'No. In a cellar, actually. The cellar of the house of one of Archie's patients. He'd gone down to find a bottle of wine, as instructed, and there this thing was, covered in rust, lying on an old mattress. And Colonel Chambers said he could have it. So he put it in the car with its great metal feet hanging out of the tailgate and we went at it with wire wool; boxes and boxes—' She stopped.

'When you are the right size,' Marina said to Mikey, 'you must try him on.'

Mikey's eyes bulged.

'Me, too,' said Imogen.

'You're a *girl*—'

'Marina,' Sir Andrew said serenely to Liza, 'is an art historian.'

'Andrew,' Marina said with equal composure, 'I am nothing of the sort. I did a six-month course on the decorative arts in New York and I spent a summer at I Tatti. I'm no art historian.'

Liza stood up.

'Would you excuse me a moment? I must just peer into the oven—'

'I shall come and peer with you,' Marina said.

'You can't.' Liza was genuinely horrified. 'Not wearing that—'

Marina rose. 'I most certainly can. I want to see every inch of this delightful house.'

Followed by Mikey, they left the drawing room.

'I wanted to take you all *out* to lunch,' Marina said. 'I

didn't want you going to all this trouble. But Andrew was adamant. I feel I should just have been more adamant still.'

Liza opened the kitchen door and a rich waft of roasting meat came out to meet them.

'It's so nice of you, but really, I don't mind. I'm quite used to it and my sister Clare is coming. She's divorced and she gets a bit depressed, living on her own. Now, stay right over there while I open the oven door. Mikey, guard Mrs de Breton. I'm so worried about her beautiful suit.'

Mikey herded Marina against the kitchen dresser and spread his arms wide to defend her from the menace of flying fat.

She said, laughing, 'Oh, this is just adorable. I love the whole thing.'

Liza put the roasting tin on the table and began to baste the meat.

'You did all that?' Marina said.

'Oh yes. I quite like cooking—'

'So do I,' Mikey said.

'Mikey is a whizz at pancakes.'

'If I was very nice to you, Mikey, would you someday make me pancakes?'

Mikey nodded vehemently.

'And you have an elder brother?'

'He's at boarding school,' Mikey said, dropping his arms but not moving away. 'He cries there.'

Marina looked at Liza.

'He cries?'

Liza said unhappily, 'It was so kind of Andrew to send him. And I'm sure he'll be fine. But he's taking a bit of time to settle down.'

'It was Andrew's idea?'

'It was a kind one. It was to get Thomas used to the idea of being away at public school.'

'And what,' Marina said, taking a slow sip of sherry, 'do you think?'

43

Liza put the lamb back in the oven.

'I didn't want him to go,' she said with her back to Marina.

'And did you say that?'

'Sort of—'

'My dear Liza. This isn't fair of me at all. It's none of my business. But I'd have felt just as you feel. Mikey, would you know where there was more ice for my drink?'

When he had sped off, Marina said, 'Would you like me to speak to Andrew?'

Liza was startled. She thought of Thomas's letter which she had intended to produce in front of Marina. It now seemed a shabby little scheme, and in her shame she said, too abruptly, 'Oh no—'

Marina went over to the sink and looked through the window at the leaf-strewn lawn and the half-bare beeches and the pale autumn pastureland rising to the pale autumn sky.

'What a lot you achieve,' she said to Liza, over her shoulder.

No-one had ever said anything of this kind to Liza.

'Do I?'

Marina turned round.

'Husband, house, children, garden, teaching, cooking. I'm bowled over—'

Mikey came back with an ice tray.

'Clare's come. Imo's being stupid and jumping on the sofa.'

'Isn't Daddy stopping her?'

'He's talking to Grandpa.'

Liza ran back to the drawing room. Imogen had fallen off the sofa and was crying in Clare's arms. Over by the bay window, which overlooked the lane, Archie and his father were deep in conversation.

Liza took Imogen from her sister and put her firmly on the floor.

'Looks like you had a lovely welcome—'

Clare was taller and thinner than Liza, with large anxious eyes and hair drawn back into a black velvet bow on the nape of her neck.

'They're talking about cot deaths.'

'How cheerful. How are you?'

Clare made a balancing movement with her hand.

'So-so.'

'Clare,' Liza said, 'this is Marina de Breton.'

'I am afraid,' Marina said, taking Clare's hand and smiling, 'that they are talking about cot deaths because of me.'

Politely the sisters waited to be enlightened.

'My late husband left a trust to be used for the promotion of humanity's understanding of itself. Mostly it goes on schemes for schools and colleges, and some educational scholarships. But I saw the last series of *Meeting Medicine* and just *knew* that's where Louis would have wanted his money put. And his youngest daughter lost a baby that way, so the only condition I made to Andrew was that at least one programme—'

Clare's eyes were immense with sympathy.

'Your grandchild?'

Marina raised her eyebrows.

'No, indeed. Louis de Breton changed wives like other men change their shirts. This daughter was a child of his second marriage. His funeral was bizarre. The front pews of the church were solid with his widows, *solid*. Children and grandchildren as far as the eye could see.' She winked at Liza. 'I wore scarlet. And a hat as big as a wheel.'

They stared at her. Archie, turning from the window, caught them at it, gazing, silent, his wife, his sister-in-law and his second son. Only Imogen, doing unsuccessful headstands on the sofa cushions, was outside the spell.

'Darling,' Archie said, 'shall I carve?'

*

Sir Andrew was enormously happy. He looked about the dining-room table and felt a rich pleasure in everyone round it and everything on it. To him, each person, each dish, each glass and fork, seemed to have an extraordinary value and vitality, reflecting his own sudden and miraculous sense of not just being alive, which he was used to, but of living, down to each last nerve end, which he was not. He had been disconcerted, even embarrassed, by this uncharacteristic exuberance at first, had been afraid he was going to make a fool of himself, and, in the process, destroy the sober esteem in which, he knew perfectly well, the world held him. But his confidence had grown with the realization that he was not, as he had feared, a victim of elderly and absurd folly, but, rather, one of the chosen; a man – a little late in the day, perhaps – chosen to have his half-empty cup suddenly filled until it brimmed and spilled. All over his mind and body and heart, doors, long shut, some never even opened previously, were swinging wide. Looking down at his plate of lamb and vegetables, Sir Andrew was shaken with a shudder of unquestionable ecstasy at the recollection of being in bed with Marina de Breton.

'Oh dear,' Liza said anxiously. 'Are you cold? I'll get an electric fire. The radiator in here never works properly—'

'I'm not cold in the least,' Sir Andrew said, turning upon her a radiant smile.

She said in amazement, 'You look so happy!'

'I am.'

She blushed. He did not. He continued, with great dignity, to look unabashed and radiant.

'Liza,' he said teasingly, 'have I shocked you?'

'Not shocked—'

'Your stiff old Scots pa-in-law shouldn't fling his cap over windmills, eh?'

'Don't,' she said.

He was laughing gently. Suddenly furious with him

for not having the decency to be self-conscious, she looked away and briefly caught Archie's eyes across the table. He raised one eyebrow.

'More peath,' Imogen said, beside her mother. 'Heapth and *heapth* more peath.'

'Only when you have eaten everything else.'

'This,' Marina said to Archie, 'is some of the best lamb I have eaten in my life. And being Greek, I do know about lamb.'

'Greek?'

'Greek. I only put the accent on for customs officials and traffic wardens and inattentive shop assistants and anyone else tiresome. I left Athens when I was three. I had charming and unsatisfactory parents who thought New York was simply waiting for them with bated breath, which of course it was not. I do believe outrage and disappointment killed my mother. She was an early dope fiend, in the days when it was still chic. Ikons and cocaine and Fortuny evening dresses – the last word in dated debauchery. Poor Mamma.'

'You are making it up,' Archie said.

'My dear. It is far too outrageous for that.'

She gave him a quick glance. He was looking away from her, towards Clare on his other side.

'Do you believe her?' Archie demanded.

Clare, whose susceptibility to male physical charms, even the familiar ones of her sister's husband, always threw her into confusion, said, 'I – I think so.'

Marina burst out laughing.

'That's adorable!'

Archie took Clare's hand.

'Don't be bullied—'

'You see,' Clare said, gathering courage from his grasp. 'Liza and I had such an unutterably boring upbringing that we can never believe it when other people tell us how fascinating theirs was. I used to pray and pray to be kidnapped and then, lo and behold, Liza was. By Archie. So unfair.'

47

'And did nobody kidnap you later?'

'Oh yes,' Clare said, looking down. 'Robin did. But having me wasn't as exciting as chasing me. So he went off to chase someone else.'

'That's too bad,' Marina said. 'I hope she made him perfectly miserable.'

'She does. But he likes it. I suppose it's a sort of permanent chase.'

Marina turned to Archie.

'And are you a chaser?'

'No.'

'With all these women patients Andrew tells me of, feigning illness like crazy for two seconds of your undivided attention?'

'Even,' Archie said composedly, 'with all of them.'

He stood up to carve second helpings. It looked to him as if Marina was going to throw him another challenge, so he said deliberately, 'I like being married.'

'You and your father,' Marina said, 'are remarkable men.'

She turned to Mikey, diligently eating beside her.

'And will you be a doctor, too?'

'I'm going to be a cook.'

'A cook?'

'And live here always,' Mikey said.

'You are a very unusual boy. Boys commonly can't wait to leave home. I have eleven stepgrandsons in America and they leave home all the time.'

Mikey thought about this. He thought about his bedroom and the picture of Superman over his bed and the torch he had under his pillow to flash signals on the ceiling with, after his light had been turned off. And he thought of Thomas.

'If I leave, you see, I mightn't like it so much.'

'So,' Marina said, 'will you bring your wife back to live here, too?'

'I don't want a wife. I want a dog.'

'I'm not sure that's quite the same,' Clare said quickly.

Marina waved a hand.

'He's on to something, you know. Louis de Breton's dogs had a much better time than his wives. Archie, if you were going to offer me more of that sensational lamb, I shall save you the trouble and say yes please. And I never have second helpings. Never in this world. Do I, Andrew?'

And she looked across the table at him and together, wrapped in some intimate and delightful joke, they began to laugh.

Much later, Liza said she and Clare would do the washing up, and why didn't Archie make a bonfire? Sir Andrew had driven Marina de Breton away with mysterious indications of pressing things to be done in London, and Archie had not uttered since their departure which inhibited Liza from saying all the things she was bursting with. When she suggested a bonfire, Archie just nodded and collected up his children and the spaniel and old newspapers and matches and went out into the dying afternoon. From the kitchen window, Liza watched him with a mixture of sympathy and exasperation. Clare, struck by the effortless glamour of his appearance in tall Wellington boots and an immense and dishevelled Aran jersey, felt his evident dejection to be almost tragic.

Archie himself was chiefly consumed with self-disgust. His own view of love was founded upon generosity, and, while he was well aware that clumsiness and pure maleness often prevented him from fine-tuning this outlook, his every basic instinct in love was bent upon giving. A colleague of his, whose wife had become entirely swallowed up by her Open University course in psychology, had said fretfully once to Archie, 'In my view, the least she *owes* me is a decent dinner at night.' Archie had been both struck and shocked by this. Obligation did not come into his emotional scheme of things – responsibility, yes, contributions from both sides, certainly, but never a feeling of being beholden, of being in someone's debt. Looking at Imogen now, picking up spiky beech nut shells and putting them into a broken flowerpot, made him realize the extent of her dignity and, even at three, her separate valuable power to love without abasing herself or compromising herself. He, her father, wished to give her emotional space. He wanted her love, but he wanted it freely given. He wanted his father's love in the same way, and he had always had it. He had it now. His father had, today, been demonstrably affectionate. But he had also shown that he was full of another kind of love, full of it. Archie plunged his fork into a mound of garden rubbish and flung it to the top of the bonfire.

'Jealous bastard,' he said to himself. 'Childish, shameful, jealous bastard.'

Thick, unecologically sound, blue-grey smoke uncurled itself slowly into the air and filled Archie's eyes with the blessed excuse for tears. Mikey came drifting up through the gauzy air and held out his closed fists.

'What have you got?' Archie said, smearing his jersey sleeve across his eyes.

Mikey opened his fists and revealed a pound coin in each.

'One for me and one for Imo. I'm holding on to hers because she thought it was chocolate.'

'From Grandpa?'

'No,' Mikey said. 'From Mrs de Breton.'

Archie looked unhappily down at the fat golden coins.

'Did you like her?'

'Of course,' Mikey said.

'Why?'

Mikey looked away, his face contorted with the

50

impossibility of describing his susceptibility to her charm.

He said uncertainly, after a while, 'I liked her earrings.'

Archie held his arms out.

'Come and give your old da a hug.'

He lifted Mikey up so that his rubber-booted toes bumped against his knees. Mikey put his arms out stiffly behind Archie's head, still gripping the money.

'I'm going to save up for a guinea-pig. One of the ones with whirly bits in its fur.' He bent his head back to look into his father's face. 'You can share it if you like.'

'He's wonderful with the children, isn't he?' Clare said, rinsing wine glasses at the kitchen sink and gazing out of the window. 'Perhaps if I'd had a baby, Robin wouldn't have left.'

'He would, you know. He'd have left just the same and it would be worse for you, now, with a baby.'

'Nothing could be worse,' Clare said.

Liza was stretching plastic film over leftover helpings of lunch.

'Clare, you are not to talk like this—'

'I swore I wouldn't,' Clare said. 'I absolutely swore. But listening to Marina at lunch made me so depressed and sick of myself. I mean, you simply can't imagine her letting life get her down, can you? I thought she was amazing. And she looked so wonderful. How old do you think she is?'

Liza, who was full of the same envious admiration of Marina, said she supposed about her mid-fifties.

'But she was so sexy. Wasn't she? I mean, you and I will never be that sexy. We never have been. Have we?'

Liza was impelled to say that she thought Archie found her sexy, but stopped herself in the nick of time because it struck her that, whatever he felt, she didn't feel herself to be sexy. She picked up a cloth and began to dry the glasses Clare had washed.

She said in a very sensible voice, 'She's much more exotic than us. And sort of international. And rich. Being rich is supposed to be very sexy.'

'And all that suede, and gold jewellery. And her wonderful shoes. I bet they were Italian. Liza, did you notice Andrew could hardly keep his hands off her?'

'Of course I noticed.'

'Is that what's the matter with Archie?'

Liza began to put the polished wine glasses on a tray.

'Well, it is a bit unhinging—'

'Telling me,' Clare said. 'She filled me with dissatisfaction. You're so lucky, she might become your mother-in-law and give you lunch at the Connaught and lovely presents. She looks that sort of person. Robin's mother can't see anything wrong with Robin. It has to be my fault he left. That's what she thinks.'

'Marina understood about Thomas,' Liza said. 'She offered to speak to Andrew and my first reaction was to say no, but I wonder—'

Privately, Liza thought there were other things Marina might understand about, too. 'The first of many meetings,' Marina had said to Liza before she was driven away. And she had smiled. There had been an edge of female complicity to that smile.

'I'm taking a rice pudding down the lane to old Mrs Mossop,' Liza said. 'Want to come?'

'Not really. But I don't want to go home either.'

'Clare,' Liza said warningly. She opened the bottom oven door and took out a Pyrex dish.

'I'm three years older than you,' Clare said. 'And we might almost be different generations. Look at you. All this domestic bliss and a job and village life—'

Liza wrapped a clean dishcloth round the Pyrex dish.

'Hold that.'

On the way down the hall, they passed through a lingering breath of Marina's scent and stopped to sniff.

'Honestly,' Clare said. 'It's like having a crush at school.'

Liza began to giggle.

'Aren't we idiotic?'

'No, no, I love it; I love this carried away feeling—'

'Me, too.'

'Think of what life is like for Andrew, I mean, just think—'

'I know. I simply didn't know where to look at lunch.' Liza opened the front door. 'Do you think they just drove straight back to London to go to bed?'

'Yes,' Clare said, 'of course they did. And left us all here, years younger, simply green with envy—'

'Speak for yourself!'

'Can you,' Clare said, stepping carefully down the drive because of carrying the pudding, 'can you talk to Archie about it?'

Liza thought.

'No,' she said, 'I don't think I can. Not about that.'

'But I thought you talked about everything. Sex and everything—'

'But not Andrew and sex.'

'No,' Clare said, 'perhaps not. But will Archie think about it?'

'Yes,' Liza said slowly. 'I don't see how he can help it,' and then she took the pudding from her sister and they went away with it down the lane to old Mrs Mossop's cottage, and found her there, alone in her darkening room, watching the empty Sunday lane.

'When I want charity,' Granny Mossop said, 'I'll ask for it.'

But she grew cross when Liza offered to remove the pudding and, when the sisters peered back in through the window as they left, she was hunting for spoons.

Chapter Four

On Monday morning, Liza accused Archie of behaving like a child. She did this over breakfast, causing Mikey to weep and remember he had not done his violin practice, and Imogen to refuse, flatly, even to look at her breakfast. They were all late and a faint disheartening drizzle was misting the kitchen windows. Archie, whose provocative crime had been to remark that the sitting room still smelled like Harrods, got up in silence, kissed his children, and went off to his car. Liza was impressed to find that she felt buoyed up by indignation rather than borne down by tears, as was her wont in such situations, and merely said to Imogen as Archie's car could be heard revving in the garage, 'Eat that up when you are told.'

The car went down the drive and Imogen picked up her cereal bowl and held it upside down over the floor.

Driving down the lane towards the village, Archie wrenched his mind on to the day ahead. Surgery, visits, an hour or two at the local cottage hospital (saved from the great central state crushing machine only by relentless local effort), a practice meeting, more visits and evening surgery. The practice meeting would, he knew, be about the installation of computers at the health centre. Intellectually he was all for this but emotionally he rebelled. One of his colleagues had described him as a refugee from an A. J. Cronin novel which Archie thought, on the whole, pretty accurate. He also knew, without complacency, that diagnostically and in human terms he was the best doctor in the practice. His colleagues, with varying degrees of good and bad grace, knew this, too, and would in consequence emphasize their own additional roles as, for instance, anaesthetists at local hospitals. Archie had no wish to be anything other than a rural general practitioner and, when it was pointed out to him that he was bound to get the fidgets at forty, he said he was planning a really big break-out then, so as not to disappoint them. The pharmacist at the health centre had overheard him say this once, and had endured several terrible nights subsequently, plagued by impossible fantasies of which she was later ashamed.

Because he was early, on account of the incident at breakfast, Archie paused at Stoke Stratton post office. This was run by Mrs Betts, a formidable widow from a Southampton suburb, who used it as a power-base from which to shape and control the village. She was secretary to the Women's Institute, founder of the rambling club and organizer of the village fête. She had also revived a gardeners' group and was Clerk to the Parish Council. Tall, solid and handsome, Mrs Betts had brought to Stoke Stratton a very clear idea of what English village life should be like and a strong determination to impose this vision on the few hundred people who came to buy stamps at one end of her shop and throat lozenges, birthday cards and potting compost at the other. Progress, in Mrs Betts's view, meant power in the hands of the bourgeoisie and the neatening of sloppy agricultural ways. On her counter stood a homemade advertisement enticing her customers to sign a petition asking the local farmer not to drive his tractors down the main street of the village. As the farm lay above Beeches House, and the lane leading to it was usually liberally strewn with succulent chunks of mud, Mrs Betts was very pleased to see Archie as an early customer.

He asked for a dozen first-class stamps, some brown envelopes and a packet of peppermints.

'And you'll sign my petition, Dr Logan.'

'Sorry, Mrs Betts. No go. I've no objection to mud.'

'Come now, Dr Logan. Think of Mrs Logan. I saw her and her sister coming down your lane yesterday with the greatest difficulty.'

'It's a natural hazard of country life—'

'Only because no-one has thought to do anything about it. Where would we be if we all just accepted things? Dr Logan, there are seven old footpaths now open again round this village thanks to me and my ramblers.'

Archie folded his stamps and slid them into his wallet.

'Richard Prior is a good neighbour to me, Mrs Betts. I'm not going to provoke him and I don't mind his mud.'

Mrs Betts laid her large capable hands on the counter.

'Dr Logan, it's you professional people who must take the lead. It's not like the old days when there was a squire to turn to. It's up to people like you and Mr Jago now to preserve our heritage.'

Archie gave her an enormous smile.

'Do you know, I think mud *is* part of our heritage.'

In the road outside, the Vicar was parking his car behind Archie's. Colin Jenkins was a narrow, pale man in his thirties with a passion for committee work, who was to be seen driving into Winchester for diocesan meetings of one sort or another far more often than around his parish. On the rare occasions when he and Archie had coincided at a sickbed, Archie had felt strongly that, should the patient die, Colin Jenkins would regard his soul as one more convert to the egalitarian and socialist bureaucracy which was his evident notion of the hereafter.

'You can't talk to him,' an unhappy patient of Archie's had once said. 'When my son was killed, I couldn't talk to him at all. If I'd tried, I'd only have got an anti-government tirade.'

This morning, Archie was in no mood for Colin Jenkins. As the Vicar slid out of his car, Archie gave a preoccupied smile and wave intended to indicate his hurry, and climbed into his own. Reflected in his mirror, he saw Colin standing in the road, looking after him, a figure at once self-satisfied and forlorn. Archie put his foot down. He suddenly wanted a telephone.

He rang from his room at the health centre.

'Sorry,' Sally Carter said, 'Mrs Logan's gone. She went twenty minutes ago. If you ring the school, you might get her before lessons.'

He rang Bradley Hall. The school secretary, a kind, confused woman with a sweet telephone manner and an aptitude for muddling bills, said Liza was in prayers.

'I'm so sorry. They've just gone in, only just. I can hear them singing "When A Knight Won His Spurs". Shall I ask Mrs Logan to ring you when she comes out?'

'No,' Archie said. 'No, thank you. It isn't urgent. It can wait.'

'But I'll tell her you rang—'

'No,' he said again. 'No. Don't bother.' And then he put the receiver down and wondered what on earth had impelled him to say no, and not just once, but twice. A dull misery collected in his throat and settled there. He cleared it decisively once or twice, but to no avail. He leaned forward and pressed his intercom button.

'Mrs Hargreaves for Dr Logan, please. Mrs Hargreaves.'

Liza sang enthusiastically. All around her the children, who liked the hymn and its clear images of storybook chivalry, sang with equal fervour. Above the altar, Albert on his tortured cross seemed to be wincing at the jovial atmosphere of folksy Protestantism in which he found himself, an atmosphere June Hampole was careful to encourage so that no enraged father could possibly accuse her of Popery. Looking across at Liza singing innocently of the death of dragons, June observed how well she looked, how happy. Liza Logan, June Hampole thought, shuffling through her pockets for the prayer she had chosen and now seemed to have mislaid, was a prime example of middle-class excellence, an unshakeable rock of competence and decency and endeavour. As she grew older, her experience would give her authority and she might well, June thought, surprise herself by her own strength. June found her piece of paper and went up to the lectern below the altar.

'Let us pray.'

The children rumbled to their knees on the floor of the chapel. June put on her spectacles and unfolded the paper.

'Dog biscuits,' the piece of paper said. 'Blankets from dry cleaners, gin, telephone tennis court people for resurfacing estimate.'

'Today,' June said, 'we are going to pray to St Anthony of Padua. He liked pigs and he is the patron saint of lost things. I am tempted to rename the lost property cupboard The Cave of St Anthony. Close your eyes and pray for something you have lost. I have lost this morning's prayer.'

And I, Liza thought, putting a restraining hand on the restive small boy beside her, have lost something, too. Something I did not much want. I have lost some of my inadequacy. The small boy twisted himself free and hissed in a stage whisper that he had lost his recorder.

'We'll find it after prayers,' Liza said softly, sure that she would.

'Now,' he said. 'Now—'

'No. After prayers.'

He subsided against her and put his thumb in his mouth. She put her arm round him and thought of his parents, a tough self-confident pair who ran a small racing stable and were friends of Simon and Diana Jago. Her arm round their child, Liza reflected that today she could cope with them too with perfect assurance.

'Our Father,' June Hampole said. 'Which art in heaven, Hallowed be Thy name—'

The familiar rhythms rolled round Liza: the daily bread and the trespasses, the temptation and the forgiveness. From now on, she would forgive Archie, she would be very understanding about his attitude to Marina, she would make a huge imaginative effort to put herself in his shoes. This was difficult since she could not imagine caring much, one way or the other, if her own father produced a substitute for her mother, but not, she told herself, impossible.

'Amen,' said June Hampole and the staff and children with emphasis.

They rose, whispering, to their feet.

'No talking!' Commander Haythorne bellowed.

They began to shove each other instead until the neat lines of children bulged and swerved like serpents.

'No pushing!' shouted Commander Haythorne.

'Isn't this,' Blaise O'Hanlon said, materializing at Liza's side, 'just your best moment of the day?'

'I always rather want to join in—'

'Exactly. We are doing break duty together. I have engineered it with Gaelic cunning. What is your first lesson?'

'A passage from *Lettres de mon Moulin* with the sixth form.'

'Isn't that dreadfully advanced? Why aren't they allowed *Madame Bonnard Va au Marché*?'

'My *recorder*—' a voice pleaded, three feet from the floor.

'Justin, I'm coming to look for your recorder. Because sometimes I simply can't bear her. Little dollops of Daudet and Fournier and Verlaine keep me sane and stretch their tiny minds.'

Two girls flattened themselves elaborately against the frame of the chapel doors to let Liza and Blaise go through.

'Thank you, Sophie. And Tamsin.'

'What I'd really like,' Blaise said as they emerged into the school hall floored in forbidding, gleaming squares of black-and-white marble, 'is to be in your class and be ticked off by you.'

'Go away,' Liza said. 'Go away and don't be creepy.' But she was smiling.

In the lost property cupboard Justin's recorder lay where Liza had visualized it, in a box among other recorders, hockey sticks, pens, pencils and a butterfly net – the principle at Bradley Hall being to sort lost objects according to shape rather than category.

'There,' she said. 'What did I tell you?'

He blew into it experimentally to see if it remembered him.

'What do you say?'

He glared. He was at an age when manners seemed almost an hypocrisy.

'Thank you,' he said, but he was scowling. Then he went scuffing off down the passage, tooting intermittently, and Liza withdrew to the drawing room.

The sixth form liked their Daudet, after the initial and ritual complaints. For most of them, their only contact with the French was quarrelsome little episodes in queues for ski lifts in the Trois Vallées and thus they were incredulous of Daudet.

'Are you sure he was French?' one of them said.

'Absolutely.'

At break time, Liza made them all zip up their parkas before they lined up with the rest of the school in the orangery for milk and a biscuit and were subsequently released into the damp grey air. Herding them towards the old orchard – where they were not permitted to eat the apples since a seven year old had bitten inadvertently on a sleeping wasp – Liza was joined by Blaise O'Hanlon, wearing round his neck the whistle he used for football coaching. He simply walked beside her, saying nothing but listening to what she was saying to the children around her.

'Our baby's come home. Mummy brought it. It's got no hair and red feet.'

'I expect you had red feet when you were that little.'

'Mrs Logan, Simon's got my Snoopy and when I tried to get it he done bashed me in—'

'Simon—'

The toy came whirling through the air.

'Stupid Snoopy, stupid, stupid, stupid—'

'What is your baby's name?'

'Oh, it doesn't have a name. It's just a baby.'

'Our baby's called Oliver—'

'We had one but it grew up and now it's Naomi—'

'Snoopy's got a poo-face—'

'Mrs Logan, Simon said poo—'

The crowd jostled its way through the orchard gate and dispersed to race about and scream in obedience to expectations. Liza and Blaise strolled to a central position and waited for someone to fall off something or be knocked over, and Liza, in addition, waited for Blaise to flirt with her. He did not. He said, instead, rather sadly, that he had been homesick for Ireland all weekend and couldn't seem to stop thinking about it.

'Not Dublin so much, as the West. My father has a house in Connemara. I kept wanting to be in that house by the peat fire with proper Irish rain outside, not this milksop stuff.'

'Well, why don't you go? At half-term. Why don't you fly to Shannon and go?'

'I might,' Blaise said, and looked straight at her.

Two boys, in pursuit of a battered Bramley apple they were using as a football, came careering past, missed their footing in the slippery grass, collided and cannoned into Liza. She staggered back, off balance, and was caught deftly by Blaise.

He said, 'You idiotic, clumsy little sods,' and restored Liza gently upright. Then he did not take his arms away.

She said, 'Oh, thank you, Blaise, but really I'm fine.'

He said, 'Me, too,' still holding her.

She twisted to look in his face and it wore a new and serious expression. He made a tiny movement and, realizing that he was about to kiss her in the midst of a hundred and eighty-three children, she made a sudden and determined effort and broke free.

'*Blaise.*'

He said nothing. He merely gave her a long, hard look and then moved away, blowing his whistle to round up their charges. Liza felt breathless and strangely daring, a feeling not unlike the one she had experienced at breakfast when she told Archie he was behaving like a child. The two boys with the apple came up and said, looking at their feet, that they were sorry.

'It's all right,' Liza said. 'You slipped.'

They gaped.

'Didn't you?'

They nodded.

'Well, then. Off you go. End of break.'

They cantered off, howling. Liza thought of Mikey doing the same thing on his well-ordered Winchester playground. Then she thought of Thomas.

'What is it?' Blaise said, coming up.

Her eyes were huge.

'Thomas.'

'May I comfort you?'

'I – I don't think you'd better.'

He took her hand. She removed it.

'No.'

He sighed.

'Do you think I'm different today?'

Liza shot him a glance.

'A little gloomier—'

'The thing is,' Blaise said, 'that serious lust has turned into serious love. I'm in real pain.'

'Nonsense.'

'Liza—'

'Come on,' she said repressively, but her heart was very light. 'Come on. We have to get this lot unbooted and into class.'

Driving home after lunch, Liza stopped in the village to buy a postal order for a set of rubber dinosaurs Mikey had saved up for, from the back of a cereal packet. He had taught Imogen a dinosaur song that began 'Hocus, pocus, I'm a diplodocus' which she sang with the relentless repetitiveness of the Chinese water torture. When Thomas had had his dinosaur phase – as inevitable a part of childhood, it seemed, as losing milk teeth – he had suffered nightmares about a *Tyrannosaurus rex* which he could see circling in the beech trees on windy nights, clashing its leathery wings and gnashing its terrible teeth.

Mrs Betts liked Liza. She approved of her clean, pretty appearance, the deference she showed to senior Women's Institute members, and her suitable, socially responsible job. Liza, in her turn, tried not to be put off by Mrs Betts's refinement, bossiness and mauve mohair jerseys (today's had a pie-frill collar and three glass buttons) and to remember that Mrs Betts encouraged the kind of village community rallying that Colin Jenkins's wife declined to do.

'Now, Mrs Logan,' Mrs Betts said with an arch smile. 'I know you're not going to fail me.'

'I hope not,' Liza said.

Mrs Betts made a flourishing movement towards her anti-mud notice, and her coloured glass bracelets chinked together playfully.

63

'Naughty Dr Logan wouldn't sign this morning. Said he wasn't upset by Mr Prior and he didn't mind mud. All very well for you, I said, but what about poor Mrs Logan, visiting the old people down the lane that looks more like a field? To be perfectly honest, Mrs Logan, Mr Prior is taking more and more liberties with this village. I hear a nasty rumour that he wants to sell off the field next to your house for development. People like that have to be stopped early on, Mrs Logan. And that's where my petition comes in.'

Liza, who didn't in the least mind about the mud, but was alarmed at the threat of development, said, 'Are you sure about that? About the field next to us?'

Mrs Betts leaned forward.

'Between you and me, I've a friend on the local planning committee and he,' she paused so that Liza could draw interesting inference from the pronoun, inference flattering to Mrs Betts, 'gave me to understand that an application has been submitted by Mr Prior. No more than a hint, mind you. Just giving me fair warning.'

'When did you hear this?'

'Saturday night.'

Liza thought of Mrs Betts and her friend in the lounge bar of The Keeper's Arms, the pub in King's Stoke, their neighbouring village. It had wall-bracket lights, shaded in red imitation silk, and fake-tapestry cushions, and kept a range of country wines which proclaimed themselves to be made from elderflowers, and wheat and whortleberries. She could imagine Mrs Betts saying, 'Mine's a small port, please.'

'Oh dear,' Liza said. 'Have you told anyone?'

'Just yourself and Mrs Jago when she popped in for a "Get well" card. I would have mentioned it to Dr Logan but he was in such a rush—'

'Surgery,' Liza said appeasingly.

'Of course, Mrs Logan.'

Liza looked at the anti-mud petition. The Jagos hadn't signed nor had old Mrs Mossop's family, but everyone else down her lane had spelled themselves out in capital letters. Mrs Betts held out a menacing pen.

'Thank you, Mrs Logan. Such a help to have your support.'

Uncertainly, Liza signed. Mrs Betts pushed the postal order across the counter.

'I don't know who imagines we have a quiet life in the country, Mrs Logan. In my view, you can't let up for a minute—'

The door from the road opened and admitted a decisive-looking woman in a waxed cotton jacket and corduroy trousers tucked into shapely rubber riding boots. Mrs Betts smoothed her mohair bosom and braced herself.

'Good afternoon, Mrs Prior.'

Liza gathered up her postal order in panic. Her signature on the petition seemed twice the size of anyone else's.

'Hello, Susan. What a dreary day. Would you forgive me? I must dash. Imogen—'

The door banged behind her. Susan Prior glanced after her, glanced back at the counter, took in the petition and moved to the far end of the shop to examine, apparently, a rack of birthday cards.

'It is quite beyond me,' she said carelessly, her back to Mrs Betts, 'why people with the mentality of garden gnomes ever want to live in villages in the first place.'

At home, Sally was vacuuming the sitting-room carpet and Imogen was rushing at corners with a flamingo-pink feather duster.

'Thpiders, thpiders!'

Sally switched off the machine.

'There's two telephone messages on the kitchen table. And Mrs Mitchell says she'll bring Mikey back

65

as she's got to go into Winchester anyway.'

Imogen dropped the feather duster with a scream. A real spider, small but stout of heart, was advancing up the bamboo handle.

Sally said, 'Don't be silly, Imogen. Spiders are nice. Come and help me put him outside.'

Imogen scuttled behind Liza and buried her face in her skirt.

'Oh, Imo, what a cowardy—'

Sally carried the duster to the window and shook the spider out into the air. With Imogen still glued to her skirt, Liza hobbled away to the kitchen and discovered that one of the telephone messages was from Marina: 'Mrs de Breton says she will ring again later.' Good, Liza thought, attempting to detach Imogen with one hand while carrying the kettle with the other. Imogen, in order to show that this was a game, not a spider panic, would not be detached, however, but dragged herself behind Liza, clutching her skirt.

'Don't, darling.'

Imogen clung harder.

'Imogen, let go.'

Gripping the folds of brushed cotton in limpet hands, Imogen buried her face and shoved it hard against Liza's thigh.

'Stop it, Imogen. Let go and don't be such a stupid baby.'

Imogen pretended she could not hear. She breathed a hot damp patch through the fabric against Liza's thigh. The telephone rang. Dragging Imogen crossly behind her, Liza limped across the room.

'Hello?'

'Liza? My dear. It's Marina. I have to thank you for possibly the best Sunday ever. I detest Sundays but yesterday I adored.'

'We adored having you.'

Imogen opened her mouth wide, braced her teeth against Liza's skirt and bit as hard as she could.

'*Ow—*'

'My dear,' Marina said in alarm. 'What is happening?'

'My horrible little daughter. Wait a moment—'

Liza put down the receiver, seized Imogen and ran with her out of the room. Imogen was bawling now, her face scarlet and furious.

'Stay out there,' Liza said. 'Stay out, you beastly little girl.'

She shut the kitchen door and wedged a chair-back under the handle.

'I'm so sorry,' she said to Marina. 'Imogen suddenly bit me. I suppose it's her revenge for my going out to work.'

'Imogen? That angelic baby?'

'Not angelic,' Liza said. 'An angelic-looking fiend.'

Imogen was crashing some object on the far side of the door.

'Stop it!' Liza shouted.

There was a pause while Imogen considered the effect she was having, and then the crashing began again.

'Excuse me,' Liza said desperately.

She put down the telephone, moved the chair, opened the door and seized Imogen, running with her down the hall towards Sally. As she ran, Imogen tried to bite her again.

'Sally, I'm on the phone and she's being frightful—'

Sally, with whom Imogen was seldom frightful, put down her duster and took the child from Liza.

'Heading for a smacked bottom, I see.'

Liza ran back to the telephone

'Hello? Oh, I'm so sorry—'

'What would you say,' Marina said, 'to a day in London with me? Lunch, and perhaps an exhibition. Or a movie. I'd come down to you, but I'm sure it would be better for you to come up to me. I just feel—' She paused and then said with great warmth, 'I just feel you and I have a great deal to say to one another.'

'I'd love it,' Liza said, smiling into the telephone.

'Would you?'

'Oh yes—'

'Then,' said Marina, 'go get your diary. Right now. And we'll make a date.' She paused again, and then she said, 'It's time you had someone spoil you.'

Archie did not come in until twenty past ten. He had telephoned to say he would be late, and so Liza had eaten her share of supper after she had put the children to bed, and put the rest in a low oven for Archie. Then she took her marking in by the sitting-room fire and corrected seventeen dictées and fourteen comprehensions. When those were done and stowed efficiently away in the red canvas bag she used for school books, she made herself a mug of coffee and settled down to think what she would wear to go to London and have lunch with Marina. She had reached the guiltily excited conclusion that she had nothing suitable, and must therefore go shopping, when Archie came in, having organized an emergency ambulance to take a child with suspected meningitis into Winchester hospital. Having announced this, he pulled Liza out of her chair into his arms and said he was sorry about this morning. Liza said so was she. Then Archie kissed her and said he was starving, so Liza went away to the kitchen and returned with his supper on a tray.

Archie said, 'Why are you looking so pleased with yourself?'

'Am I?'

'Yes. Something nice happened?'

Liza thought of Blaise and of Marina.

'No. The reverse really. Imogen was ghastly while I was on the telephone and Mrs Betts told me Richard wants to build on the field next to us. Scared me, rather.'

'Why?' Archie said with his mouth full.

'Why?'

'It wouldn't affect us. We've got the trees between us.'

'Archie—'

He cut a canyon in his potato and wedged in a piece of butter.

'I've no objection to Richard making a bit of cash. And why shouldn't more people have the chance to live in the country?'

'Archie, it would ruin living here. Horrible little houses and horrible suburban people keeping themselves to themselves—'

'You little snob,' Archie said without heat.

She was pink with indignation.

'I'm not! How dare you? How can you be so obstinate? It would be awful to have the field built over. It – it would devalue the house—'

'I don't think so.'

'Archie,' Liza cried, standing up. 'Why don't you care?'

'I do,' he said. 'But not about this sort of thing. I care about people.'

She shouted, 'You are so bloody pleased with yourself.'

He put his knife and fork down and looked at her.

'You know I'm not.'

'Yes, you are. You are! Well, I'm sick of it. I'm sick of doing everything *you* think is right. I'm sick of being treated like a child. I'm sick of you being so patronizing and I'm sick of doing every damn blasted thing to please you all the time!' She paused for an angry breath and then she shouted, 'And I'm spending the day with Marina next week. In *London*.' And then she rushed out of the room.

When she had gone, Archie took two more increasingly unenthusiastic bites of supper and put the tray on the floor. He sat with his elbows on his knees and stared at the rug between his feet, half-thinking about Liza and half-wondering why these curious shapes and patterns should occur so naturally to the Afghan mind. After a moment or two the spaniel, who was called Nelson after an enthusiasm of Thomas's, inspired by seeing the Admiral's tiny embroidered swinging cot aboard the *Victory*, pushed the door open and began to take a powerful discreet interest in the remains on Archie's plate.

'Leave it,' Archie said.

Nelson sat down two feet from the tray and longed for it with every fibre of his being. Archie picked the tray up and carried it out to the kitchen, pausing on his return to listen up the stairwell. There was silence. Part of Archie had hoped for the excuse of hearing Liza crying, but there was no sound of any kind. He went to the telephone and rang Winchester hospital and was told that his child patient was about to have its lumbar puncture. He said he would ring back in an hour. Then he went back to the kitchen and made a mug of coffee and carried it back to the sitting room. As he crossed the hall, the bathroom door above him shut with decision.

He turned on the television, and then he turned it off again. He read the leader and letters page of the newspaper without absorbing any of it. He drank his coffee. He had a conversation with Nelson and disentangled several burs from his extravagant ears. Then he leaped up, crossed the room and bounded up the stairs two at a time, bursting into their bedroom to find Liza sitting up composedly in bed with her hair brushed, reading an article on the Church of England's neglect of the successful, in a Sunday paper. She did not look up.

'Liza,' Archie said.

'Mm?'

He sat on the edge of the bed.

'What is it?'

She looked at him briefly, then returned to her paper.

'I explained. Downstairs.'

'But it isn't true. I don't patronize you. I depend on you.'

She looked up again.

'You make me,' she said, 'feel limited and suburban and narrow. I might be all those things and I might, too, be fighting like anything against them.' She shook the paper slightly. 'It would be nice to be given a bit of credit now and then.'

'But I don't think these things. I don't think the same way as you about this development, but I can't see what that has to do with all these accusations.'

'That's exactly what I mean,' Liza said.

He put his hand out to her.

'Liza.'

'No,' she said. 'Just because you have the upper hand in bed—'

'But you like me to have the upper hand in bed—'

She turned her face away.

'Perhaps you shouldn't take so much for granted.'

He stood up.

'Jesus,' he said. 'This conversation might be happening in Hebrew for all I understand it.'

Liza said nothing. He lifted his fists and beat them lightly against his temples.

'Can you tell me, very simply, what we are talking about?'

Liza laid down the paper and folded her hands on it.

'You and me. Your attitude to me. Your assumptions about me. My self-knowledge telling me that many of those assumptions are unfair.'

'I see,' Archie said. He walked slowly round the bed, thinking, and came to a halt, looking down on Liza.

'And all this grew out of my not sharing your abhorrence at the prospect of new houses in the field next door?'

Liza bent her head.

'Oh God. Archie, you are so obtuse—'

He waited. She offered no further explanation.

After some moments he said, 'Clearly,' and then he went downstairs to telephone the children's ward at Winchester hospital once more.

Chapter Five

Marina de Breton took great trouble over Liza's day in London. She explained to Sir Andrew that it was sheer self-indulgence, plotting a treat for someone sufficiently unspoiled to appreciate one. All her stepgrand-children, a Kennedyesque brood of talent, instability and unceasing problems, had grown up so accustomed to the cushioning effect of the de Breton fortune that they were immune to the luxury of being imaginatively indulged. It had not taken her long to realize that her best gift to them was a brusquely humorous refusal to treat them as moneyed little stars, and an accompanying insistence on speaking to them as if they were both unremarkable and tiresome. This approach had won her a surprising amount of affection, but it did not allow her natural generosity much room for manoeuvre.

She was the only one of Louis de Breton's wives whom he had not divorced and she knew perfectly well that she owed this dubious distinction purely to the fact that he had died before he got round to it. She was quite clear in her own mind as to why she had married him which was that like some gifted, exhausted, moneyless Edith Wharton heroine she was absolutely sick of the brave struggle of managing on her own. Clever but inadequately educated, without family in America after the early deaths of both her improvident parents, she had married once, very young, a law student who had abandoned her a year later for the fellow student who was about to bear his baby. After that, she moved precariously from job to job, usually fund raising for, or promoting, small orchestras and ballet companies, or organizing minor exhibitions in out-of-the-way New York galleries, the unsteady pattern of this being given brief respites by a series of lovers, all of whom she managed to retain as friends after their return to their wives or the discovery of another mistress.

Louis de Breton arrived as a most unlikely fortieth birthday present. Large and overbearing, with all the outward mannerisms of a Tennessee Williams bully-boy, he came to a gallery opening Marina had organized because his oldest granddaughter had contributed the sculpture that stood in the centre of the main room, an angular column of rusting spears and pikes entitled *Woman With Two Horses* and priced at ten thousand dollars. Marina, dressed in narrow black trousers with a scarlet matador jacket she had made herself from a *Vogue* pattern, offered a glass of champagne to the burly man in a tuxedo standing in front of the sculpture. He looked at the champagne and said did she have any bourbon.

Then he waved a hand at *Woman With Two Horses* and said, 'Is this garbage?'

'Yes,' Marina said. 'I am afraid it is.'

'Overpriced garbage?'

'That, too.'

'My granddaughter made it.'

'In that case,' Marina said, 'I sincerely regret that it is garbage.'

Louis de Breton bellowed with laughter. Armed with his bourbon, he went round the gallery repeating Marina's remark. Particularly to the sculptor's mother, his daughter-in-law, who, he told Marina later, was a scheming bitch. Next day he sent Marina a coffin-sized box of orchids and asked her to dine with him. She agreed, on condition that he never sent her orchids again. So he sent her roses and lilies and stephanotis in pots and branches of forced lilac and posies of violets every day for six weeks. And then he married her.

She was not in the least in love with him. She found

him excellent company, generous, domineering and selfish. His physical appetites were both large and fickle, and he had never troubled to control his temper. For the first year he was willing, and at times even eager, to be both companion and confidant, but, if ever, unlike Scheherazade, her capacity to entertain him brilliantly and with novelty flagged even a little, he grew morose and then took himself off in search of more dissolute pleasures. Marina did not suffer too badly. In her mind, she had made a form of bargain with Louis de Breton, and was well aware that she had deliberately made her bed and must now lie on it. So, as far as possible, she relished her security, got to know as many of his exaggerated family as she could, enrolled herself in art history courses and took herself travelling. On the whole she declined to allow herself to feel lonely.

After eight years of this curious life, Louis de Breton died of a heart attack, and Marina could then confront the fact that he had wished to leave her for a Filipino beauty queen. The immense and infinitely complex will took almost four years to disentangle as past wives and mistresses emerged from the woodwork in a seemingly endless stream of claim and counterclaim, but Louis de Breton's wishes for his fifth and last wife were one of the few unequivocal elements in it. Marina was left with a substantial apartment on the Upper East Side, a sizeable income, and the administration of the Louis de Breton Foundation, which its founder had originally set up as a tax dodge but had then become irrationally fond of and had wished to be used for its true purpose. It became, for Marina, her first real career. It brought her occupation, preoccupation and a chance to exercise both her administrative skills and her long-unrequired benevolence. Then, in quest of Sir Andrew Logan, it brought her to London.

She telephoned him and asked him to dine with her. He said he would be delighted, and suggested the

Savoy Grill. They met at eight, drank a glass of champagne together and dined at Sir Andrew's usual table. They talked of everything except the purpose of the dinner which had been for Marina to suggest the funding of a *Meeting Medicine* series. When the bill was brought, Sir Andrew deftly removed it to his side of the table and extracted his cheque book.

'If you are going to behave like this,' Marina said, 'you will make talking business impossible.'

'Exactly.'

'Then please give that check to me.'

'If I give the bill to you,' said Andrew Logan, who had never made such a remark to a woman in his life before, 'then I shall not have a clear conscience about taking you to bed.'

She had blushed.

He finished writing the cheque, capped his fountain pen, put it away in an inside pocket and looked at her over his half-moon spectacles.

'Is there anywhere else you would prefer?'

She shook her head. She was speechless. He rose from the table, came round to move back her chair and offered her his arm.

'Then we should waste no more time.'

He had needed, as Marina put it to herself, a good deal of relaxing. But once relaxed, he had, in one of Louis de Breton's phrases, moved a mountain or two. Marina had arrived in London in late August and two months later she was still there. As far as she could see, there was no incentive to return to East 62nd Street and every incentive to remain in London. She moved out of her room in the Connaught and took a small serviced flat off Eaton Square where she and Andrew Logan conducted an infinitely pleasurable love affair, only interrupted by his work and visits to his flat in Victoria to take the telephone messages on his answering machine.

When he proposed marriage to her, he did it with

none of the assurance with which he had first proposed bed. It had been a most unhelpful time of day, just after breakfast, and it was plain that he had not meant to say anything so momentous, but she had inadvertently alarmed him, as she took away the coffee pot, by saying casually that she thought she ought to go back to New York and see how things stood.

He seized the coffee pot from her and then, still clutching it absurdly, said, 'You would not go for long—'

She looked surprised.

'No,' she said. 'I shouldn't think so.'

'And you would come back.'

'Andrew—'

'I must tell you that I could not bear it if you did not come back. I should not know how to live any more. Don't go, Marina. Don't leave me. Marry me. I beg of you, marry me.'

She reached out and gently took the coffee pot out of his hands and set it on the kitchen counter. It was a tiny kitchen, as efficient and flexible as a ship's galley, with scarcely space for two people to pass. So Marina hardly needed to move a step to put her arms round Andrew Logan.

'Of course I'll marry you.'

'You will?'

His eyes were closed.

'I'm afraid,' she said, 'that I've assumed I was going to for at least the last month.'

He began to laugh. He said, 'Thank God. Oh, thank God,' and then he said he must take her down to Hampshire and introduce her to Archie.

'But not as your fiancée.'

'Not?'

'No,' Marina said. 'One shock at a time.'

Privately, she thought she would tell Liza first. Even, remembering the rumblings of emotional thunder she had heard in Archie's presence, ask Liza how to break the news. There was a strong possibility of a particular bond between herself and Liza, a chance of the kind of intimate female friendship that enriches all the other relationships the participants have. Marina thought, with wonder, that she was about to be very blessed, and, when she thought that, it made her cry. Andrew Logan, who had shrunk from women's tears all his life, adored it when she cried.

'You're nothing short of a miracle for Andrew,' Liza said, spearing a radicchio leaf out of her salad. 'It's written all over him. I've never seen him like this. I thought he was a dear, right from the start, but such a buttoned-up Scot. You know. And now—' She put the radicchio into her mouth and waved her fork. 'Now he's absolutely illluminated.'

Marina said, 'It's quite miraculous for me, too.'

Liza, full of excellent gnocchi and Soave and a beautiful morning of watercolours in a Cork Street gallery and taxi rides and being given a green cashmere jersey that Marina said was entirely made for Liza and which she insisted on buying ('Well, if you won't take it now, I shall simply wait and give it to you at Christmas'), said generously, 'I do hope you will marry,' and then blushed.

'Oh, we will,' Marina said. 'As soon as we can tell everyone.'

'Archie?'

'Archie.'

Liza picked up her wine glass and held it by the rim and looked down into it.

'It isn't personal, you know,' she said. 'It isn't you. It's anyone. It's having his father all to himself, all his life, and no mother.'

Marina said, 'I wouldn't dream of mothering him. Or depriving him of his father in any way that is his.'

'I know. I don't think it has anything to do with logic.'

'Of course not.'

Liza looked up.

'He's frightfully emotional, you see. He takes things to heart so much. When he loves people, he really loves them.'

She could feel silly, faintly tipsy tears pricking at the thought of Archie's loving-heartedness.

'I can see all that,' Marina said.

Liza bent her head. She was filled at once with remorse at her recent behaviour towards Archie and a simultaneous and sudden recollection of Blaise O'Hanlon saying to her, 'I'm in real pain.' Marina watched her.

'What is it?'

Liza said, 'Oh. Oh, nothing really. Just some stupid cross-purposes—'

'Your little boy?'

'Thomas? Partly. And other things.' Liza raised her head and said boldly, 'Sometimes, I feel so inadequate. Archie's so – so wholehearted, he lives so generously, he—' She made a little negative gesture. 'He's such a thorough human being, if you know what I mean. And then I feel that I can't measure up to the size of him. I am so much bolder away from him; I feel so much more confident. It's almost as if he is—' She stopped, and after a tiny pause said more firmly, 'I know he isn't judging me. I don't mean *that*.'

Marina made a competent sign to a waiter for coffee.

'What I don't see,' she said, 'is why you should want to be like him. Why you aren't pleased and proud to be yourself.'

Liza said, flattered, and thus without complete conviction, 'England is absolutely full of girls like me.'

Marina said, laughing. 'Don't be absurd,' and reached out and took Liza's hand. 'I think maybe you just need your husband to yourself. Maybe it's time Archie was weaned off his father.'

'Espresso,' the waiter said, in caricature Italian,

putting a tiny cup in front of each of them.

'It isn't that they aren't both kind to me,' Liza said earnestly. 'It's more—' She paused, anxious to be quite fair and entirely honest. 'It's more that Archie feels his father understands everything about him so instinctively and, vice versa, that he doesn't really need to try completely to understand me.'

Marina drank her coffee and wondered what it really was that Liza was trying to say. She knew from long experience what it was like to live with someone who baffled you, or denied you access to vital areas of themselves, and perhaps there were parts of Archie he had never transferred from his father's guardianship to his wife's. Perhaps, too, those things were in better hands with Andrew than with Liza? But Liza, Marina thought, watching her unwrap an almond biscuit from its tissue paper, wasn't greedy; she just wanted what most humans wanted, to be loved and also to be acknowledged.

Although she perfectly well knew the answer to her next question, Marina leaned forward a little and said, 'Do you think all this would be helped if I were to marry Andrew?'

Liza nodded vehemently.

'Good,' Marina said. 'So do I.'

'Does he talk about Archie much?'

'Not an abnormal amount.'

Liza said with a tiny pride, 'I was engaged to someone else when he met me.'

'I know. I heard. He bore you off.' Andrew had also said, 'I was so relieved it was little Liza. Archie had had such a turbulent love life, violent enthusiasms followed by violent antipathies, everything from shop-girl waifs of seventeen to a terrifying divorcee of forty-four who prowled about after Archie simply growling with lust—' Marina smiled at Liza. 'Andrew was so pleased it was you.' She leaned across the table again. 'Now, my dear, we are going to a movie in a darling little movie theatre I have discovered full of armchairs. And then I shall make you promise solemnly to come and see me again soon. And then I shall let you go home.'

'It's been *perfect*,' Liza said. She picked up the sleek carrier bag that held her new jersey and peered inside with a little sigh of contentment. 'Should I tell Archie?'

'About my marrying his father? No. No, I don't think so. Wouldn't you think it only right that his father should do that?'

Archie had resolved that he would not allow Liza's day with Marina to become an issue. If she wanted to make a private mystery of it, he would let her, and would simply hope that whatever grievance it was that she had against him would become either clear to him, or evaporate. So he asked her about the practicalities of the day, envied the acclaimed French film she had seen, said, 'Oh, Liza, it makes me think of Lucca,' when she mentioned the gnocchi, and admired the jersey which was, as he said, a dozen cuts above any jersey that had ever entered Beeches House before. Then he kissed her, said, 'I'm so glad it was fun,' and went away to read C. S. Lewis to Mikey, leaving Liza in the kitchen feeling at once slightly superior and mildly frustrated.

When he came down, they had supper together and the telephone did not, for once, ring at all. They talked about incidents in the practice and incidents at Bradley Hall and not about Marina or Andrew or the threatened development. While Archie was peeling an apple, the telephone did ring at last, unable to contain itself, but it was not a patient for Archie, but Chrissie Jenkins, the Vicar's wife, for Liza, who wanted to know if Liza would stand in for her at Sunday School this week, as her mother at Lymington was ill and she had to go down there for the day. Liza, thinking of the restaurant at lunchtime, the shop where Marina had bought her

81

jersey, the luxurious plushy darkness of the cinema, and contrasting all these with Stoke Stratton village hall on a Sunday morning, and Lynne Tyler playing the sad, damp piano with several vital notes missing, said yes, without much grace.

'I wouldn't ask,' Chrissie Jenkins said, whose whole life was dedicated to getting other people to do parish work in order to show the world that she was married to Colin and not to God, 'if it wasn't a bit of an emergency. She relies on me, you see, being a trained nurse.'

'No, it's fine,' Liza said.

'We're doing the miracles this term. I expect little Imogen's told you. It's the feeding of the five thousand this week, and we were going to act it out. Lynne says she'll bring brown bread cut into fish shapes, and will you bring white? And a little basket or two—'

'Yes,' Liza said. 'Yes.'

'Thank you ever so much,' Chrissie said. 'I know how you like to do your bit.'

'Cow,' Liza said, putting the telephone down.

It rang again at once, and this time it was Cyril Vinney, old Mrs Mossop's son-in-law, to say his sciatica was so bad he didn't know how he was going to make it through the night.

'And the awful thing is,' Archie said, collecting his bag, 'that I wouldn't much care if he didn't.'

Stoke Stratton village hall had been built just after the war. It was a wooden-framed hut, gloomily creosoted, with metal window frames painted municipal-green. It consisted of one oblong room from whose ceiling hung, alternately, ineffective electric heating bars and unenthusiastic lighting strips, and, at one end, a grim little kitchen and a pair of institutional lavatories. The Women's Institute, at the instigation of Mrs Betts, had made flowered curtains for the windows and contributed a square of orange-and-brown speckled carpet which swam, isolated, at one end of the polished wooden floor. But for all its charmlessness, Stoke Stratton was proud to have a village hall. Not only were there functions in it twice or thrice weekly – badminton, old-time dancing, Young Wives, Evergreen Club, Mother and Toddler Group, Poetry Circle, Ramblers' Club, Village Preservation Society, Gardeners' Club, jumble sales, Christmas fayres, harvest suppers, P C C meetings, Youth Group discos – but Stoke Stratton graciously rented it to neighbouring King's Stoke and Lower Stoke, neither of whom boasted such an amenity.

On Sunday mornings, Colin Jenkins turned the heaters on, on his way back from early communion, so that by the time the Sunday School assembled, they could only just see their breaths before them. It was the only Sunday School in the three villages, and provided a blessed child-free hour on Sunday mornings for parents who could be bothered to deliver and collect. Liza, armed with half a loaf – 'Shouldn't it be pitta?' Archie had asked unhelpfully – and several small bread baskets, arrived to find a dozen little children sitting at a trestle table colouring in simplistic pictures of the raising of Jairus's daughter. Imogen, who knew the form, ran to battle her way into a place at the table and corner the crayons she wanted, but Mikey hung back and said he thought he'd just watch.

'But why? Why don't you join in?'

He put his face babishly into Liza's side.

'I don't want to.'

Lynne Tyler, a valiant and friendly woman whose husband was Richard Prior's cowman, came out of one of the lavatories holding by the hand a shrew-faced child clutching a blue plastic handbag.

'We do this all morning,' Lynne said to Liza. 'In and out. She won't go alone and she won't do anything when I take her.'

'Can't you ignore her?'

'Last time I did, we had a disaster. Now come on, Kirsty. You sit down and do your drawing.'

'Wanna wee—'

'No, you don't,' Liza said, lifting her firmly on to the bench next to Imogen. Imogen clamped a hand on the nearest pile of crayons.

'Mine,' Imogen said.

Kirsty began to cry.

Liza said, 'Let's just start. Mikey, let go. Do you usually start with a prayer?'

'Oh no,' Lynne said, almost shocked at such a pedestrian idea. 'We have a little song. Don't we? Imogen, you tell Mummy what we sing.'

Imogen fixed Liza with an implacable stare.

' "Jethuth," ' said Imogen clearly, ' "wanth me for a thunbeam." '

'There now,' Lynne said, and went to the piano.

All the children climbed off the benches and clustered round her, all except Kirsty, who sat where she was and watched a trickle of pee run from under her skirt on to the floor. Sighing, Liza went to the kitchen for a bucket and a cloth.

'Jesus wants me for a sunbeam,' the children sang unevenly. 'Jesus wants me for a star. I am Jesus's little rainbow. Shining, shining from afar.'

They subsided raggedly on to the Women's Institute carpet.

'Hands together, eyes closed,' Lynne said, swivelling on the piano.

'We pray for our homes and our families. Sit still, Adam. And for our mummies and our daddies and our brothers and our sisters—'

'And our dog.'

'And our dog, Stephen. We thank you for the lovely countryside. And our food and drink. And all our friends. And we ask you to look after everyone we know who isn't well. And now,' said Lynne, 'Imogen and Mikey's mother is going to tell you the story.'

84

'Wanna wee,' Kirsty said loudly.

Lynne got up patiently, but Liza seized Kirsty and dumped her on the bucket she had brought from the kitchen.

'You can sit there and pee to your heart's content.'

Kirsty hit Liza with her handbag. Lynne looked deeply shocked at the whole episode.

'Is she a Vinney?'

'Yes,' Lynne said.

'That explains it then,' Liza said heartlessly. 'Don't worry. I'll face any music there is. Don't move,' she said to Kirsty. 'Until I say.'

Kirsty subsided slowly down into the bucket until she was doubled up. Then she began to howl. At this moment, the door at the end of the hall opened and Blaise O'Hanlon came in. Everybody stared, particularly Liza.

'Hello,' Blaise said. 'Hello, kiddiwinks. Hello, Liza.' He held a hand out to Lynne. 'Hello.'

'What are you doing here?'

'I came with a message from June,' Blaise said. 'About Tuesday. Dan has ploughed up the telephone cable with the rotavator so she couldn't ring. I went to your house and your nice doctor husband said you were here with loaves and fishes. Why is that child in a bucket?'

'It's the best place for her,' Liza said.

Blaise went over and pulled Kirsty upright.

'You are very unattractive,' he said to her with enormous charm. 'And you smell like a fishing smack. But I don't see why you should be condemned to a bucket.'

Kirsty gazed up at him with rapture.

'This is Mr O'Hanlon,' Liza said to Lynne. 'He teaches at Bradley Hall School.'

Lynne smiled at him, partly out of natural friendliness and partly because he had been kind to Kirsty.

'What message?' Liza said.

Blaise was wandering about among the children.

'I'll tell you afterwards. Mayn't I stay and help? I say, are you Mikey? I remember you from a football match. You run like the wind.'

Mikey blushed and nodded vigorously.

'We'd be only too pleased if you'd stay, Mr O'Hanlon,' Lynne said. 'Now, hands up who's going to be Jesus.'

'I'll be Jesus,' Blaise said. 'And then I can get this lot organized. Now, come on. I'll have you, and you, and you over there in green trousers, as disciples, and the poor bucket child can be the boy who brought the fishes. And the rest of you can be the multitude. Who can tell me what a multitude is?'

'I'm so sorry,' Liza said to Lynne, 'I really am. He's being impossible.'

'Oh no. No, he isn't. You can see he's a born teacher. I think it's lovely he wants to help.'

Liza went over to a grey plastic chair and sat down, half indignant, half enchanted. In a matter of moments, Blaise had the multitude seated on the carpet – 'Now don't go near the edge because it is the sea and you will drown' – and was standing before them with his arms outspread and the disciples jostling each other to be the ones completely next to him.

'It had been a long, hot day,' Blaise said, half an eye on Liza. 'And you lot in the crowd had been wandering about after Jesus all day without a *thing* to eat or a *drop* to drink—'

Lynne tiptoed round to sit next to Liza.

'He has a real gift, hasn't he?' she whispered. 'And he's ever so young.'

'He's ever so naughty,' Liza said with emphasis.

'Sweet face—'

'And then one of the disciples – it'd better be you, Green Trousers – said, "Master, there's a boy here with two loaves and five fishes." Or was it five loaves and two fishes? Can't remember. Doesn't matter. And then you, little Miss Bucket, come up – come on, come here – and show me and all the others what you have got in your basket.'

Kirsty held up her basket so high that nobody could see.

'Can't see, can't see,' complained the multitude.

'If you are tiresome, Miss Bucket,' Blaise said, 'I shall deprive you of your starring role and dump you back in the chorus.'

Kirsty knelt on the carpet and put her basket on the floor and the multitude crowded round and pawed it and spilled the loaves and the fishes.

'Pick it all up,' Blaise said. 'Or I shall go away and leave you unprotected from frightening Mrs Logan.'

'Poor little Kirsty,' Lynne said. 'It's lovely to see someone take notice of her.'

'And of course all the disciples said there won't be anything like enough for five thousand people and Jesus said just you *wait*. Now, Green Trousers, you take a basket, and Mikey another, and little Ginger Specs, you have this one, and take them round the multitude – and do you know, there was heaps and heaps, the baskets were always full and everyone ate so much they had to lie on the ground groaning like you do at Christmas. Oh dear, Miss Bucket, what are you snivelling about now?'

Kirsty held out a diamond-shaped slice of brown bread.

'I don't like fish—'

'Brilliant!' Blaise said. He spun round on Liza. 'Hear that? Amazing. Oh, the power that is mine—'

Liza got up.

'Which I'm now going to take away. Go and sit down and let Lynne and me finish in peace—'

'I'm sure you're very welcome,' Lynne said loudly, rising too and determined to show Blaise some Christian courtesy. 'Very welcome to stay, indeed. Isn't he?' she said to the children who all chorused enthusiastically in agreement. 'Shall we teach him our butterfly song? Come along, Imogen. You show Mr O'Hanlon the movements we do.'

She went over to the piano and struck a chord.

'If I were a butterfly, I'd thank you, Lord, for giving me wings. And if I were a robin in a tree, I'd thank you, Lord, that I could sing—'

Waving his wings and opening and shutting his beak, Blaise O'Hanlon smiled in triumph at Liza over Imogen's energetic head.

'Well,' Liza said later, in the lane, 'what was the message?'

'What message?'

'The message you came with so urgently from June who cannot telephone because Dan has inadvertently ploughed up the cable.'

'There isn't one. And actually, the telephone cable at Bradley Hall is overhead and a very unsightly thing it is too.'

Liza stopped walking.

'Then what is this pantomime all about?'

'I wanted to see you. I couldn't wait until Tuesday. I had to see you. I had to see where you lived.'

'We live at Beeches House,' Mikey said helpfully.

'I know that now,' Blaise said. 'But I didn't before and I longed to. So I came.'

Grasping Imogen's hand tightly, Liza began to walk very fast up the lane. Blaise and Mikey ran to keep up with her.

'I can't think about anything else,' Blaise hissed.

Imogen began to grizzle and drag backwards.

'Imo, come on. Blaise, I can't have this kind of conversation here. I can't have this kind of conversation anyway, I mean. Imogen, I shall spank you.'

Imogen wrested her hand free and flumped down on the road. Blaise dropped back and picked her up.

'I won't embarrass you,' he said, hurrying after Liza

with his burden. 'I won't hang around. I just had to have a sight of you, that's all. Couldn't you just say one nice thing to me to keep me going until Tuesday?'

Liza said nothing.

'It does seem a bit hard,' Blaise said, panting slightly. 'You could spare me a crumb, really you could.'

Liza said, 'You're making a fool of me—'

'No,' Blaise said. 'No.'

He stopped and set Imogen abruptly on her feet.

'Look at me.'

Liza halted and slowly turned to face him six feet away.

'You're not just lovely,' Blaise said almost diffidently, 'but you're different. You're special. And the thing that turns my heart over is that you don't realize that you are.' He put a hand on Imogen's head. 'If you only knew the power that is yours.'

Liza gazed.

After a moment, Blaise sighed and took his hand away from Imogen and said to Mikey, 'I ought to go, you know. Would you like to look at my car before I do? It's a Morgan and although I terribly disapprove of showing off, I must tell you that it has wire wheels.'

Chapter Six

Stratton Farm lay a few hundred yards up the lane from Beeches House. The farmhouse was an amiable building on to whose Tudor and Jacobean ramblings a prosperous eighteenth-century owner had slapped a graceful Georgian façade. It was constructed of comfortable pinkish brick under a mellowed tiled roof, and, at a respectful distance from it, across a space of admirably kept garden, lay the farmyard and the stables. The whole looked thriving and unpretentious, a working farm whose owner's chief interests lay in horses and herbaceous borders. Even the pig unit – highly successful and the reason for the briskly authoritative columns that Richard Prior contributed to country magazines – was hidden behind a line of stalwart Victorian barns, and veiled in Virginia creeper.

The Priors had lived at Stratton Farm all their married life. The house and four hundred acres had been a joint wedding present from Richard's father and uncle, whose sole descendant he was. Twenty-five years later, the acreage had grown to over seven hundred, and pigs had brought Richard prosperity. Susan Prior had borne him two laconic sons and was an admired horsewoman and trainer of gun dogs. Richard, a lean, lounging man, was renowned for his lack of sentiment. 'If it doesn't work,' he would say candidly at parochial church council meetings, of motions whose inspiration owed more to emotion than pragmatism, 'then scrap it.'

The Priors' social moral code was essentially Whiggish. Their farm workers lived in sound cottages and

90

were expected to return good labour for fair treatment. The Priors could always be relied upon in a crisis and equally to be very plainspoken about any kind of dishonesty or slacking. This paternalistic attitude spread to their view of the village. 'I don't mind a few city ponces like you,' Richard often said to Simon Jago, who was a senior merchant banker. 'But only a few. Villages are for villagers.'

'Mr Prior,' Mrs Betts of the post office would confide to her planning officer friend on Saturday nights, 'lacks what I call common courtesy. He may have been born a gentleman but I'm afraid you'd often never know it. Quite frankly, I wouldn't address a dog in the way Mr Prior sometimes speaks to the Vicar.'

'Frightful woman,' Richard Prior said of Mrs Betts. 'And as for Jenkins, you could wring him out. No wonder the Church of England is going to the dogs, full of lefty wimps like him.'

When he submitted his planning application for developing the field below Beeches House, Richard Prior knew exactly what his motives were. Half of them were businesslike – the best economic use for an awkward field that had never proved successful for grazing or planting – and the other half were social. Watching the Stoke villages fill up with weekenders and commuters to Southampton and retired people had disturbed him greatly. The miscellaneous cottages, which had once sat realistically and appealingly in gardens where cabbages, dahlias, washing, hens and motorbike spares jostled for space among the nettles, were increasingly being bijoued up into Hansel and Gretel dwellings, gleaming with new paint and fresh thatch and sprouting incongruous carriage lamps and fanciful name-plates. The gardens, fenced, hedged, trimmed up and squared off, were disciplined into anonymity, the flowerbeds dug so assiduously as to resemble chocolate-cake crumbs.

And with the refinement came price rises. Children

91

born in Stoke Stratton cottages and wishing, in turn, to raise their own children there, were driven by the cost of it to the faceless housing estates on the edges of Winchester and Southampton. Old Mrs Mossop and her Vinney children only remained where they were because Richard Prior owned the cottages and would not turn them out in Mrs Mossop's lifetime on account of her dead husband who had worked tirelessly at Stratton Farm all Richard's time there, refusing to take any holiday that did not coincide with those dictated by the Church calendar. Even when Granny Mossop died, Richard did not plan to turn the Vinneys out. He was well aware that their shiftless, expedient way of life was as much a part of the village as old Mr Mossop's obdurate industry had been; all he would actually draw the line at was employing a Vinney.

Indeed, in his view, the Vinneys and the Mossops, the Carters and the Durfields, and all the other village families whose ancestors lay in Stoke Stratton church-yard, should all be able to remain living among their roots. It was, in his opinion, both right and natural. To this end, he proposed to build on the controversial field one substantial house which would make a fine profit, and, at the opposite end, half a dozen simple, two-bedroomed cottages to be let to young couples who had not been born more than ten miles from the village.

'It's the only way,' he said to Archie Logan, 'to keep this village going and to defeat the electric lawn mower brigade.'

They were sitting at the kitchen table at Beeches House, with Richard's plans spread out on the table between them, weighted at the corners with tumblers, and a jug of water and a bottle of whisky.

'I'm afraid it'll mean a bit of mess and noise for you for a year,' Richard said without adjusting his tone to apology. 'But we'll try and minimize that.'

Archie bent over the plans. He was doing his best to

ignore Liza, who sat at the other end of the table, sewing name tapes on to Mikey's new games clothes, and pointedly not saying anything. Richard, who was used to living in a household where people only spoke if they had something constructive to say, was perfectly used to silence and saw nothing sinister in Liza's. She sewed with little quick jabbing stitches, occasionally pausing to give the plans and Archie a look of contempt.

The plans showed the big house at the Beeches House end of the field, and cottages clustered at the far end. A belt of trees would screen the one from the other, and all they would share would be the access entrance from the lane. The big house would have an acre of garden and a pleasant, unremarkable view across fields and hedges to the church tower and some jumbled village roofs. The cottages would each have an oblong garden at the back and a communal space of grass between them for their children to play on together.

Archie said he thought it all looked jolly good. Liza thought it looked horrible. The big house would attract people of the mentality she had grown up with, and now thoroughly despised, and the cottages would blare rock music all weekends and their inhabitants would hang their washing out permanently and let their children scream like a school playground. She did not wish to say any of this in front of Archie or Richard, both of whom would think her very uncharitable and small-mindedly snobbish, and both of whom she might resentfully think were right. So she sat and sewed and thought, as she did a great deal, of Blaise O'Hanlon, and, as she did only slightly less, of Marina.

It was, quite literally, spell-binding to have someone so in love with her. She was quite sure she was not in love back but she was absolutely fascinated by Blaise's feelings. She went over and over them with wonder and, when she looked in the mirror to brush her hair or put on her ear-rings, she tried to see herself as Blaise saw her, tried to see both the freshness and the mystery he said she had. Her consciousness of his infatuation – she was determined to label it sensibly so – made her feel different physically: elated, shining-eyed, power-ful. And everything Marina had said to her confirmed these sensations. 'I don't see,' Marina had said to her, 'why you aren't pleased and proud to be yourself.'

'Mrs Betts,' Richard Prior said to Archie, 'is forming a Stoke Stratton Preservation Society.'

Archie made a face.

'She's a powerful lobbyist,' Richard went on. 'She'll rally all her ramblers, you know. I just have to make sure I've got quality and leave quantity to her. I thought I'd start with you and Simon Jago. And I might succeed with the Vicar on sociological grounds.'

'I'll see Simon,' Archie said. 'I don't think Simon will be any problem.' He looked at Liza. 'Do you, darling?'

She gave him a blank look. He raised his eyebrows and shrugged, but said nothing. If Liza wished to score off him – as she so often seemed to, just now – then he would not give her the satisfaction of doing it in front of Richard Prior.

Liza raised her sewing to her mouth and bit off a thread, saying between her teeth as she did so, 'I don't suppose Simon Jago would disapprove of any money-making scheme.' She emphasized the 'money'.

Richard Prior looked at her briefly, and without admiration. Then he said to Archie, 'I thought we'd plant a hedge the far side of your beeches, to give you a bit of cover. And I'll stick up some hurdles until it's grown.' He stood up and put his tumbler down on the part of the plan where the cottages would stand. 'I'll leave these with you for now to ruminate over.'

'I'll ring you,' Archie said. 'I'll ring you when I've had a think.'

Richard Prior went to the outside door, the steel rims to his brogue heels ringing on the floor.

'Good man.' He nodded minimally at Liza. 'Thanks for the dram.'

'Why,' Liza said when the door had closed behind him, 'why do you have to be so wet? Why agree? He's heaps rich enough. Why help him to be richer?'

'That isn't the point.'

'Oh. Really.'

'No,' Archie said. 'No. The point is what he is trying to do for the village.'

'But he doesn't have to live with the results! He won't have a Vinney-type slum on his doorstep! It's easy to be so noble from the safe distance of Stratton Farm.'

Archie began to fold up the plans with elaborate carefulness.

'The cottages,' he said in the level voice he used in practice meetings when he was, as he usually was, in a minority, 'the cottages will be at least a hundred yards away. There will be our belt of beeches, a new hedge, a new house and garden, and a new stand of trees between them and us.'

Liza said, 'Don't speak to me in that awful voice.'

'I don't know how to speak to you,' Archie said.

Liza took a breath. How to tell him, how to reach his true understanding and tell him that she had come to the end of a particular road on the map of their marriage, the road along which he had so far led her – lovingly, generously, but led her – by the hand. She had drawn level with him now and sometimes she wanted to step off the road for a moment and be alone. And she wanted him to recognize this, to recognize that things did not always stay as they always had been, that needs changed and so did capabilities. Liza wanted Archie to recognize *her*.

She said, in as gentle a voice as she could manage, 'You speak to me as if my point of view couldn't possibly have the validity of yours because I'm me and you are you and all that that implies. Why can't you speak to me with the courteous interest you speak with to other people?'

Archie said, 'I was under the impression that I was being perfectly polite. And of course I am interested in what you think. I just don't think you have thought far enough or widely enough.'

'And I,' said Liza, 'think you are a pompous prig.'

He waited, out of hope and long experience, for her to cry. If she cried, then he could go round the table, and kneel by her chair and hold her and kiss her bee-stung mouth and comfort her. Comforting her was a way of getting close to her and Archie relied upon being close to her. But Liza didn't cry. She did not even look remotely as if she might. She folded the last pair of marked socks into a tube, put them neatly beside the others on the pile of shorts and shirts and rose to carry them to a chair by the door, ready to go upstairs.

Then she walked back to the oven, opened the door and said to Archie without turning round, 'Perhaps you would lay the table. It's fish pie and salad, so we only need forks.'

'I love your fish pie,' Archie said.

He began to open drawers and cupboards in search of glasses and forks and plates, and then to put them on the table with uncharacteristic precision. Lining up a fork parallel to a plate, he said, 'Liza—'

'Yes?' she said, without turning from the stove.

'I don't quite know how to put this, but I haven't changed. I love you and I esteem you, as I always have. None of that has changed.'

She came forward to the table with the fish pie between her hands, swaddled in a cloth. The top was golden-brown and speckled with parsley.

'Oh yes,' Liza said lightly. 'I know that. In fact, it's part of the trouble. It's me who's changed. That's the difference, now.'

*

96

Even though they were brother and sister, it was rare for June and Dan Hampole to eat together at night. For one thing, June preferred a tray on her knee in her sitting room with the basset hounds and absolutely anything that happened to be on television, while Dan, having spent such days as he did spend at Bradley Hall, drifting about tinkering and fiddling with the electrics and the plants in the conservatory, wanted the evening to be something of an occasion. And for another, June liked eggs and baked beans and toast and anything else she could eat without looking at it, and these tastes offended Dan. He liked to take a great deal of trouble over complicated food, and then, having donned an elderly black velvet dressing gown that made him look like a decadent prior, to eat it at a proper table with wine and candles and conversation. As the Hampoles had been brought up to regard cleanliness as suburban rather than godly, these stately evenings of Dan's, smeared with candle-grease and spilled wine, resembled Miss Havisham's mouldering wedding breakfast. The food was always excellent but it was imperative that no non-Hampole observed the extreme casualness with which Dan cooked it in a kitchen where cats roamed unchecked across the table tops and mice grew stout and brazen in the unswept corners. Once a month or so, spurred on by something particularly successful he had achieved with a rabbit or a partridge, Dan would invade June's study and say, 'Tonight's a night, old duck,' and she would reluctantly abandon her burrow and pin some of her mother's brooches on her jerseys and cardigans, and join Dan in what was originally the dining room but was now given over to history lessons.

Since Blaise's arrival, world history had taken on a wild and romantic aspect, with a strong bias in favour of bloodshed and Irish struggles. The long wall that faced the windows had been stripped of its pictures – these were now hanging densely in Dan's private apartments – and made into a giant pinboard for pictures and posters of great battles with the Battle of the Boyne in prime position in the centre.

Spooning an orange and port sauce over June's partridge, Dan waved at the wall above him and said, 'You'll have to speak to him, you know.'

June, who was thinking how comical it was to be sitting at a Regency snap-top table in a sea of pupils' desks, before a great branched candelabra and a decanter of claret, said rather absently, 'Speak to whom?'

'To Blaise.'

'Why must I speak to Blaise? He's being very peaceable just now. How inky this room smells.'

'He's being very peaceable because he is up to something.'

'But you're always up to something and I never speak to you, although I often think I should.' Dan put a glistening plateful down in front of her. 'Oh, poor little bird. I do wish partridges didn't mate for life. Out there, there will be a sorrowing widower.'

'Oh no, there won't because here he is. June, the things I get up to, I get up to miles away from Bradley Hall. Blaise is getting up to his thing right under your dear but unobservant nose.'

June stared.

'What thing?'

Dan settled himself opposite her and flourished open a huge and dingy napkin.

'Darling June, Blaise is trying to persuade little Mrs Logan to fall in love with him.'

'Nonsense.'

'Not nonsense. Fact.'

'Perfect nonsense. She is an irreproachable wife and mother and she has far too much sense. Anyway, Blaise is very annoying and not at all seductive.'

Dan said, with his mouth full, 'You are not Mrs Logan. You are his exasperated aunt.'

98

'I think this is all mischief. I expect he has a crush and it will wear off, like all crushes. In any case, what evidence have you?'

'My eyes,' Dan said, in the voice of Long John Silver. 'I saw her swoon in the orchard and be clasped in his arms.'

'*Swoon?*'

'She was knocked flying by some rampaging little toads. But she stayed swooning for far longer than was decent and eluded being kissed by a hair's breadth. And he hangs about for her and whispers to her and writes her torrid letters.'

'Dan,' June said, putting down her knife and fork. 'How do you know that?'

'Because I went to his room on Sunday morning when he had mysteriously vanished, and not to Mass, in search of my field glasses which he had borrowed and not returned, and there on his table lay a letter, which I read, in which he told Mrs Logan that he knew he was in love because he wished for her happiness even more than his own and that this had never happened to him before.'

'Bosh,' June said.

'Too true.'

June thought for a moment, chewing, and then she said, 'Of course, it's very isolated here for a boy used to a city, so I suppose you can't blame him for daydreaming. But I absolutely refuse to believe that Liza Logan encourages him in any way. She might be kind to him but she wouldn't let him take a single liberty. I am quite sure of that.'

'I think,' Dan said, spooning up his gravy with loud slurps, 'I think you should ask her if Blaise is being a nuisance. And see if she blushes.'

'I'll do no such thing! She is a valued member of staff and I wouldn't insult her. But I will keep an eye on Blaise. Can't you take him up to London with you sometimes?'

'The whole point about London,' Dan said weightily, 'as you well know, is that nobody knows where I go or what I do. Blaise tagging along would be a nightmare.'

'Where is he now?' June said suddenly.

'Gone to the pub. He's a great hit at the pub. Why? Did you fear he'd gone to moon about under Mrs Logan's windows?'

'Certainly not.'

'I'd keep an eye,' Dan said, tipping the decanter to pour wine inaccurately into both their glasses. 'It's your school and your staff and all that, but I'd keep an eye, if I were you. Young men can be so – so *rapacious*.'

On one of her days off school, while Sally oversaw Mikey's homework and put Imogen to bed, and Archie was still doing evening calls, Liza went round to see Diana and Simon Jago. She did not tell Archie she was doing this and she did not yet know what she would say when he discovered she had been, but neither consideration deflected her. Diana Jago was a friend, a true friend, and Simon, inaccessible behind his carapace of English public-school blandness, was always very gallant to her, and she did not doubt her welcome.

The Jagos lived at Stoke Stratton House: pink brick and long sash windows and porticoed porch in the best eighteenth-century tradition. Inside, it was furnished and decorated with expensive confidence, particularly at the windows, which were hung with heavy silks and chintzes under elaborate pelmets of swags and tails. Diana's horsiness gave way indoors to a penchant for great splendour and great whimsicality so that in the drawing room, nestling in the rich folds of the yellow silk curtains, crouched a family of American porcelain frogs as big as small cats, their backs patterned with daisies.

Diana Jago did not take Liza into the drawing room but into a small red sitting room with a sophisticated carpet and an immense fire. In front of this, Simon sat in an armchair with the newspaper and a drink, and, when Liza came in, he got up and said, 'I say, my reward for coming home early,' and kissed her with a blast of gin and British Rail.

'She's come to bend our ears,' Diana said. 'You start on him,' she said to Liza, 'and I'll get you a glass of wine.'

Liza sat on the club fender.

She said to Simon, 'It's about Richard Prior and his development.'

'Ah,' Simon said. 'Then it depends upon which way my ear is to be bent.'

'Away from letting him build.'

Simon took a gulp of drink.

'Good girl.'

'Heavens,' Liza said. 'I thought I'd have to argue.'

'So did we,' Diana said, coming back into the room with a glass of white wine and a dish of peanuts. 'Here. That do? Liza, I had a smallish dust-up with the divine Archibald in the surgery this morning because he's all in favour, so I assumed you'd be too.'

'No,' said Liza, very decidedly.

'Can't understand it,' Simon said. 'Hybrid piggies keep the Priors more than comfortable and the village is quite big enough as it is. And if he's going to build cottages on the cheap, they'll be frightful to look at. Probably look like the piggeries.'

Liza turned her glass slowly round.

'I thought you'd be *pro* it for the same reason as Archie is. I see what he means about helping the village young, but I think the price is too high.'

'It's the thin end of a very nasty wedge,' Diana said, sitting on the arm of Simon's chair. 'Next thing you know, we'll be a suburb of Winchester. It drives me witless to have to agree with Mrs Betts, but I do. Got a cigarette?'

'No,' Simon said. 'Buy your own.'

'I do. And then you smoke them. Liza, I hate to quarrel with the blessed Doc, but I simply have to. Think who'll get those cottages. Probably that hopeless Durfield boy the Army threw out for drugs, and a dreaded Vinney or two. The whole thing is all too easy for Richard, stuck up there at the farm out of sight, sound and smell.'

'That's what I said to Archie,' Liza said.

'Christ,' said Diana, kicking a slumbering Labrador by the fire. 'If you're going to fart like that, for God's sake go and do it in your basket.'

The dog sighed but did not stir.

Simon said, 'I fear the whole thing might be rather unpleasant. Feelings running high and so on. Liza, have the other half.'

She shook her head.

'I must go back and grill a chop.'

'More than I'll get—'

'Too right,' Diana said.

Liza stood up.

'I wish you'd ask us to dinner again soon,' Simon said. 'It's the only decent food I get. Correction. It's the only food I get.'

'Take no notice,' Diana said, ushering Liza towards the door. 'Nobody got a paunch like that on a starvation diet. Give Archie my love. I thought he looked a bit crestfallen this morning.'

When Liza got back, Archie was in the kitchen, on the telephone.

'Look, darling, it's only until Sunday. We'll see you on Sunday. And if you're in the rugger team and second in French, it really cannot be the end of the world.'

There was silence, and then a faint cheeping began, the far end of the telephone line. Liza mouthed, 'Thomas?' and made a movement to take the receiver, but Archie motioned her away.

'What do you mean, picking on you? Oh. Yes, that is rather horrible, but if you are having a dormitory fight, you do get a bit bashed up; it isn't necessarily deliberate. Are you sure? I mean, are you sure someone has taken him and you haven't just lost him? I see. Look, we'll be down on Sunday and we'll see Mr Rigby. Yes. Yes, Mummy is here. All right, darling. Chin up. Bye, Thomas—'

Archie passed the receiver to Liza.

'Darling? Thomas—'

'Someone's stolen Blue Rabbit. I know I didn't lose him. He's always on my bed. And then they got me on the dorm floor and pulled my hair and when I went to cry in bed Rabbit wasn't there and they laughed. Mummy,' Thomas said, his voice catching in his throat, 'I really am trying to bear it, but bits of it, I can't.'

'Oh, darling—'

'I've only got one more 10p. If it goes pip-pip, will you ring back?'

'Thomas, love, we'll be seeing you in three days—'

'That's so long—'

'Look. I won't ring you, but we will ring Mr Rigby. How's that?'

'No!' Thomas shouted.

'But if you feel bullied—'

'No! No, you mustn't!'

The telephone pips began, and over them Liza called, 'Only till Sunday, darling. Only till Sunday!' and heard Thomas saying urgently, 'Don't go, don't go, don't go—'

She turned to Archie.

'Should we ring back?'

He opened his mouth to say he thought that ringing Thomas's form master would be more constructive, when the telephone rang again and Liza snatched it up.

'Thomas?'

'I'm afraid not,' Sir Andrew said. 'Only your old pa-in-law.'

'Andrew!'

'Do Thomas and I sound so alike?'

'We've just had Thomas on the telephone in rather a state, and then his money ran out and I thought he had found another ten pence and rung again. How are you?'

'Extraordinarily well.'

'I'm so glad. Would you like Archie? He's actually right here.'

Archie came over to the telephone with uncharacteristic reluctance.

'Dad?'

'I'm sorry about Thomas. Is it something serious?'

'Impossible to tell, particularly over the telephone. But unnerving enough.'

'Of course. Poor little fellow. Archie, I shall be in Winchester next Monday. Could you have lunch with me?'

'Lunch?' Archie said in amazement.

'Yes. Lunch. Don't you eat lunch?'

'Of course I do. But why are you asking me to have lunch with you in Winchester? Why not here?'

'Archie,' Andrew said patiently. 'Will you have lunch with me in Winchester on Monday?'

'Yes,' Archie said. 'Of course I will—'

'And you see Thomas on Sunday?'

'Yes—'

'Then you will be able to tell me what is the matter and what you have been able to do, won't you? What about the hotel in the Close, about one? I'll see you in the bar.'

'Dad—' Archie said.

'Love to Liza. And the little ones. I'll see you on Monday, and I'll write to Thomas.'

Archie put the telephone down and turned to Liza.

'What is going on?'

She was standing by the table, leaning against it with

one hip. She was wearing jeans, a blue shirt and a cream wool jersey, and she looked about sixteen. She put a hand out to Archie.

'Nothing sinister—'

'He's getting married. That's it, isn't it? He wants to marry Mrs de Breton and he is taking me out to lunch to tell me so.'

He stopped. Liza waited. After a while, she came away from the table and put her arms round him. He did not respond.

She said gently, 'Be sensible. What could be better for him? Why should he live alone? Why shouldn't he be in love? It's so unreasonable to be so resentful.'

He looked down at her, but not in the least as if he was seeing what he looked at.

'It's the unreasonable things,' he said, 'that wrench your very guts.'

Chapter Seven

'I spent a good deal of your childhood,' Sir Andrew said, pouring Chablis, 'trying to get married again. I was lonely, certainly, but I was also convinced that you needed a woman about. A woman to relate to. The trouble was that I couldn't find her.'

Archie, sliding his knife along the backbone of a Dover sole, said nothing.

'And then, after a while, I stopped trying. I suppose it is the usual human ability to adapt to what one has, or hasn't, got. If you cease to look at women simply as potential wives, and instead look at them as women, the field obviously becomes much broader. Yet, at the same time, the emotions involved become much shallower, rather as talking requires much shallower breathing than singing. For long stretches of time, I simply did not sing.'

He picked up his glass.

'While you were at home or at university, this state of affairs did not seem significant. Indeed, it was not significant. Though anxious not to be a preoccupation to you, I lived a very satisfactory emotional life with you and through you. As you got older, and started to manifest characteristics quite unlike my own, that satisfaction grew deeper. But nobody can, or should, live vicariously through another, particularly not parents. When you fell in love and married, it was with my absolute blessing, but for all that, it reminded me, for the first time in a long time, that I had my own life to live. It was not easy. I was out of the habit.'

He paused, took a swallow of wine and then said,

106

'Are you going to sit there in silence, chewing, until the end of lunch?'

Archie sighed.

'I am listening.'

'Good. Do you have any comments so far? Does what I am saying seem to ring true and to chime with what you remember?'

'I don't remember any women,' Archie said.

The waiter, who had recognized Sir Andrew, came up with an air of elaborate discretion and put a dish of potatoes at his elbow. Sir Andrew said, 'Thank you,' and then to Archie, as if the waiter had already moved away, 'I seldom brought any home. If I'd met a woman that I had loved enough to propose to, I should have.'

'And now you have.'

'And now I have.'

Archie moved his glass of water slightly so that the ice cubes in it clattered together.

'You have never talked like this before. Not remotely. You have never talked about feelings.'

'I know.'

'I thought that you didn't like it. I thought you were contemptuous of people who talked about their feelings.'

'I am contemptuous,' Sir Andrew said, 'of people who can't face bearing painful feelings and try to off-load them on to others. And I think that the people one discusses one's feelings with should be few, and dear, and the occasions upon which one does it, seldom.'

'And this is one.'

'Yes. And you are one of the two people in my life that I would, or could, talk to in this way. The other is, of course, Marina.'

'Of course.'

Sir Andrew pushed the dish of potatoes across to Archie.

'I want you to understand me, Archie. I want you to understand both the kind of life I have lived and the

107

kind of life I have found. And, in return, I very much want to understand you. I want to understand your reluctance.'

'I'm not sure,' Archie said, 'that I understand it myself.'

'Sometimes, you know,' his father said with this astounding new ease of his, 'I was so envious of you and Liza. Not of you having her, love her as I do, but of what you had together. Now I am on the brink of such a relationship myself. Do you think that somehow wrong?'

'No.'

'And do you think it, in some instinctive way, disloyal to your mother?'

'No.'

'And do you very much dislike Marina?'

Archie coloured.

'I hardly know her.'

'And your every vibration indicates to me that you neither wish nor intend to.'

Archie hunched over his plate. After some seconds he said, 'You are wrong to suppose that.'

'Then help me,' Sir Andrew said.

Archie pushed his plate aside. He said with difficulty, 'I have – always had you. And then I had Liza. Between you, you know me. You know that, despite outward appearances and some very strong convictions, I am not as confident as I seem.'

He stopped.

'And?'

'I don't seem to have men friends,' Archie said. 'I mean, I get on with the members of the practice all right, but I don't need them, I don't want to do jolly boys' things with them.' He broke off and then he said directly, 'I am afraid of losing you.'

'How can you lose me?'

Archie began to marshal the stray forks and spoons around his place mat. He was simultaneously stricken by feeling something painful, something enormous and nameless, and by knowing that what he was about to say was but a slim excuse for the truth.

'You'll belong to – someone else,' Archie said, boiling with shame.

The next table, who had also observed Sir Andrew and were pretending they had not, were startled to hear him say with vehemence, 'How? How will I? How can Marina's husband cease to be Archie's father when both he and she are bent upon family bonds? How,' said Sir Andrew, growing angry, 'how can you say such foolish, childish things?'

Archie shook his head wordlessly. The waiter came up and began to slide plates and dishes off the table.

'What is the matter with you?' Sir Andrew said, when he had gone. 'How can you object to a situation which will only affect you for the better, because I shall be happy, but will also avoid your having to look after me when I start falling to bits?'

Archie looked up. His father, who had always looked the same to him, restrained, well cared for, controlled, but always, chiefly, his father, now looked different. The outward things were all the same: moustache, shirt-cuffs, breast-pocket handkerchief, were all as precise as usual, but beyond them there was an unfamiliar energy, a new vitality. Gazing at his father, Archie perceived that he suddenly looked not just happy, but blazingly male. Deep in Archie, a profound longing stirred like a long unsatisfied hunger. He bent his head. Tears were pushing behind his eyes.

He said gruffly, 'I'm so sorry.'

Sir Andrew put a hand out across the table.

'You'll see. Give it a few months and you'll see how you will benefit. You can't fail to. You know better than I how generous love makes one.'

Archie nodded. He grasped his father's hand. The waiter, appearing with a trolley laden with undesirable puddings, was entirely unnerved by this and crashed his cheesecakes into the neighbouring table.

'In any case,' Sir Andrew said, taking no notice and smiling at his son, 'what makes you think I could do without you?'

The cathedral was full of Monday afternoon quiet. By several pillars, the flower ladies were assiduously topping up the water levels in great pyramids of chrysanthemums and the odd subdued autumn tourist drifted round the nave in gentle quest of Jane Austen's memorial. In a side aisle, dwarfed by a baroque monument, a College boy, illicitly away from the sportsfield, was having a tense and unsatisfactory conversation with a girl in black suede thigh boots whose stance alone indicated her desire to get away. As Archie passed them on his way to the choir, she gave him a pleading glance.

The choir stalls were quite empty, except for a solitary man in a mackintosh gazing at William Rufus's tomb. Archie climbed up to the back row on the south side and subsided against the screen to give himself a satisfactory view of the royal chests of the Saxon kings of England. He stared at them for a long time. A woman came up to join the man in the mackintosh.

'Can't be the real thing. Not *the* William Rufus. Must be a copy.'

'It's real,' the man said. 'That's the whole point. It's him.'

'Doesn't seem possible.'

'That's the point,' the man said again. 'It is possible. It's real history.'

The woman straightened up.

'Can't take it in.' She moved away a little. 'Coming for a coffee?'

'In a minute. I'll follow you. I'll only be a minute.'

When she had gone, he leaned forward and laid a hand on the tomb. His eyes were closed. Then he opened them and saw Archie watching him. He smiled. And then he took his hand off William Rufus and put it in his pocket and went slowly out of the choir as if he were reluctant to leave it. As he went into the north aisle, he turned for a second and Archie raised his hand. For a moment, the man remained, looking back, and then he moved slowly away down the north aisle and Archie's hand fell back into his lap.

What, he wondered, was he going to do? How had it come about that he, Archie Logan, liked and loved all his life, should now feel himself to be wandering alone in some darkling place? And, what was worse, a darkling place with no map. He had always had a map. He had always known, with a benign, unpushy certainty, where he was going; he had been conscious, ducking into Granny Mossop's low doorway, that she was truly worth more to him than his father's public glories ever could be. Even now, he knew he did not want those glories, and he knew that, at least, with an energy that was familiar to him.

But, despite that energy, he felt helpless. All around him, those people, those precious people, who had wheeled like planets round his central earth, seemed to have changed. His father, Liza, even Thomas – stoutly declaring on his Sunday visit that they must forget his wound-up telephone call from school – all seemed to him to have found maps of their own, maps that led them away from him and into territory where he was reluctant to follow. In Liza's case, would she even allow him to follow wherever she was going? And, if she beckoned to him, could he come and be the led rather than the leader?

He slid forward until his knees were resting on the low carpeted bench in front of him. He was willing, he told himself, to be taught. He was willing to change. That was not the problem. What was the problem was the sense of being immobilized, as if the understanding of being alive, which had always come to him as naturally as breathing, had suddenly vanished. If he was his own patient, he thought, laying his head on his folded arms, he would tell himself that he was profoundly depressed. But he could not do that, somehow. What was there to depress him? Thomas was not being bullied. His father was, as he said, not removing himself, only adding to himself. Liza had every right to remind him that she was changing and developing; indeed, it shamed him to think she had had to point it out. She had also pointed out, and so had his father, that he was behaving like a child. Was that it? Was some childhood spectre of a lost mother and a thus doubly precious father stealing out of the past and his subconscious to haunt him now? Or was it just being about to be forty? Or was it both, everything?

In the choir stalls below him, a woman slipped into a pew and knelt and bent her head. She had brown hair, held back above her ears with combs, and a dark-blue overcoat whose folds crumpled softly over the pew behind her. She could have been any age between thirty and fifty. Was she, too, Archie wondered, down some cul-de-sac without any idea of how to turn round? Or perhaps her husband had run off with her best friend; or she had a child in hospital; or she had found another man and wanted to be comforted into feeling easy about it. She turned her face a little, towards the altar, and Archie could see that she was in her forties and that she looked quite composed. Perhaps she had just come in to say thank you. Archie reflected with some despair that he had much to be grateful for, but that he simply did not seem able to reach that gratitude. He knew it but he could not feel it. He could feel nothing except that he was trapped, and full of longing.

He stood up. Dim, respectful lights were being switched on down the aisles. The woman in the dark-blue coat rose from her knees, smoothed and shook herself into place and set off towards the west door

112

with the air of a person with the right amount of purpose. William Rufus was sinking into shadows. Why, Archie said to himself, why am I not at peace?

Crossing the Close back to the hotel car-park, Archie was intercepted by his sister-in-law, Clare. She worked for the city archivist, a job she claimed any filing clerk could do. She was wearing a grey flannel skirt and a navy-blue blazer, and was carrying a shopping basket containing files and a tin of cat food.

She said, 'Oh, Archie!' in the breathless way she usually greeted people, and he kissed her and asked her how she was.

She said, 'Oh, you know. Dusty and depressed.'

'Don't always be depressed, Clare.'

'I know. It's so boring for everyone, isn't it? Have you got time for a cup of tea?'

'Not really. I've been playing truant for lunch.'

She drooped.

'Walk back to the car with me,' Archie said. 'I'll drive you home.' He took her basket. 'You and the medieval records.'

'Saxon, actually. It's amazing how fascinating it ought to be and how boring it is.'

'What would you like to do instead?'

He began to move away and she took a few quick steps to keep up with him

'I think Liza's life looks pretty good.'

'I'm not sure she'd agree with you.'

'Archie?'

'Country doctor's wife,' Archie said a little wildly. 'Village life. Three children. Local job. I suppose it must seem a bit confining sometimes.'

Clare said nothing. A small nausea of apprehension knotted her stomach. Did Archie know about Blaise O'Hanlon? Clare herself did not know from Liza, who had not even hinted at him, but from Blaise, in person. Blaise had turned up at her house one evening the

113

previous week and told her, almost before introductions were over, that he must talk to her about Liza.

'There's nobody else, you see. And I must talk. I knew you existed because Liza told me, and I thought you would talk to me. I can't talk to Liza because she is so adorably resolute, so please, please can I talk to you?'

He had stayed to supper. Whisking up a soufflé, Clare reflected that it was probably a year since she had cooked for a man, and it was absolutely typical that when she did it was for a man who was not in love with her, but with her sister. He ate ravenously and was full of praise.

'Oh, this is so delicious. Are you sure there's no more? Not even crumby little edge bits? Wouldn't it be easy if you could be Liza?'

She believed in his love completely. She could not bring herself not to. But even Clare could see that for Liza Blaise was no match for Archie. To Clare, Liza and Archie had one of those rare relationships where mutual roots seemed tangled round each other.

She said to Blaise, 'There isn't any hope, you know.'

'Then I'll make there be some.'

'You mustn't be so destructive,' Clare said, excited in spite of her better sense.

'I only want to give,' Blaise said, finishing the wine. 'And I need her. Need is so different from want.'

Clare was alarmed.

'What are you planning?'

'Persuasion,' he said. 'A long, loving campaign of persuasion. I want to persuade her to see how different she is. She has no idea. She's like the Sleeping Beauty.'

'And is Archie the thorny hedge?'

'Archie?' Blaise said, briefly bemused. 'What about Archie?'

'She's married to him. He's her husband.'

Blaise looked directly at Clare.

'He doesn't see her as I see her.'

114

'You don't know that! You don't know her at all!'

'I do,' Blaise said. 'I knew her at once.'

'Reverting to me,' Clare said now to Archie. 'Do you think I'm emotionally retarded because I always want what I can't have? Or at least, I think I do.'

They had arrived in the car-park. Struggling to find the right key and to open the passenger door for Clare and to stow her basket on the confusion of the back seat gave Archie a few moments to wrestle with the memory of the jealous longing that had stricken him during lunch with his father.

When he at last answered Clare, he could say with some cheerfulness, 'Heavens, no. It's only another form of words for striving. If we all liked the status quo, think what a plodding life we'd lead. It's—' He paused, and then said with more seriousness, 'It's the – dissatisfaction and the hunger that keeps us exploring.'

He started the car and slid it out from the ranks of other cars into the narrow street leading away from the city centre.

Clare said, 'I think that sounds very insecure.'

'Of course it does. It is.'

'Robin was like that. Always exploring. His wasn't striving, it was just self-indulgence.'

Archie said, changing gear to swing steeply uphill towards the prison, 'That's another thing altogether. That's a fear born of getting to know someone and realizing that they know you.'

'I thought that was love,' Clare said.

'It is. At least, it's part of love.'

'Then—'

'Clare,' Archie said, fighting with conflicting messages from his head and his guts. 'I don't think I can quite cope with this topic at three-thirty on a Monday afternoon in heavy traffic.'

'Sorry,' Clare said at once. 'Sorry.' She pressed herself back into her seat. 'I only ask you things because you look as if you know.'

Archie said with vehemence, 'I know nothing.'

Clare lived in a narrow Victorian end-of-terrace house, which stood on the edge of a rough little green below the prison. A low wall and a square of paving divided it from the road in front, and a brick path led up to the door. Archie followed Clare, carrying her basket, and waited while she put the key into the lock and turned it and swung the door open to reveal a narrow hall and a narrower table bearing a letter rack and a china dish for keys and an arrangement of dried flowers.

Clare said, 'Are you sure about tea?'

'Quite sure. But thank you.'

'Give my love to Liza.'

'Of course.'

'And thank you for the lift.'

He bent and kissed her cheek. She smelled of L'Air du Temps. Liza used to wear it once. Sweet, schoolgirl scent; the scent, Archie had once said teasingly to Liza, of tennis-club socials in Haslemere. Liza had never worn it since. Clare waited until Archie had walked down her path and closed her gate after him, and then she shut the door and walked along the hall to the kitchen which looked, dispiritingly, exactly as she knew it would, since she had been the last person in it.

Archie drove out of Winchester, endeavouring to fix his mind resolutely on nothing at all but the remainder of his professional day. What was to be gained by letting his mind slip back into that turbulence which seemed, all at once, to freeze him and to churn him up? Better by far to think of things he could affect than things he was powerless to affect. Better, but impossible. Impossible to keep his imagination and thoughts in check, just as it would be impossible to go home to Liza and say, Look, I don't know what is the matter with me but it's acute, and can you help? He had never said such a thing to Liza. He would feel, he told himself, that it was letting her down, to saddle her with

116

his misery. What could she do, poor girl? We all survive, he told himself, on a mixture of self-knowledge and self-image, a balancing act of how things are and how we wish they were. But what, oh what, Archie thought, gripping the wheel, is it that I am so ardently wishing for?

He drove the car into the health centre car-park and brought it efficiently to rest in the rectangle marked out by painted lines and 'Dr Logan' lettered neatly on the tarmac. There was an hour before surgery, an hour with his dictating machine and then letters to consultants about ruptured Achilles tendons and chronic back pain, malfunctioning livers and nasal washes. He spread his hands out across the steering wheel. They might, at that moment, have been the hands of a stranger. Could it be . . . ?

Someone tapped on the driver's window. The pharmacist was mouthing through the glass at him. He wound the window down.

'Dr Logan. Thank goodness you've come. There's no doctor here, they are all out on call, and Mr Barrett has just been brought in by his daughter. Why she did not take him to hospital I can't imagine. It looks to me like a heart attack. Could you—'

Archie seized his bag from the back seat and flung the door open, almost knocking her over.

'Coming,' he said. 'Coming.'

Blessed emergency, blessed Mr Barrett. Leaving the car door swinging wide, Archie leaped out and ran. The pharmacist closed it behind him gently, and then leaned against it for a moment, and dreamed.

'Thing,' Imogen said commandingly.

She lay on her tummy in the bath in a flotilla of plastic boats and dolls.

'Look,' Liza said, kneeling by the bath with a soapy sponge. 'I've been singing to you for hours.'

Imogen rolled over and lay luxuriously on one elbow.

'Daddy come. Daddy thing.'

'Daddy is doing surgery.'

'Thally thing.'

'Sally has gone home with a headache. I expect you gave her a headache by screaming.'

Imogen considered this. She had screamed at teatime when Liza's appearance from school had put paid to her plan of playing with the telephone while Sally was occupied with the ironing. Once, she had randomly dialled a number and a woman had answered, so now she dialled and dialled, when she thought no-one was noticing, and whispered fiercely, 'Hello, lady, hello, lady, hello, lady,' into the receiver. She loved it.

'Not headache,' Imogen said defiantly, rolling over again.

Liza gazed at her perfect little bottom.

'You are an awful child, Imogen.'

'Mummy thing.'

Liza got up from her knees.

'No. No more singing.'

In her skirt pocket lay a letter from Blaise. She had not opened it. Half of her thought she would throw it away unopened; a quarter of her thought she would read it the moment Imogen and Mikey were safely in bed, and the last quarter of her thought she would simply carry it about, unread, like a little phial of magic whose potency vanishes when opened.

Mikey, undressed down to his socks, appeared in the doorway.

'Daddy's come.'

'He's doing surgery. He won't be back for hours.'

'I am back,' Archie said. 'It wasn't my night. I forgot.'

He stooped to kiss her, and then lower for Imogen, dipping his tie in the bath water.

'Thing,' Imogen said.

'Thing yourself,' Archie said, and picked up Mikey. 'If you're going to be a success with the girls, M.

Logan, you must always take your socks off first, not last.'

'Why?'

'So as not to look ludicrous. Don't fiddle with your willy.'

Mikey lay back against his father's shoulder, and closed his eyes.

'Willy likes it.'

'How was lunch?' Liza said.

'It was what I thought it would be. He is getting married.'

'Who?' Mikey said.

'Grandpa.'

Imogen stood up in the bath and flapped her arms for attention.

'Out, out, out, out, out—'

'So?' Liza said.

Archie looked at her.

'Out!' shouted Imogen.

Liza stooped to lift her out into a bath towel.

Archie said to her back, 'He was very affectionate.'

'Of course he was,' Liza said, towelling.

Archie peeled off Mikey's socks and lowered him into the bath.

'It's cold,' Mikey said. 'I don't want this doll thing. Or this.' He began to throw toys out of the bath.

'Stop it!' Liza said.

A purple plastic hippopotamus hit Imogen's leg and fell on to Liza's foot.

'Ow!' Imogen shrieked. 'Ow! Ow! Ow!'

'Shut up. It didn't hurt. If your father was affectionate, why are you looking like that?'

'Ow,' Imogen sobbed, clutching her leg theatrically.

'Like what?'

'Gloomy.'

'And,' Mikey said, 'I don't want this stupid crocodile.' He picked it up and hurled it over his shoulder. It struck Archie in the groin.

119

'There's no point,' Archie said. 'There's just no point.'

He stooped over the bath and gripped Mikey's arm.

'Stop that at once.'

Imogen bounced upright on Liza's knee and made the letter in her pocket crackle faintly.

'No point in what?'

'Trying to talk to you. Trying to explain.'

Liza began to pull Imogen's nightie over her head.

'Bath time isn't the perfect moment, certainly—'

'Not pink one!' Imogen shouted from inside the folds of brushed cotton. 'Not pink! Not pink!'

Archie, heedless of his sodden tie and his jacket cuffs, began to soap his son. I'm lonely, he wanted to say to Liza. I'm lonely and I'm ashamed of it. Come back, Liza. Come back where I can reach you.

Mikey squealed.

'Don't tickle!'

'I have to. Your feet are so disgusting. Why do you have such disgusting feet?'

'They are sweet feet,' Mikey said stoutly.

'Now they are. They weren't two minutes ago.' He turned to look over his shoulder. 'Liza?'

She was buttoning the last of the buttons up Imogen's back. The nightie, to Imogen's disappointment, was blue.

'Yes?'

'Hello.'

She smiled at him. It was a kind smile but not a loving, surrendering smile.

'Hello.'

'Forget it,' Archie said. 'I'm being an ass. Just forget it. I won't mention it again.'

'I do understand,' Liza said, standing up with Imogen in her arms. 'It's just the difference between mountains and molehills. That you have to see, I mean.'

Archie turned away and looked down at Mikey.

'Precisely,' he said. Precisely, he thought. Except that our definitions of mountains and molehills are in exactly opposite proportion to one another.

Mikey reared up out of the bath and put wet arms round his father's neck.

'I just did a fart,' he said and collapsed into peals of laughter.

Chapter Eight

His first wedding ceremony, Sir Andrew recalled, had
been a pawky Scottish business. A red sandstone
Glasgow church, a scattering of pursy Logan aunts, an
apprehensive collection of Welsh relations of the
bride's, bemused by the lack of spontaneity and
singing, drizzle, and the burden of the participants'
double dose of virginity, had made it a day not to be
remembered. He had felt so responsible for it all, so
much the engineer, so much the one who must create
any happiness or security they might hope for, that he
had been quite bowed down by his burdens. What a
bridegroom, he thought forty years later, what a grim
and corseted prospect for a girl! Poor little Gwyneth.
Poor, bewildered Gwyneth, trying to find some path
through to me, and I couldn't help her because I didn't
know the way myself. All I could do was be loyal and
hardworking and let her buy things for the house,
things after things: cookers and chairs and vases and
rugs and pictures. I hope they comforted her. I hope,
he thought, tying a silver-grey tie on the morning of his
second wedding, I hope she has forgiven me. If she can
see me now, I earnestly hope she will understand why
this morning, my second wedding morning, I want to
sing and sing. If she has kept her sense of humour in
Paradise, perhaps she will only remind me that I can't
and never could. She sang like a bird; it was agony for
her to hear me try. So I stopped. But today I shall start
again. To celebrate this day, I shall open my mouth to
myself in my dressing-room mirror, now, and I shall
sing 'Jerusalem'. I shall even sing the second verse
twice.

*

Marina lay in her bath. It was her last bath in this bath. Today she would give up the flat and move in with Sir Andrew until such time as she could find them a pretty house, with a garden; a house, she hoped, somewhere near Campden Hill. On the morning of her wedding to Louis de Breton she had showered in her minute, cardboard-walled apartment, then been married, wedding-breakfasted and carried aboard an aeroplane for the Caribbean, all before eleven in the morning. It was eleven now and she was still in the bath, independent rather than dependent, choosing not chosen, a possessor rather than possessed. The dignity I have this morning, she thought, surveying her painted toe-nails pushing above the bubbles of the bath essence, is the result of the indignity I had that other morning. I so disapprove of marrying for money, but I did it. I should have been punished for it, and I have been rewarded. Here I am, about to dress myself in clothes I have paid for myself to go off and marry my perfect companion. That strikes me as a gorgeous combination. That satisfies me through and through. I am my own mistress where I should be, and his mistress where I should be. If I never have such a bath again, Marina told herself, drawing out the bath plug with her toes, I shall always remember this one with gratitude. I shall always remember that, for twenty minutes, an hour before I married Andrew Logan, I felt that the balance of my life was perfect. I control the things that are natural and proper for me to control, and I am at his disposal for the rest.

'Thank you,' she said out loud, climbing out of the bath and picking up a towel. 'Thank you very much indeed. And I mean it. Cross my heart and hope to die, I mean it.'

Because it was the first weekend of the Christmas

holidays, Thomas was at home for the wedding. He wore his school suit. It was grey flannel and poorly proportioned and he didn't care for its associations, but he saw, after a term's acquaintance with the proprieties, that it was the correct thing for him to wear to his grandfather's wedding. Without being asked, he added his school tie and black school shoes. He thought Mikey, wearing sandals and a new jersey instead of a jacket, looked very wrong. Imogen, in a plaid smock frock with a white lawn collar, looked like a tartan robin. A tartan robin who would steal the show. Thomas hoped she would not get over-excited and out of control. Boarding school had suggested to him that to be conspicuous was pretty terrible. Imogen, with her penchant for screams and somersaults, could do with a dose of boarding school. Now that he was away from it, Thomas could look at his tie in the mirror with something approaching pride. It was a badge, after all, a badge that separated him from younger boys like Mikey, who had to wear sandals and who could not tie a tie properly. The envy with which Thomas had thought of Mikey while he was at school turned to pity now he was away from it. Mikey was so young, such a pest. When Mikey had said, 'Anyway, you don't know Mrs de Breton and I do, she gave me a pound,' Thomas had been full of rage, but it had soon turned to pity. In a proper suit and a school tie, he, Thomas, could hold his own against Mikey with Mrs de Breton. He had spoken to her on the phone. She had said, 'Next to marrying your grandfather, the best thing about my wedding day will be meeting you, Thomas. And you must call me Marina.' He had kept that a secret. After a term at school, he had got good at keeping secrets. His head was full of them. And because he was only nine, his privacy was a consolation to him, a refuge, and not yet a lonely burden.

Liza had a new suit for the wedding. It had a velvet

collar and cuffs, and gunmetal buttons like regimental buttons, and it fitted her like a glove. It had been very expensive. Liza had wanted a dress, a dress with a full skirt and then, perhaps, a jacket that would go with it, and afterwards with lots of other things. But Diana Jago, who had been shopping with her, had said, 'Come on, come on – what do you want to look like? A country doctor's wife?' It had been fun, shopping with Diana; far more fun than shopping with Clare, who had expected to be asked and had been aggrieved when she wasn't. Diana whirled through shops like Marina did, saying, 'Don't touch that, too dire for words,' and, 'Put that straight back, common *and* boring,' while the assistants loved her and stopped making hopeless suggestions. And here Liza was in her curvy little suit, and a small hat with no brim and a feeling that today would cement the new dimension she was developing. It was giving her such strength, this dimension. Blaise's letter lay, still unopened, in the kitchen drawer where she kept the cellophane circles for jars of jam, and freezer bags, and the icing set – a kitchen drawer, not even a romantic drawer full of underclothes or handkerchiefs. At the end of term, Liza had said to him, 'Happy Christmas,' and kissed his cheek in full view of Mrs West and June Hampole, and had then done the same to Commander Haythorne. That was three days ago. Turning slowly in front of the mirror, Liza thought that he would probably telephone soon.

Archie, hosing mud off the car to make it more suitable for London, resolved to stand no nonsense from himself today. He had kept his word to Liza and had not referred to the forthcoming wedding again, and had endeavoured to look as he wished he felt. He had bought a silk Paisley tie. He had not only taken his one good suit to the dry cleaners but had collected it, too. It hung upstairs now, waiting for him, to be worn to his

father's wedding. In a drawer or a cupboard somewhere, he had a photograph of his father's wedding to
his mother. He hadn't looked at it for years, but he
remembered it as both poignant and dismal, as
amateur a business as today's promised to be polished.
The spaniel came out of the house and stood looking
despondently at the car. How do dogs always know,
Archie thought; how much do they suffer from these
huge instincts that dominate them so?

'Nelson,' he said. 'We will not be long, and when we
come back it will all be over. For me, it will be like a
headache lifting. I'm sure of it.' The spaniel sighed.
'Don't sigh,' Archie said. 'It's catching.' He splashed a
last sweep of water across the windscreen and turned
off the tap. Liza was calling. 'Coming,' he shouted.
'Coming.'

Accept things, people said; don't break the rules. But
who, except the unhappy, should ever want to do
otherwise?

The Register Office was full of flowers and smelt of furniture polish. The registrar had a perfect hair cut and an
irreproachable suit. Archie, Liza and the children stood
in a row slightly to Sir Andrew's right, and behind
Marina was one of Louis de Breton's grandsons, who
had flown over from America especially, and the
woman from whom she had rented her flat, who made
an exhausting point of never doing business without
friendship. The grandson wore a pink carnation as big
as a small cauliflower in the lapel of a plaid wool
jacket, and the muscles of his jaw flickered faintly over
the chewing gum inside. Liza thought it was perfectly
sweet of him to come. She planned to make her
thought very plain to him over lunch. She felt excited,
standing there behind these two people sounding so
positive in their promises, excited with a breath of
anticipation as if a hidden door was about to open and
she, in her new chic suit, could just slip through. Who

knows, she thought, admiring Marina's graceful back, who knows what may happen now?

Even Imogen was being good. There was enough to look at, enough amusement to be gained from standing on a chair seat (usually forbidden), which made her taller than Mikey, to distract her. There was also her father, just beside and half behind her. She could feel her father going up for ever towards the ceiling and all the way down to the floor. If she jiggled too much his hand came down on her like a clamp, but, when she tossed a glance at him, he wasn't even looking at her as she expected, he was looking straight ahead out of a window criss-crossed with little black lines. She beamed at him, waiting for his response. Then she shut her eyes and opened them up at him very, very slowly. He never moved. Nobody was looking at her; not Mikey, not Thomas; nobody. Imogen bent her gaze and stared down over the gathered curve of her front to the just-visible toes of her patent-leather shoes. In their shine, she thought she could see the ears of her hair ribbon. She leaned forward, a little bit, a little bit. 'Stand up,' Archie hissed. Imogen leaned a fraction more and fell forward with a crash.

Archie had seized her and was hurrying her from the room almost before she had breath enough to scream. The scream burst from her as she and Archie burst out on to the pavement.

'Stop it,' Archie said. 'Stop it. You aren't hurt.'

'Knee,' Imogen wailed. 'Knee. Knee.'

They inspected both.

'Not a mark,' Archie said. 'You are a hellkitten.'

'Bang,' Imogen said, still sobbing. 'Bang knee.'

'I told you to stand upright. If you had done what you were told, you would not have fallen.'

He set her on her feet.

'Kith knee,' Imogen said hopefully.

'No,' Archie said. 'You kiss me for causing all this trouble.'

Imogen rubbed her wet face against his hand.

'Is that a kiss?'

She nodded, curls and ribbons bobbing.

'Good now,' Imogen said doubtfully.

'Are you sure?'

He stooped to pick her up again.

'Imo,' he said. 'I love you.'

She regarded him. She put her thumb in.

'Blow nose,' he said, fumbling for a handkerchief. 'Isn't it odd to think that one day you'll have an awful Imogen of your own?'

She leaned into the handkerchief and snorted. He carried her up the steps and in through the double doors, past the waiting room and in, once more, to the room where his father was being married. Had been married, in fact. They were all kissing each other and shaking the registrar by the hand. They were laughing. It was over. I want to go home, Archie thought, clutching Imogen, I want to drive out of London, away from all this – this cold, urban competence. I want to go home.

Lunch was very glamorous. It was in a hotel, with velvet armchairs for everyone, even the children, and tablecloths that came right down to the floor, and napkins so big, Mikey discovered, that he could cover himself completely with his from his head as far as his knees. He let its starched folds slide down until he could see over the top, until he could see Thomas sitting between Marina and the young American. '(Hi, you guys,' he had said to them. 'We're all in it together now.') Thomas's ears were red. Thomas was excited.

'Sit up,' Archie said.

Imogen was next to Liza, on an extra cushion. Liza was not paying her much attention because she was being nice to Marshall, Marina's stepgrandson. He was in law school. He had had a narcotics problem but he was all straightened out now, he said. He thought

Marina was a great lady, the kind of lady, he said, who was rare in our country. He said that a good deal, 'in our country . . .' His clear blue eyes were blank and mad.

'Hi, sweetheart,' he said to Imogen, craning round Liza.

She turned her head away flirtatiously.

'She's in deep disgrace,' Liza said. 'She disturbed the wedding.'

'You don't have to pay attention to weddings,' Marshall said. 'They come and go. In my family they have them all the time.'

'Have you had one?'

'I'm celibate,' Marshall said seriously. 'Since Aids.'

'But that doesn't prevent you marrying.'

'I can't test for sexual compatibility. Not any more, since Aids.' He looked at the smoked salmon on his plate. 'Does this have chemical colouring?'

Miriam Bliss, who owned Marina's flat, told Archie that there was no profession she admired as much as medicine.

'People only say that,' Archie said, 'when they have been lucky enough not to have to test our limitations.'

'But you see, you and your father,' Miriam went on, ignoring him, 'represent medicine's private and public faces between you. That's what I find so thrilling. Don't you agree? I mean, here you are, the hands-on GP, and there's your father, an absolute laboratory wizard. And we couldn't do without either, could we? So fascinating.'

Archie leaned his chin on his hand and looked at her.

'Is property owning fascinating?'

She coloured.

'Are you making fun of me?'

'No,' he said. 'But I fidget when people begin on the fascination of medicine. They get reverent. I can't bear it.'

129

'But, my dear,' said Miriam Bliss, recovering herself, 'there is a magic to medicine; you can't deny it. You aren't just engineers, you are engineers with hearts. Don't you agree? And in this caring age—'

'It isn't,' Archie said, craning towards her as a plate of duck-breast slices, fanned out in a shiny pool of russet sauce, was put before him. 'It isn't caring. We have compassion instead of religion, but it's a social compassion. It's guilt.'

Miriam Bliss said to herself that for such an attractive, articulate man he was strangely difficult to talk to.

'Guilt?'

'Over losing God and finding Mammon.'

'Is this chicken?' Mikey hissed.

'No. It's duck.'

'Duck!' He paused. 'Do I like duck?'

From across the table, Thomas said clearly, 'When I went out to lunch with Fanshawe we had duck his father had shot.'

Mikey began to eat voraciously.

'Adorable children,' said Miriam Bliss.

'I adore them,' Archie said. 'I don't really expect anyone else to.'

'Marina does. My dear, you should hear her talk about them.' She looked at Imogen who was eating matchsticks of carrot with her fingers. 'Divine. Really divine.'

'Am I what you expected me to be?' Marina said to Thomas.

He thought not. He had been expecting someone more grannyish, with grey hair and boring shoes.

He said aloud, 'I didn't think you'd laugh so much.'

'I used not to. It's what happens when you are happy.'

'Sometimes,' Thomas said, 'I laugh when I'm frightened.'

'People, I mean grown-up people, make the great mistake of thinking that being very young is amusing.

It isn't. I remember, as a child, being mostly excited or afraid. Do you feel that way?'

Thomas nodded.

Marina said, 'If you had your eyes closed, would you know you were eating duck, not chicken?'

'Not really.'

'I don't know,' Marina said. 'These fancy places. Think that they can get away with anything. What is your absolutely best food?'

'Baked potatoes,' Thomas said.

'With sour cream and crispy bacon bits and chives?'

'I've never,' Thomas said truthfully, 'had them like that.'

'I'd rather have a baked potato right now, wouldn't you? Look at Imogen. She's flirting with the waiter.'

'Don't look,' Thomas said. 'It makes her worse.'

'Do we dare give her a mouthful of champagne with pudding?'

'Champagne!'

'Certainly.'

'I've never had champagne,' said Thomas with glowing ears.

'I don't expect you have been to a wedding before. There's usually champagne at weddings. Look.' She held out her left hand to Thomas and showed him a thin band of pale, shiny gold. 'I'm married to Grandpa now. I am your stepgrandmother.'

She bent and kissed him.

'And I'm so pleased about that.'

The champagne came in a bottle as tall as Imogen. She stood up on her chair and squealed. Then a cake came, a frothing white meringue cake with a silver vase of white freesias on it.

'You are so sentimental,' Sir Andrew said to Marina. 'How could you order such a fearful thing?'

'For Imogen. And she loves it. Look at her.'

A waiter lifted off the vase of freesias, and put it down in front of Marina. Then he removed a single flower and went round the table and threaded it into Imogen's hair ribbon. Rapturously, she lifted her skirts to stuff them into her mouth and revealed her ruffled petticoat. From the next table came a round of applause.

Marina cut the cake with an immense silver scimitar. It was pale inside, speckled with glacé fruits. The children watched with intense interest. Archie watched Marina. In a moment he would have to propose a toast to the health and happiness of his father and stepmother. It seemed superfluous. They were both way beyond needing the gentle benison of others' good wishes.

The waiter was filling tall glasses from the extraordinary bottle. Mikey counted. There was one for him. Imogen poked her finger into the soft sweet mess of her cake and then sucked it loudly. Marshall de Breton told Liza that he didn't eat sugar any more. Liza was tired of being kind to him and said that there was sugar in champagne.

'Natural sugar,' Marshall said reprovingly.

'Only a sip,' Liza said to the waiter putting a glass in front of Imogen.

'All!' Imogen shouted, leaning forward. 'All! All!'

Archie pushed her glass out of reach. With one hand holding Imogen hard against the back of her chair, Archie raised his own glass with the other.

'Could you all listen? For just one moment?'

He rose to his feet, holding the glass.

'Will you all join me in wishing Marina and my father a long, happy, healthy life together.'

There was a cheer. Tables round theirs took up the cheer. Everybody stood up, holding their glasses high. Imogen jumped and squealed. All round the table, people turned to each other to hug and kiss. Archie kissed Miriam Bliss and then moved round her to put his arms about his father. Sir Andrew's eyes were full of tears.

132

'God bless,' Archie said, kissing his cheek. 'All blessings. Really. Truly.'

He let his father go. Marina was stooping over Thomas, saying, 'I'm so glad you like it. It's so sophisticated to like champagne.' Archie put a hand on her shoulder. She straightened and turned to him.

'Archie. Dear Archie—'

He took her in his arms.

'Marina.'

'I'll do everything in my power to make him happy. I don't want to change any of the good things—'

Archie felt tears rising. He said, 'Marina,' again and then he bent his head and kissed her on the mouth.

It was a soft night, for December. Archie put Nelson on to his lead, pulled on Wellingtons, and went off into the damp sweet air that still smelled of autumn over winter.

'There you are,' Liza had said to him when they got home. 'You've lived through it. Haven't you? And really, it wasn't such a big deal, was it? It was just a lovely wedding.'

Archie had smiled. Liza had taken off her suit and was standing there in just her petticoat, rounded and sweet. She came over and kissed him, such a kind little kiss with just the smallest, faintest edge of condescension.

'Silly Archie.'

'When I have feelings,' Archie said, taking her wrists for one last try, 'they are very real to me. And strong. The fact that they look trivial from the outside doesn't alter that, nor does any effort I might make to hide them.'

She sighed. She said, 'I know all that.'

He let go.

'No, my darling. You hear me and you dismiss it.'

'Don't quarrel,' she said pleadingly. 'Not after such a lovely day. You were sweet today. You were lovely to Marina.'

He said, 'I want to make love to you.'

She started laughing.

'Oh-ho. All this romance is so catching—'

'Come here.'

She skipped sideways.

'Let me just see if Thomas is asleep—'

When she came back, he was naked. She let him undress her, which they both liked, and then she waited to be kissed, as she usually was, all over. But tonight Archie was perfunctory in his kissing. Not only that, he was rough. 'Ow,' Liza said once or twice, sounding like Imogen. 'Don't. You're hurting.' He came very fast, not waiting for her. And when he had come, he did not say in her ear as he usually did, More, more, more. He simply lay with his face buried in the pillow beside her neck for a few moments, and then he levered himself up, and out of her and said, 'I'm sorry. That wasn't exactly a masterpiece of finesse.'

'It's a bit much,' Liza said, 'to take your anger out on me.'

'Yes. I'm really sorry. I did want you. I do.'

Liza rolled sideways off the bed.

'I'm going to have a bath.'

Archie stood up.

'I'll take Nelson out. It's my Sunday on tomorrow.'

'It's dark. He's been out—'

'I want to,' Archie said, struggling into clothes. Liza gave him a quick glance and pulled on her dressing gown.

'How awkward you can make our lives when you try,' she said.

For a split second, he thought he might hit her. He held his breath. She gave him a tiny, fleeting look of triumph, as if she had guessed, and went off to the bathroom. Archie went downstairs and took a courteously astonished Nelson out into the dark.

He crossed the lawn and went through a gap in the hedge to the field where Richard Prior planned to

134

build his houses. The darkness gradually resolved itself into greater and lesser densities, trees and bushes, and through them the lights of far houses, and the bungalow next door where the Pinkneys crouched in terror of being involved. Nelson strained at the lead, the night being loud with the scent of rabbits.

'Sorry, old boy,' Archie said. 'If I let you go, you'll be gone for hours.'

A pheasant rose whirring out of the darkness ahead.

'Painted foreign hen,' Archie said to Nelson. 'Take no notice.'

They crossed the space where the big house might stand, Archie stumbling in the rough grass. It irritated Liza that he would never take a torch, but he said he preferred to stumble; a torch spoiled the darkness. Nelson made little hopeful darts here and there, stirring up the scents of earth and leaf. The dark air lay softly on Archie's grateful face. Above him, a blurred moon hung among pale stars and from all around came the faint settling-down cluckings and twitchings of hedgerow life. He lifted his face, eyes closed.

I must go back, he thought. I must go back and apologize properly. For behaving like a brute. Why did I? Why did I want to be violent? I did want to. I felt fierce and hungry. Liza seemed too small, too sweet for what I wanted. What happened? Why should I be like that? It's over, today is over; I was dreading it but it seemed to pass me at a distance and now it's over. I should have taken Liza to bed, laughing; I should have been full of relief. God, Archie thought, opening his eyes, my God, how I detest people who take themselves so seriously. Am I having a severe sense of humour failure? Am I going mad?

'Am I going mad?' he said to Nelson.

He turned towards home. A light shone in the kitchen and above it another from their bedroom, and beside that the landing. While he watched, Liza came to the bedroom window and drew the curtains across.

135

Typical, she would be thinking, typical of us to draw them only after we have made love. That kind of abandonment always used to make her laugh; she loved to be lured into carelessness. 'Let go,' he would say to her. 'Go on. Trust me. Let go.' Perhaps she hadn't really liked it, only the idea of it. Perhaps it was in her nature to keep something back, not to chuck herself off cliffs with him as he wanted her to do, as he could do himself. Perhaps, Archie thought, moving unevenly towards his house, perhaps taking life in great gulps as he had always done was wrong because it tore roughly at the edges of other people's more delicate lives. Maybe he was paying for past greed with present misery.

'Do you suppose,' he said to the spaniel as they pushed through the hedge, 'that this is a kind of growing up?'

Liza was rummaging in a kitchen drawer. She had a fistful of jampot covers in one hand. She did not look up as Archie and Nelson came in.

'Do you really want to make jam now?'

'No,' Liza said calmly. 'I'm looking for a letter. A letter from a friend.'

Archie said, 'I am genuinely sorry I behaved like a rugger scrum just now.'

She turned. Her face was clean of make-up and her hair was pinned on top of her head with a plastic clip.

'Oh, Archie—'

'I mean it.'

'I know. Please don't start all over again. I know. It doesn't matter.'

She put the jampot covers back in the drawer and pushed it shut.

'I just wish you wouldn't make such a meal of everything. It all has to be a big issue with you, doesn't it? Everything has to be a big deal.'

'Some weeks ago,' Archie said, 'you complained that I didn't make a big enough deal of you. That I belittled you. What is it that you really mean?'

Liza put her hands over her ears.

'No more—'

'Talk to me,' Archie shouted. 'Talk to me. Please.'

Nelson crept to his basket. Liza took her hands away and put them in her dressing-gown pocket. The letter met her fingers.

'No, darling,' she said. 'No more talking. Not now.'

And then she smiled at him again, and went up to bed.

Chapter Nine

The Stoke Stratton Preservation Society had its first meeting the week before Christmas. It took place in the village hall, decorated since late November with tired paper streamers, an unenthusiastic Christmas tree and drawings, done by the Sunday School, of Baby Jesus, mostly coloured bright pink with yellow hair.

Simon Jago was chairman, Mrs Betts secretary and prime mover. Mrs Betts had stationed Sharon Vinney – seasonally out of work from the local watercress beds – in the shop-end of the post office to give herself time for Society paperwork. The night before the meeting she had arranged chairs in rows in the village hall, each one bearing a fact sheet on the development and, on a table for the committee, in front of them, a scarlet poinsettia in a pot, a carafe of water and several glasses. Behind the table stood a blackboard with a map of the field pinned to it.

Now, dressed in a knitted frock of lilac wool with a scalloped hem and a tie-neck, Mrs Betts stood inside the village hall door, and welcomed people in. She wore pearl and diamante ear-rings and was very gracious.

'I can't stand,' Diana Jago whispered to Liza as they came in together, 'being in the same boat as her.'

'She's loving it,' Liza said.

Mrs Betts shook their hands warmly.

'So good to know people are really prepared to stand up and be counted!' She turned to Archie. 'Well, Dr Logan, I never expected to see you here.'

Archie smiled at her.

'I am a man of infinite surprises, Mrs Betts.'

138

He went past her to the back row of seats, and chose one. Diana and Liza, with Diana making mock-furious faces at him, went past him, up to the front, and sat in a prominent place. After a while, Richard and Susan Prior came in, and went to sit either side of Archie.

'Mrs Logan,' Mrs Betts said, bustling up. 'Mrs Logan. I really must protest. This is not a public inquiry. This is a private meeting for like-minded people. I really cannot have Dr Logan and Mr Prior making difficulties.'

'Oh, I don't think they will. I'm sure they are just here as observers—'

'Would you be so good as to make sure of it? I really haven't gone to all this trouble to have my efforts undermined.'

Liza went pink.

'Mrs Betts, I can't possibly—'

'Have a word,' Mrs Betts said. 'Just a little word. Please, dear.'

Diana stood up.

'I'll come with you.'

They walked to the back of the hall.

Diana said easily to Archie, 'Old Ma Betts is worried about barracking from the back row.'

'I'm here to listen,' Richard Prior said.

'That's what we said.'

'Do you think,' Susan Prior said to Liza, 'that it's a good idea to run errands for that woman?'

'I wasn't. I simply—'

'It's all of a piece, of course,' Susan went on, across her. 'All of a piece with you worrying about the class of neighbour you might get.'

Liza gave a little gasp. She looked at Archie. He should defend her! But he merely said, 'Trading insults won't help anyone.'

'Archie!' Liza said.

'I can't sit with you,' Archie said helplessly, 'because you are the opposition.'

139

Liza was close to tears.

'But she—'

'Is a rude cow,' Richard Prior said. 'Always has been.' He looked up at Diana. 'I came to hear you, actually, Mrs J. Are you as good on your feet as you are in the saddle?'

'One squeak out of you,' Diana said, 'and I'll ask for you to be ejected. All three of you. Come on, Liza. Back to the front with me.'

Liza was glaring at Archie. His face registered nothing.

'See you later,' he said to her.

'He should have stuck up for me,' she cried to Diana, following her back up the hall. 'Why did he let Susan snub me?'

'She didn't snub you.'

'She did! She said I was suburban.'

Diana turned and looked at Liza.

'No. No, she didn't.'

'She implied it—'

'Liza,' Diana said, pushing her down into her chair. 'Liza, look. You and Archie don't agree over this. You can't expect him to rush to your defence when you say things he believes are wrong. You *do* mind about your neighbours. So would I in your position. Well, out with it, then. Say yes, Susan, I do care who lives next to me and it's all very well for you to sneer, living half a mile from anyone. Fight back—'

Mrs Betts stepped forward from the table, ear-rings sending forth whiskers of rainbow light, and cleared her throat.

'Ladies and gentlemen, I must first say how thrilled I am—' She glanced behind her. 'We are, to see so many of you this evening. I think I may safely say that such a number indicates the strength of feeling that this proposal has aroused. Mr Jago will outline the development plans for us, and then what I – we – would like is to hear points from the floor.'

How could he, Liza thought, how could he let her be so rude to me? And in front of Diana. My view is just as valid as his. I know it is. In fact, it's more so because he isn't thinking of me and the children and our quality of life, and I am. He's just following out some impersonal social principle. And he's doing his usual things. Liza's a darling, she imitated Archie to herself, but she has no brain. He doesn't look at me, Liza wailed silently, he doesn't see me, and yet he demands that I look at him, that I corkscrew myself into understanding his adolescent self-absorption, his unreasonableness . . .

'What I want to know is,' Cyril Vinney said, heaving himself and his beer gut roughly upright, 'what these houses are going to cost?'

'Mr Vinney, that is not perhaps relevant—'

'A million quid!' someone shouted from the back. 'That's what that field's worth, as a site! A million quid!'

'Half,' Richard Prior called without heat.

'I'm not moving,' Cyril Vinney said, 'until I get an answer to my question.'

Why do I bother, Liza thought, watching Simon Jago attempt to talk Cyril Vinney down. Why do I care what Archie thinks? 'You have such power,' Blaise had written. 'It's the power of someone both mysterious and honest. What a combination! I admire you so. Can't you see?'

Archie was saying, 'I do think we should get off the question of money, and on to the question of the preservation of village life.'

'Tell that to old Prior!' Cyril Vinney shouted.

Simon Jago said that he would like all remarks addressed to the chair.

There were some sentences in Liza's letter from Blaise that she knew by heart, even though she had only read it a few times. I deserve this, she told herself; I deserve to be recognized for myself at last. Archie doesn't see me for what I am, he only sees me in relation to himself. 'You are changing me,' Blaise had written. 'I am different, I have a different vision because of you.' Liza looked down at her lap. Simon Jago was explaining how the field in question was the end of a long green corridor running out from Winchester, and, if it disappeared, the remaining strip could then be considered an infill all the way to the industrial estates on the edge of the city. 'That field,' said Simon, 'may not look like much to you. But to planners and developers it is a last bastion, a bastion they want demolished.'

Archie, at the back, stirred uneasily. He did not in the least want to continue sitting next to Susan Prior, but he felt both that Richard was right and that to move seats now would create more rifts than ever. He glanced at the back of Liza's head. It looked extremely indignant. He could not blame her, and yet he felt, with a sinking heart, that she was not handling her opinion well, that she might humiliate herself. He also felt, almost above anything, that he had not moved because he could not. An alarming inertia, the inertia that seemed to lie in wait for him these days like a migraine, filled his mind and limbs with lead. His glance strayed back to Liza. She couldn't help him, could she? Or wouldn't she? He must not think about it. He must divert his mind.

Between Liza and Archie, in the crowd, sat the Vicar, Colin Jenkins, who ostentatiously expressed no opinion on the development, but who was quite unable to resist a meeting. Archie's roving thoughts swooped down on him like a bird of prey. Colin's wife was out on night duty, no doubt, bent upon her relentless task of asserting her independence from Colin's spiritual master. Archie thought He probably got entered on Chrissie Jenkins's kitchen calendar on a weekly basis, along with nursing shifts and parish meetings. Pop God in for ten minutes between the Thursday Club for

142

young mums and a trip to Tesco, and that's Him dealt with until the weekend.

Mrs Betts was handing out forms. They were forms for enrolment in the Society. She swept deliberately past Archie and the Priors.

'May I have one?' Archie said. 'I'd like to see—'

'Never too late for a change of heart,' Mrs Betts said.

Susan Prior leaned to look at the form with him.

'I'm sorry if I upset your wife.'

'Would you say so to her?'

Susan got up and walked to the front of the hall. Everyone was standing now, Liza with the Jagos, and Susan said to her, without preamble, 'I'm sorry if you thought I was rude.'

'You were rude,' Diana Jago said.

'I don't have to agree with you,' Liza said, wishing she had not said it the moment it was out and then, making matters worse, 'I am perfectly entitled to my own opinion.'

Susan looked at her.

'So you are,' she said, and moved away.

Simon Jago put a hand under Liza's elbow.

'Forget it.'

'She always sounds so sneering—'

'No, no. Just blunt. Calls a spade a spade.'

Liza said, 'I'd better find Archie—'

'Of course.'

'Thank you. Thank you for standing up for me.'

She pushed through the disorderly crowd of chairs and people.

'Poor little thing,' Diana said, watching her go. 'I don't suppose she's ever said boo to Archie before.'

'Come on. Archie wouldn't be hard on her. Not Archie . . .'

'Every marriage,' Diana said surprisingly, 'has its own balance. It's a natural balance. Liza's tried to tip theirs a bit, that's all.'

143

'Good God. Has she? Why?'

'Search me. I just know—'

'Forty-seven members,' Mrs Betts said triumphantly, steaming up to them. 'And eleven more promises. Now, Mr Jago, we really can get started.'

There was a crush to get out of the hall. In it, Liza lost Archie and found herself next to Colin Jenkins who said he hoped she didn't mind him saying so but he was a bit concerned about the fire hazard of the Sunday School carrying real candles at their crib blessing service.

'Twelve children,' Liza said. 'Or fourteen. A dozen little candles. Parents all round. I'm sure it will be perfectly safe.'

'There ought to be a code of practice about these things,' Colin said. 'Then we'd know where we were.'

Liza stared. Ahead of her in the crowd she glimpsed Archie, head and shoulders above the rest. She saw Sharon Vinney pluck at him as he passed, and mouth something, and she saw Archie bend swiftly towards her and then, as if she had hit him, jerk away from her and shove his way forward into the night outside.

'Excuse me,' Liza said to Colin Jenkins and began to press forward herself. She had to pass very close to Sharon Vinney who wore a quilted skiing jacket and swinging ear-rings in the form of crucifixes.

'You can tell him,' Sharon said loudly to Liza as she went by, giving out a blast of fried food and old cigarette, 'you can tell him that I'm not the only one. The whole village thinks the same. The whole place—'

In the lane outside, Liza could find no Archie. She called him, self-conscious at the sound of her voice and his name. After a while, Mrs Pinkney from the bungalow crept up and said she had seen Archie walking away a few moments ago, in the direction of home.

'Quite fast, Mrs Logan. I think he thought you were ahead of him. At least, I wouldn't like to be definite, but I think—'

Liza set off, running. At the Beeches Lane turning, she caught Archie up.

'I'm here!' she called. 'Archie! Wait!'

He took several more strides before he halted.

'Mrs Pinkney said you thought I'd gone—'

'No,' Archie said.

'But why did you rush off, then? Why didn't you wait? It's dark, Archie, it's a dark night—'

'Sorry,' he said. 'Sorry.'

His voice sounded half strangled.

'Was it Sharon? I came ¬ushing out after you, just in case, and here you are stampeding off and just leaving me—' She broke off. She couldn't see his face. She took a deep breath and said loudly, 'Well, whatever she said to you, you bloody well deserve!'

Archie began to walk again. She hurried to keep up with him.

'What, Archie, what is it, what did she say? What—'

'She said,' Archie shouted, 'she said I was neglecting her mother and that I was not fit to be a doctor.'

Liza drew a huge breath.

'But that's nonsense. Take no notice. You know it isn't true—'

Archie swung round in the lane, almost on the spot where Blaise had said, 'If you only knew the power that is yours,' and gripped Liza's shoulders.

'It is not nonsense. It is true.'

Oh, my God, Liza thought, I can't stand any more of this. It's always been bad, Archie's violent over-reaction to things, but this autumn it's got really out of control. And I haven't got the energy to humour him any more, really I haven't. She drew a breath.

'Sharon Vinney,' said Liza in the level, quiet voice she used in class, 'is a mischief-maker. You've said it yourself, often. There's nothing she likes better than a bit of trouble to stir. And it isn't as if she does anything for her mother herself. She expects the Health Service to do it all. She expects you to do everything she won't. I'm sorry I shouted,' Liza said with great kindness. 'Really I am. But you mustn't be a silly Archie.'

He drew his breath in sharply. Liza tried to take his hand in the darkness and found his fist was clenched.

'Archie, please—'

'I'm hungry,' he said. 'I'm terribly hungry,' and began to walk away once more, up the lane, leaving her no alternative but to follow.

'I don't know what's the matter,' Liza said to her sister on the telephone. 'It's like living with some mad stranger. He sat miles away from me at the meeting. Then he just let Susan Prior be frightfully insulting without even attempting to defend me. And then he took some stupid village remark to heart and rushed off home leaving me to follow on my own. In the dark.'

Clare, whose genuine sympathy was not unmixed with a small pleasure at Liza's dismay, settled herself more comfortably by the telephone and said, 'Does he know about Blaise, do you suppose?'

There was a brief, complete silence.

'How do you know about Blaise?'

'From Blaise.'

'What?'

'He came here,' Clare said, while the pleasure grew and began to dwarf the sympathy. 'He came here because he was desperate for someone to talk to.'

'I don't believe it!'

'It's true. Of course,' Clare said, ignoring the huge excitement she had felt when Blaise described his love for Liza, 'I didn't encourage him at all. I mean, I'm sure he's as much in love with the *idea* of being in love as he is with you. I'm sure you see that.'

Liza said nothing.

146

'After all,' Clare said, sensing a tiny triumph, 'he can't hold a candle to Archie. And it's just a crush, really, isn't it, a schoolboy crush?'

Liza took a deep breath.

'Archie knows nothing about Blaise, because there is nothing to know.'

Clare's triumph began to deflate.

'Liza—'

'I can't help Blaise's feelings. I can help my own and they are under perfect control. I don't need you to point out what the matter with Blaise is.'

'No,' said Clare, drooping.

'You're as bad as Archie,' Liza said, gathering strength. 'You imagine all kinds of awful things that couldn't possibly happen. Do you really think I would risk all I've got for something so silly?'

'No,' Clare said.

'Let's stop talking about it,' Liza said, generous at the approach of victory. 'I tell you why I really rang. It's about Christmas. Will you come and have Christmas Day here? Please. We'd love it.'

Typical, Clare thought miserably, putting down the telephone. I have the upper hand for the first time in ten years and I lose it in three sentences. Not just that, but Liza's right. She was justified in being cross. Who, in their right minds, would risk Archie for Blaise? She got up and went along the hall to her sitting room. On the table in the window she had put a neat, small Christmas tree, carefully decorated in gold and silver and scarlet. Archie would laugh at that tree. He'd think it half-hearted, inhibited. No wonder Liza had strength, living with someone of such appetites. It gave you confidence, being with Archie. Her tree had no confidence, poor thing, sitting neatly on its table, obediently glowing with symmetrical fairy lights. She leaned against the wall and looked at it.

'Sorry,' Clare said to her Christmas tree.

*

On Christmas Eve, Sir Andrew and Marina telephoned from Kenya. They were in the last week of their honeymoon. The children, dressed for bed, had a minute or two each on the telephone to them. Imogen was very excited.

'Hello, lady, hello, lady, hello, lady,' Imogen shouted to Africa. From Africa, Archie could hear his father laugh.

It was paradise, they said. They were at Malindi and had been on safari. Marina was beside herself about the birds. They had been on a private safari and had been given breakfast out in the bush, breakfast with napkins and Cooper's Oxford marmalade and eggs and bacon cooked on a bonfire.

'But no *Times*,' Sir Andrew said. 'All that was missing was *The Times*.'

'Are you brown?' Liza asked. 'Are you brown as nuts?'

'As cornflakes—'

'Oh! Oh, it sounds so marvellous!'

'It is,' Sir Andrew said. He was laughing. 'It is. Her ladyship shot a guinea fowl. Lovely shot. We'll bring the cape back, for salmon flies. For Archie.'

'Can you hear that boom-crash?' Marina asked, coming on the line to Thomas. 'Can you hear? That's the Indian Ocean. I'll bring you shells—'

'Yes,' Thomas said, cramming his ear to the receiver. 'Yes.'

'Happy Christmas, darling. Give them all a hug from us. A big Christmas hug.'

It was quiet and dull when they put the receiver down.

Mikey said sadly, 'They saw a lion.'

Christmas seemed suddenly commonplace, beside a lion.

Liza said, 'Everything she touches becomes special, doesn't it? You can't have ordinariness, not with Marina—'

'Sh—' Archie said.

She flashed him a look of irritation.

'Not *still*—'

He crossed to the kitchen door.

'I've got a few calls, I won't be long.'

'Granny Mossop?' Liza said unkindly, to punish him for his persistent unacceptance of Marina.

Archie paused, his hand on the doorknob. He seemed about to say something noisy, but then he changed his mind and said in a perfectly normal voice, 'I sent Granny Mossop into hospital two days ago.'

'Oh, good, good—'

'Not good,' Archie said. 'She won't speak to me. Or the nurses.' He looked at the children. 'Into bed, you lot. Or You Know Who'll never come.'

Abruptly, Imogen remembered.

'Chrithmath!'

She went scuttling up the stairs, squealing like a piglet.

Colin Jenkins disliked Christmas. At Christmas and Easter, he was quite unable to control the parish, which took the bit between its teeth and plunged into the festivals with a lavishness which Colin felt was both wrong in itself and mainly attributable to the materialism of the present government. Chrissie had, as usual, declared the over-excitement of the parish not to be her responsibility.

'Sorry, dear, but it really isn't my business. I've done my organizing. I did it in November. What with Mother and the hospital, I've got my work cut out as it is. You should just put your foot down. Really you should.'

The interior of the church was flagrant proof that he had not. It was crammed with as much decoration as it could hold: windowsills furred with pine branches, pillars wound with ribbons, pedestals in every corner bearing explosive arrangements of greenery and scarlet

149

silk poinsettias, six inches across, bought by Mrs Betts from her wholesalers in Southampton. From the chancel arch a gold cardboard star spun on a chain of tinsel, and, below the lectern, illuminated by miniature electric light bulbs rigged up by Lynne Tyler's husband, stood the Sunday School crib, the cast only lacking the three kings, who lay in a shoebox in the vestry, awaiting Twelfth Night.

It not only irritated Colin to see the church turned into some ceremonial garden centre, but also to see it full of people who never came to church otherwise. They'd come at Christmas because it was quite jolly; they would telephone for wedding or funeral or christening arrangements in the faintly imperious manner of people booking holidays; they were full of inflexible theories about the way vicars – and, even more, vicars' wives – should live their lives, but any suggestion that they might use the church for its regular and intended purpose caused indignation and resentment. When he was a young man, Colin had once been so stirred by a speech given by Bishop Trevor Huddlestone that he had, for at least a month, determined to become a missionary. Christmas at Stoke Stratton made him regret with particular energy his failure to keep that resolve.

He expressed his disapproval by refusing to dress up for Christmas. They could have him simply in a surplice and black stole, and, if he stuck out like a sore thumb in all the gaudy nonsense, so much the better. Maybe that would get the message home. The church, of course, was packed, from the Jagos in the front pew with their two languid daughters tossing sweeps of blonded brown hair from their faces, to Lynne and Robbie Tyler at the back with their brood of children and a clutch of aunts and grans. Mrs Betts, who believed God to be primarily the President of the Women's Institute, wore a fancy tweed coat with matching hat, and was accompanied by a daughter and a son-in-law so suitable in dress and demeanour that they might have been designed for her, as fashion accessories.

About halfway down, sandwiched between pews full of Christmas strangers staying in the village, Liza, Archie and Clare had penned the children between them. Archie was not on call again until Boxing Day, but his morning of Christmas freedom had begun at ten past four when Imogen had appeared, covered in chocolate and strenuously wishing to play post offices. By nine o'clock, the day had felt already done to death, and when Clare appeared at ten-thirty, in time for church, both Liza and Archie had fallen upon her like castaways sighting a sail. Clare, who could not help drawing comfort from other people's misfortunes, was heartened at the sight of them and began to feel a dim glow of appropriate enthusiasm. Anything, after all, was better than waking alone to a silent city that was bound to be full, just bound to be, of blissful couples in bed together, opening stockings crammed with senti-mental, intimate jokes.

Liza was wearing a cream jersey that Clare knew, after she had hugged her, was cashmere, It was from Marina. So was the beautiful brown snake belt she had on, and the computer games for the boys and the princess dressing-up clothes for Imogen and – what for Archie?

'A rod,' he said, gesturing towards it. 'A trout rod.'

'But it's a beauty!'

'Yes,' he said flatly. 'Far too much.'

Liza seized Clare's arm and mouthed silence. In the kitchen, alone for a moment, she had shown Clare a tiny box with a garnet-and-pearl pin in it, a heart on a golden bar.

'Who's it from?'

'Shhh. Guess.'

'No,' Clare said, eyes enormous.

'Yes. Silly ass. I shall give it straight back.'

'It's awfully pretty.'

Liza put the box back in the kitchen drawer. The card that had come with the box lay under the drawer's lining paper.

'What did Archie give you?'

'A picture. A Victorian watercolour of the Stoke river.'

'It sounds lovely!'

'It's sweet,' Liza said, thinking of the garnet pin.

Archie had been very kind to Clare. He had made her coffee and talked to her all the way down to church and given her Thomas to sit next to. Above the carols, and the readings, delivered at top-speed in an incomprehensible scream by the older members of the Sunday School, Clare could hear Imogen's intermittent grizzling. She was not the only one. Dotted around the congregation, the child victims of Christmas hype whined and fidgeted. Clare, without responsibility for any of them and pleased to be in this comfortable, celebratory, unspiritual gathering, briefly felt quite happy.

But for all that, she could not help perceiving that Archie was not. Finely tuned as she was to notice every quiver on the seismograph of her own feelings, Clare had become morbidly sensitive to atmosphere. Archie was smiling certainly. He sang the carols, admonished Mikey for wriggling, glanced with affection at Liza, at his children, at Clare. But he was not happy. Just below the surface, Clare thought, lay some trouble, manifesting itself in glimmers of tension and defensiveness. She worried that it was Blaise. It was not reasonable to worry about Blaise, she told herself, but instinctively it was not to be avoided. Liza had said someone in the village had upset Archie. Could it be that? Or could it be that Liza's new little manner with him, a kind of condescending little manner, thinly masking a sizeable impatience at his attitude to his father's marriage, was affecting him more deeply than anyone suspected? Oh

152

dear, Clare thought, how awful, how interesting, how consoling. Should she say anything about Blaise? Heavens! Should she?

Thomas seized his *Songs of Praise* and riffled through it officiously.

' "Hark the Herald",' he hissed. 'There you are. Seventy-four.'

Two days before the New Year, Sir Andrew and Marina came home. They had a horrible flight, they said, delayed and rough, and Sir Andrew was feeling a bit battered by it, but all they needed was a good night's sleep and they would be down, as planned, on New Year's Eve.

Archie was on duty throughout the New Year. When Liza had suggested asking his father and Marina, he had said do, yes, do, with unexceptionable enthusiasm, but of course I shall be in and out a lot. That did not seem to Liza to matter. Indeed, it might be easier to have only his intermittent presence for the first staying visit. She, on the other hand, was excited about it. She and Sally cleaned the spare room, and she put on new white linen pillowcases and sheets with embroidered hems. She made lists of meals and, as she did it, imagined how warm Marina would be in her praise of them.

Early on the morning of New Year's Eve, the telephone rang. Liza, thinking it would be a patient, picked it up preparing to say that Dr Logan was already at the health centre.

'Liza—'

'Marina!'

'My dear,' Marina said. 'Liza. I've called – I'm so sorry, but I've called—'

Her voice sounded light and faint.

'Marina,' Liza said, alarmed. 'What is it, what has happened?'

'Forgive me. It's a little difficult. One moment—'

There was a pause.

Then Marina said, 'Liza. Dear, I'm afraid I have to tell you that Andrew is dead.'

Chapter Ten

Stuart Campbell, senior partner in the practice, was very delicate with Archie. He had met Sir Andrew himself a couple of times, and had felt admiration for him both professionally and privately. He also felt that Archie could have gone much further and faster in his own career if only he had chosen to, and had said to his wife, once or twice, that Sir Andrew's fame inhibited his son. So, while he wished to condole most seriously with Archie, he also felt his junior partner's life might now begin to blossom. Archie, after all, he repeatedly told colleagues exasperated by Archie's impulsiveness or forgetfulness, had the human touch.

Dr Campbell's habits were stately. He was in his late fifties and enjoyed the image of an old-fashioned rural general practitioner, invariably tweed suited, comfortable in farm kitchens, regarding the weather from the exclusive point of view of a fisherman. Grey summer days, to Stuart Campbell, were good days, because they cast no shadows on the water. When he spoke to his colleagues, he liked to summon them magisterially into his own room at the health centre and speak to them, very genially of course, from the far side of his desk. The other doctors sat the same side of their desks as their patients. They said it inspired confidence. Stuart Campbell said it did precisely the reverse.

He did not, however, summon Archie to him, but went instead to find him after surgery. Archie was scribbling notes in his immense black hand but stopped as Stuart came in, and instinctively rose, like a schoolboy. Stuart waved a hand.

'My dear fellow—'

He put the hand on Archie's shoulder.

'You have all my sympathy. Betty's, too. A great shock.'

Archie, though drawn, looked perfectly composed.

'Thank you.'

'Wonderful life,' Stuart Campbell said, removing his hand. 'Wonderful to know how much you've done in life, how much you've given. I feel very privileged to have met him.'

'Thank you,' Archie said. 'Thank you for coming in.'

'My dear boy. It's the very least – And of course if there's anything at all that any of us can do, here, you've only to say the word.'

Archie gave a small sigh.

'There's very little to do, actually. Being my father, everything is in apple-pie order.'

'If you want more time off—'

'No,' Archie said quickly. 'No thank you. I shan't want that.'

'I thought perhaps your stepmother might like—'

Archie looked down.

'She's a very independent woman.' He looked up again and gave a little smile. 'I'm sure she'll make her own decisions.'

'Yes. Yes, of course.'

He paused. Then he put his hands in his trouser pockets and said, 'Coronary, I suppose?'

'Complete occlusion. No previous symptoms beyond tiredness after a long flight the day before.'

'Archie,' Stuart Campbell said with more energy. 'Archie, don't hold out.' He took his hands out of his trouser pockets and gripped Archie's arm. 'Sometimes, as you know as well as I do, it's easier to let go in front of someone whom you do not have to protect, like your wife. And I'd understand, my dear fellow, heavens, I would.'

Archie gazed at him.

156

'I'm a clumsy fool,' Stuart said. 'Spoken far too soon. Betty always says I've the tact of a rhino.'

'No,' Archie said. 'You could not be kinder. Really. And I'm so grateful. But I'm all right. Very sad, of course, but perfectly all right.'

'I don't like it,' Stuart Campbell said later to his wife. 'I don't like the look of him.'

Betty Campbell, who considered Archie a man oversized in every direction, said she thought it was a mercy he hadn't broken down. It never helped for a man to weep, anyway. Stuart was about to protest, and then recollected that Betty and her partner had lost at their weekly bridge four, and refrained. When her next remark turned out to be, 'And don't you go meddling. There's no-one like doctors for interfering,' he was glad he had.

The next day, in the post office, he met Liza. She was looking pretty but subdued and the elder boy was with her. Stuart waited until they had bought the stamps and writing paper they had come in for – Mrs Betts, heavy with genteel condolence, served Liza as if she were an invalid – and then he ushered her back into the lane to say, 'I do hope you'll let me know if there's anything we can do. We can fill in for Archie between us, you know. And there's always such a mountain of paperwork at such times.'

Liza turned to him gratefully. Large, easy, unthreatening men like Stuart Campbell brought out all that was sweetest and most female in her.

'You are so kind. But I don't think he wants anything to be different. It's his way of coping. And his stepmother is amazing: so brave, so competent.' She looked up at Stuart. 'They had only been married three weeks. A month ago on Friday. I can't bear it.'

Thomas, beside her, was again apprehensive, and then certain, that he would cry. He shuffled sideways and glared into the bare twigs of the hedge, where litter

157

had blown and hung like grimy rags. The tears rose and the rags blurred and quivered.

'You must ring me,' Stuart said, 'if you're at all worried. About anything. It wasn't – a usual relationship.'

'No.

'So very close. Most fathers and sons get on, all right. But not like that.'

'Perhaps,' Liza began and then glanced at Thomas's shaking back, and stopped. She went over and put her arms round him. 'Darling.'

'Perhaps,' Stuart said, understanding her.

She looked at him over Thomas's head.

'It's this quiet, quiet sadness. So out of character.'

Whose quiet sadness? Thomas thought, calming down a little. And what was out of character? Characters were people in plays. Cartoon ones were Mickey Mouse. He snuffled a bit against Liza's shoulder and felt descend upon him the terrible weariness that followed the bouts of weeping.

'The one thing I've learned from doctoring,' Stuart said, 'is that the exceptions exceed the rules. A hundred-fold. And trauma invariably creates exceptions.'

'I'm keeping a close watch—'

'I've no doubt of it, my dear. Just let me know if you notice anything disturbing.'

Thomas disengaged himself and rubbed his face vigorously with his anorak sleeve. Stuart put a brief hand on his head.

'Well, your father has plenty of people to comfort him, that's for sure.'

'But the trouble is,' Thomas said, 'that we're the ones who need comforting. And Marina.'

Marina. At any mention of her name, they felt filled with awe and pity and love. At least, Liza and Thomas did, and so, in his unformed gawky way, did Mikey. She had wanted them all to come to London; she had wanted them all to be as close to Sir Andrew – the last living second of Sir Andrew – as she could get them. So Liza had left Imogen with Sally for the day – 'Come too!' Imogen had bellowed, but not for long, with Sally there – and they had driven up to London on New Year's Eve and found Marina in the Victoria mansion flat, alone in the sitting room full of towering Edwardian furniture brought down from Scotland.

She did not weep although she had plainly wept earlier. She held each one of them hard, and then Archie and Liza had gone into the big, gaunt bedroom where Sir Andrew lay, in new blue pyjamas, wearing an inscrutable expression, neither happy nor sad, merely absent. Liza had never seen anyone dead before and was a little afraid of that, but very much more afraid of what the sight of his dead father might do to Archie. But it seemed to do very little. He was, after all, more than accustomed to it. He simply stooped and kissed his father's forehead, and so Liza thought she had better do so, too. The flesh was soft and cool; remote but not particularly dead. She took Archie's hand, but he did not grip hers, merely let their palms lie together. He longed for Liza to cry. She did not because it did not seem necessary; there was no reality for her at that actual, real moment of standing by the body, looking down into that familiar, dead face.

When they came out, Marina and the boys were sitting on the sofa close together.

'Would you like to see Grandpa?' Archie said.

Mikey flung himself back into the sofa cushions.

'No.'

'Thomas?'

'A bit,' Thomas said.

Marina took his hand.

'From the doorway?'

He nodded. He stood up and Archie took his hand and led him along the passage to the bedroom.

Thomas halted in the passage and looked through the open door into the bedroom, and saw his grandfather lying very neatly, with bare feet. The bareness of his feet shocked Thomas deeply. It was improper, rude to leave his feet bare.

He said roughly, 'He ought to have his slippers on.'

'Yes,' Archie said. 'Of course he should.'

Thomas pointed.

'They're there.'

Archie went across to the chest of drawers, which bore exactly the boxes and brushes he remembered from boyhood, and picked up the slippers. Thomas did not move. Then Archie went over to the bed and fitted the slippers on to his father's feet.

'There,' he said. 'Do you think that is more suitable?'

He turned. Thomas had gone. He was back in the sitting room, saying to Mikey in a voice harsh with boasting and bafflement, 'He only looks asleep.'

Mikey hid his face in the sofa cushions.

Thomas said to Liza in an incompetent whisper, 'Let's go home. I want to go home.'

'Of course you should,' Marina said. 'Of course. But you'll be glad you came.'

Liza began to pick up her handbag and look for Mikey's jacket.

Marina said to Archie, 'We'll talk tomorrow. It's all under control today.'

'Yes,' he said. He went out of the sitting room and back to his father. Marina, after a moment, followed him.

'I rang Maurice Crawford. He came at once. He is doing the certificate.'

Archie was stooping over his father.

'I'll go,' Marina said. She craved his questions.

'You don't have to.'

'But you might want to be alone—'

'Too late,' he said.

'He died in my arms,' she said. 'Literally. He wasn't

160

alone for a split second at the end. Maurice says he will have known nothing, just a stab of pain and then—' She stopped and put her hand to her face. 'I'm so sorry. I forgot you were a doctor.'

'Not at all,' Archie said. He straightened up.

'I said we could talk tomorrow. But of course we could now, if that's what you want—'

'No,' Archie said. 'No, thank you.'

'I don't want to do anything except the way you want it.'

'Thank you.'

He came up to her and gestured that she should precede him back to the sitting room. She hesitated, briefly overwhelmed with a longing to be comforted, on the very edge of flinging herself into his arms. But nothing whatever in his face or manner invited that.

So she simply said again, 'I'll do things just the way you want,' and walked ahead of him.

Liza could see they had not communicated. Archie went across to Mikey and lifted him into his arms.

'Could I have a hamburger?' Mikey whispered urgently. 'A London one?'

Liza put her arms around Marina.

'Would you like me to come up and stay? It would be so easy, with the holidays, and Sally. And I'd love to be with you. If you'd like it.'

'Dear,' Marina said, shaking her head. 'Dear Liza. I'll tell you the minute I need anyone. There's no-one I'd rather have than you. But there's so much to do just now and I'm best alone for a bit. I'm used to being alone. More used – more used than not.'

They drove home almost in silence, pausing only to buy the boys two monsterburgers in white cardboard boxes, and two drinks in lidded cups as big as buckets. Once or twice, Liza put her hand on Archie's, on the steering wheel, and he gave a cursory pat with his other one, but apart from that she gazed out of the window at the charmless suburbs and then at the

161

lifeless winter landscape that edged the motorway. In the back seat, heartened by food, the boys tussled mildly together and forgot the morning.

Colin Jenkins paid a pastoral visit. He had done this once before, on arrival in place of his mild, scholarly predecessor who had been an honorary canon of the cathedral and had retired into the heart of the city. On that first visit, Liza had made coffee and talked to him a little awkwardly in the sitting room round the bump that was to be Imogen. He had not met Archie until they had coincided at a hospital bed and he had known, with a small resentment, that Archie had had the upper hand at that meeting. Now, emboldened by the passing of time, Colin rather imagined that the ball, at this interview, would be in his court. It was not supremacy over Archie that he wanted, he told himself, but a chance to fulfil his proper role. He, the unbereaved, would be the stronger, the one able to give.

He called in the evening. Archie opened the door wearing jeans and a dark-blue fisherman's jersey. He had no shoes on, only thick white seaman's socks, and the absence of shoes was, for some reason, disconcerting. He led Colin into the sitting room where there was a fire in front of which Nelson lay on his side. Liza was watching television, but, when Colin came in, she got up and switched it off, and there was the sudden extreme silence that the banishment of television leaves.

'I've called to offer you both my very great sympathy. And to tell you that I shall pray for you. And your father.'

Archie said nothing. Liza guided Colin to a chair.

'We opened some wine. Will you have some?'

'Oh no. No, thank you.'

'Coffee?'

'I couldn't put you to the trouble,' Colin said. 'I only

162

came for a moment or two. I thought . . .' He looked at them both, Liza back on the sofa, Archie still standing up. 'I thought we might say a prayer together.'

'Good God,' Archie said.

'It is,' Colin said firmly, as if proffering an unwanted indigestion tablet, 'very comforting.'

'I'm sure,' Liza began, 'for some people—'

'But you are Christians. You are churchgoers. You are part of the Christian family.'

Liza looked at Archie.

After a pause he said, without much grace, 'I may be a religious man – I may have a deep religious sense – but I am not at all sure there is a God. Not your God, in any case.'

Colin smiled. It was his smile of patient understanding.

'But if you are religious, then surely that implies belief in God?'

Archie sat down on the arm of the sofa and put his head in his hands.

'I don't think—' Liza said.

'Christ,' Archie shouted across at her, raising his head. 'Christ! Don't you even know what religion means? Are you so hidebound by your colourless bureaucratic orthodoxy that religion only means to you this frightful modern Church with its doggerel hymns and playschool prayers?' He got up. 'Religion, Colin, is an awakened sense of some great controlling force, an awareness that above or beyond there is not just a freedom but a fulfilment. And this awareness of power and possibility makes us strive ever onwards, morally, emotionally, spiritually. What on earth has such a concept to do with the dreary pen-pushing second-rate God you want to offer me?'

And he left the room.

Liza said, 'Oh, Colin, I'm so sorry, you must forgive him. He's terribly upset, he—'

'Of course,' Colin said, all indulgence. 'It's only to be

163

expected. Quite understandable. And I gather they were particularly close. It's a hard blow.'

Liza nodded. She was torn between pity for Archie and fury with him, while at the same time realizing that his speech to Colin was the longest and most eloquent he had made since Andrew died.

'Perhaps,' Colin said, 'you and I might pray together now. For Archie, as well as for his father?'

Liza looked at him helplessly. What alternative, but to agree, had Archie left her? Colin Jenkins, victorious, smiled and closed his eyes.

'Oh, God, our Father—'

'How could you?' Liza cried. 'How could you be so rude to him?'

Archie shrugged.

'It was absolutely gratuitous! He's an annoying little man but he meant well, and he was only doing his job!'

'It was insulting,' Archie said, rolling away from her in bed. 'It was insulting to be spoken to like that.'

Liza took a deep breath. She was sitting up against the pillows. She folded her hands in front of her on the duvet. The thing to do was to keep very, very calm.

'I see. So your grief is special and more awful than anyone else's. Just as your love for your father was special and greater than anyone else's. No-one is fit to help you because you are in this special category. Diana Jago comes to see you and you just stare at her. Richard Prior, of all people, comes to see you and you look at him like a dog that's been kicked and will never trust people again.'

Archie lay listening, his eyes open.

'It's the same old thing, isn't it? It's the same old arrogance. It doesn't occur to you, does it, what hell Marina is going through or what a nightmare she had? You won't lift a finger to comfort her. Oh no. She took away Archie's daddy so she must be punished. How long are you going to keep this up? How long? Because people will get sick of your self-indulgence, and the first of them will be me.'

Archie did not stir. She looked across at his exposed shoulder and the back of his head.

She said in her most Mrs Logan-of-Bradley-Hall-School voice, 'And the children are not going to the funeral.'

There was silence. It lasted half a minute and then Archie said, 'Yes, they are.'

'Mikey and Imogen are too young. And Thomas doesn't want to.'

Archie rolled over.

'He does.'

'No,' Liza said. 'He's had bad dreams ever since you took him in to see Andrew the day he died. He's had them most nights.'

'He hasn't said anything about them to me—'

'He probably knows there's little point in saying anything to you just now. It's like living with someone deaf and blind.'

By his sides, Archie's fists were clenched.

'Have you quite finished?'

'I think so,' Liza said.

Archie got out of bed.

'Where are you going?'

'To the spare room.'

'I see,' Liza said. 'Melodrama to the end.'

Dizzy with rage and misery, Archie banged the door behind him. When he opened the spare-room door, he realized he could not sleep there. It was still waiting for Andrew and Marina, the high white pillows piled up, untouched, virgin. Choking with tears, he stumbled downstairs and cast himself on the sitting-room sofa. Alone in their bedroom, Liza slid neatly down under the duvet, turned on her side and cried and cried as if her heart would break. On the landing, crouched against the banisters, Thomas shivered in his pyjamas and listened.

*

Thomas thought St Stephen's Church in Rochester Row was horrible. It was a sad, dead colour and everything about it seemed too tall and sharp and most unfriendly. The street was horrible, too, grim and red, like a menacing great passage. Why on earth his grandfather's funeral had to happen in such an awful place was incomprehensible.

It was frightening being so few of them, just him and Archie and Liza and Marina one side and a few old men in dark suits the other. Archie had said there would be a huge memorial service later, which would be very cheerful because it would be all about the marvellous things Grandpa had done, but Thomas might not be able to come to that, because of school. He wished he hadn't come to this. He'd said yes partly to please Archie and partly to spite Mikey, and he regretted both of those reasons now, sitting between Liza and Marina in the gloomy dark with the almost unbearable sight of Grandpa's coffin there, in front of them, on a chrome trolley with rubber wheels. The trolley and the wheels offended Thomas the way his grandfather's bare feet had done.

He thought it unlikely he would cry any more. He thought he must have cried himself right out. He was sick of crying. The only thing to do was not to think about Grandpa, and not to think about going back to school, either – the other black beast that lurked about waiting for his mind to lie idle for a second. He seized his prayer book. He would count all the 'e's on one page. Liza's hand came down and turned the pages back to the correct place and ran a pointing finger along the current line of prayer. Thomas waited until she had taken her hand away and then he closed the prayer book with enormous carefulness and put it in front of him, on the polished wooden ledge. He would have nothing to do with it.

The undertaker's men came up the aisle. There were

six of them. They were not all the same size and they were not pleasing to look at. Slight quivering beside him told Thomas that Liza had begun to cry. He leaned forward imperceptibly, and out of the side of his eyes saw that his father's eyes were full of spilling tears that he was doing nothing about, just letting them brim and fall. It was terrible. The undertaker's men undid some little bolts, lifted the coffin on to their shoulders and made a wide sweep in front of the brass rods of the rood screen; then Thomas realized that they were going to walk away down the aisle. Carrying Grandpa. They were carrying the coffin away. Where? To do what . . . ? A vast black mushroom ballooned up inside Thomas's head and shoved at his skull and his tongue and the backs of his eyes.

Marina's hand appeared. It took his, very hard. Then her face followed it.

'Look up there,' Marina said. 'Go on. Look up.'

Her other hand was pointing.

'Where?' Thomas said, battling with the mushroom.

'Up there. Look up there.'

Above the choir stalls, Thomas could dimly see a faraway roof. It looked blue. It glimmered.

'Stars,' Marina said. 'Just look at that. Hundreds and hundreds of golden stars.'

January had laid its repressive hand on Stoke Stratton. It had not sent snow, but frost; frost and pearl-grey skies to brood over dark trees and dun grass. In the garden at Beeches House, only a brave eleagnus had any colour. If people had to die, Liza thought miserably, why did they do it at a time of year that seemed quite to have lost hope? She knelt on the floor of Thomas's bedroom, in front of his school trunk, with the Pinemount uniform list on the floor beside her, and a pencil to tick off the endless columns of socks and shirts and soccer boots. Thomas, who was supposed to be helping, was slumped on the sofa downstairs in

167

front of a video of *Superman*. She had neither the heart nor the energy to rout him out. They were all worn out with each other, tired of death. Pinemount might at least be a change for Thomas, a place where death and all its ramifying complications were swiftly swamped by timetables and sport.

She put her face down into the trunk. It smelled poignantly of detergent and boy. She, too, longed for term to begin, partly because she so much needed a structure once more, and partly because she wanted Blaise O'Hanlon's admiration back, an admiration that she had, magnificent in her sternness, told him he must desist from, when he had telephoned from Dublin two days before Christmas. She wanted it, she told herself, because living with Archie was so lonely just now; lonely and complicated. It was complicated because he could fill her with frustrated fury, as he did the night Colin Jenkins came, and then, as at the funeral, with real pity: he had turned to her, in that beastly church, and put his arm round her and drawn her to him, and that, for all its sweetness, was more confusing than anything.

She straightened up. She must not think about it. She must think about marked hairbrushes and spare name tapes and towels with loops on them, for swimming. On Thomas's bed, above the opened trunk lid, Blue Rabbit lay propped against the pillow and watched her lugubriously out of his brown embroidered eyes. Perhaps, Liza thought, picking up the list once more, perhaps now that Andrew was dead, the idea of Pinemount might die, too? But she would have to talk to Archie, and at the moment how could anyone, anywhere, talk to Archie?

'Old rubbish,' Granny Mossop muttered.

She lay on her side in a high hard bed in the geriatric ward and mumbled her lips about. She was so thin now that her bed had had to be padded up for her, and, because of the constant accidents of her condition, she was padded, too, a bundle of alien white hospital swaddlings out of which her little brown hands and arms crept like twigs.

'You are not old rubbish,' Archie said. He sat on a chair by her bed and leaned so he could see her. 'You are not here because you are rubbish, but because you couldn't manage at home any more.'

'Could,' she said.

Her teeth floated upside down in a jar of pink fluid on the bedside trolley. Without them, her mouth sucked and fluttered, collapsing in on itself. Archie put a hand on hers.

'Sharon was worried—'

'Ha!'

He dared not ask if Sharon had been in to see her mother. Granny Mossop twitched her hand free. She gestured feebly at the ward.

'Old fools.'

She was difficult to hear. He bent closer. She smelled of cloth and age and illness. They were afraid jaundice was setting in. She would smell worse then.

'I'll be back,' Archie said. 'I'll be back in a few days.'

'Ha,' she said again, with less emphasis.

'I will. I promise you.'

He did not want to leave her. He stood up and waited for a moment, looking down on her wasted, nut-like face and uneven tussocks of white hair. I am afraid, he thought, I am afraid that if I leave her she will die, and if I am not here when she dies, then I will never know.

He went down the polished corridors of the hospital, past screens and pairs of double doors and a mystifying complexity of green signs sending the scarcely hopeful sick down the labyrinths to a chance of cure. A good many of the staff knew him because he was a faithful visitor of practice patients, and some of them stopped him and said how sorry, how very sorry they

169

were about Sir Andrew and how much he would be missed. Thank you, he said, yes, how nice of you; no, we had the funeral quickly because it was what he wished, and there will be a memorial service later.

'It's harder, if you're a doctor,' a staff nurse he had known for years said to him. 'People don't think that. They think that because you know, you understand and so it's easier. But it's the reverse really, isn't it? It's knowing why that makes accepting so hard.'

'And unfinished business,' Archie said.

He went out to find his car. He had no desire to get into it and less to drive back to the health centre. He unlocked the door, and climbed into the driver's seat and sat for a while looking at, but not seeing, a brisk, inflexible shrub planted against an unlovely brick wall. Thomas would be getting to Pinemount now, driven by Liza with Diana Jago, whose spirits could be relied upon to remain buoyant and infectious. Was second term better than first? Or was it worse because there were no optimistic apprehensions left, you only knew the worst? He started the car. What was worst or best any more? Where was there anything but plateau? 'I remember thinking one morning,' a woman patient afflicted with profound menopausal depression had once said to Archie, 'I thought: Is this all there is?' He turned the car into the traffic. God, Archie thought. Is it?

Chapter Eleven

The distinguishing feature of spring terms at Bradley Hall School was that the temperature outside the building felt considerably higher than that inside. The boiler thundered dully away in its basement, pouring heat into the brick walls that surrounded it and only managing to send a tepid trickle through the immense old toast-rack radiators that stood so optimistically under every window. The first day of term was usually spent twisting old newspapers into sausages that could be crammed into the frames of the huge, beautiful eighteenth-century windows that now shook in the winter winds like loose teeth.

The first assembly was always rather festive, chiefly because June Hampole was so genuinely pleased to see the children back. Beaming at them over an enveloping muffler, she told them that the school cat had seven kittens – two toms, she said, and three queens, and two that seemed, however hard she peered, quite androgynous – and that the forsythia was bravely out in the central courtyard and that everyone was to wear gloves for lessons until they were told they might take them off.

'The children cannot write in gloves,' Mrs West called clearly.

'All the better. They are at the most receptive age for learning by heart.'

Liza, laughing, allowed Blaise to catch her eye. He looked older, a little thinner, and his air of dishevelled bohemian glamour was even more pronounced. He had said nothing to her yet, merely looked. Liza was wearing the green jersey Marina had given her.

'You must all sit very close to one another,' June Hampole said. 'But there is to be no touching. No silly touching, that is. And we will pause every ten minutes or so, and do a minute's jumping.'

Mrs West, a professional of forty years' experience, winced faintly. Her English classes would proceed in the orthodox manner they always did. She had brought an electric fan heater with her. Jumping would not even be considered. Liza, happy for the first day in weeks, wanted to laugh out loud at the thought of jumping. Her classes could jump to their verbs. The whole assembly was laughing.

'No laughing!' Commander Haythorne barked.

June Hampole, thoughtfully chewing the earpiece of her spectacles, said they would have a closing prayer. She had not looked one out; she merely thought she would invent one on the spot.

'Dear Father,' she said musingly, and paused, 'Dear Father.' The children, heads bowed, waited. 'Dear Father, this term is like the year, a new page. Which we are going to write on. With great kindness to one another and no fibs and no bullying. Our pens,' said June Hampole gathering speed, 'shall be our loving hearts as well as our desire to do well and to make our parents proud of us. And . . .' she paused again. 'And. And Amen, I think.'

'Amen,' the children chorused loudly.

In the crowd pushing out of the chapel, Liza waited for Blaise's voice at her shoulder. She did not hear it. She was carried out into the hall and surrounded by children wishing to tell her about Christmas presents and skiing holidays and how they thought they had a sort of pain. Across their heads, she saw Blaise herding his first football lesson down the dark passage that led to the fearsome and beetle-infested changing rooms. He did not glance at her. He had not, of course, Liza told herself, noticed she was there.

She turned sternly upon her first classful and said,

'Now that's quite enough attempts to deflect me. In you go. And we'll get the jumping over at the beginning.'

She did not see Blaise at break. She sat beside Commander Haythorne on the accommodating leather sofa in the staff room and he offered her a ginger biscuit out of his particular tin, and told her about his Christmas in Wales, and Liza was a very animated listener in case Blaise should come in and think for one instant that she was waiting for him. He did not come in. She ate her biscuit and Commander Haythorne described the majesty of the seas at Marlow Sands in winter and the atrociousness of his daughter-in-law's housekeeping skills, and her high delight in the day dimmed a little and admitted itself to be troubled.

The morning wore on, and lunchtime came, an Outward Bound exercise in the orangery where the frost still iced the glass inside, and steam rose from the mounds of potatoes and cabbage in exaggerated clouds. Liza seated herself at the head of her usual table and after a while Blaise came in with a troop of boys, and passed her, saying, 'It's murderous out there. The ground's like iron. Am I liable if they break their little legs?'

His voice was easy and conversational. It was the voice he used for everybody. He then stopped by Mrs West and said something quite prolonged to her and made her laugh. Liza turned brightly to the child beside her, a plain and eager girl of eleven who never seemed aware that her determination to sit next to members of staff at meals did not endear her to her contemporaries.

'Well, Laura. Was Christmas all it should be?'

'Mrs Logan, it was brilliant. Granny came and so did my other grandfather and we went carol singing and Mummy didn't have a headache, not once, and I had champagne and the dog was sick but not on Granny, luckily, and on Boxing Day—'

But he looked at me in prayers, Liza thought. It

wasn't an ordinary look, either. He's just being careful, he's not arousing suspicion. I must play the same game, of course I must.

'I really, really hate cabbage. It's my worst thing. Do I have to eat it, Mrs Logan? Do I really, really have to eat this cabbage?'

'Simon, I think you should eat two bites. To do you good. Then you can leave the rest.'

'But I'll be sick. I promise.'

'Eat it with something. Eat it with a bit of sausage.'

'I love cabbage,' Laura said.

'Then,' said Simon, looking at her with pure contempt, 'you can eat mine.'

The afternoon was long. The chill of the day had settled down into real, penetrating cold, and the novelty of a new term had worn off in the face of universal recollection of what school was like. Liza's classes dozed and fiddled, sucking their gloved fingers and then trying to poke woolly filaments off each other's tongues with pencil ends. They were bored with French, bored with trying to concentrate after a month's freedom. At twenty to four, the first cars appeared and the mothers got out of them to stamp about on the drive and bellow at each other about the hell of the weather and the double hell of Christmas. When the last bell went, a gasp of relief ran round the class like a gust of wind. Banging their desks and scraping their chairs, they stampeded past Liza back into their real lives.

She went slowly out to her car. She, too, was extremely cold, and fumbled to get the door open with rigid fingers. In the glove compartment lay the garnet pin. She had planned to return it to Blaise and she had planned exactly what she would say. She looked about her. Mrs West was backing her car out carefully from the corner she always used, and the part-time mathematics teacher, who found Bradley Hall's unorthodoxy quite bewildering, was loading piles of exercise books

174

into her boot. Prep already! The first day . . . There was no-one else. No Blaise. Liza waited a little. The mathematics teacher and Mrs West drove slowly past her and turned towards the main gates. Liza started the engine. She backed her car and turned it, switching the fan and the heater on to full so that the interior roared like a train in a tunnel. She drove out on to the main drive and turned for home. Across the lawn, and halfway across the adjacent field, a man was walking, away from the school. He wore Blaise's yellow muffler.

There was a notice on the door of Stoke Stratton post office. 'Appeal!' it said sternly. 'Don't give in! Lobby all officials!' It was written in thick black ink on one of the large sheets of blossom-pink paper Mrs Betts favoured for her edicts.

'What's happened?' Liza said.

Because of the cold, Mrs Betts was encased in a home-knitted Aran cardigan which gave her the contours and solidity of a hot-water cylinder.

'We shall not give up,' Mrs Betts said. 'I shall go to the House of Lords if necessary.'

Sharon Vinney, intermittently dusting the postcard rack, gave an audible snort.

'What is it?' Liza said. 'Is it the field?'

'He,' said Mrs Betts with deadly emphasis, 'he thinks he has got planning permission.'

'He has,' Sharon said. 'It's final. It'll make all the difference to our Trevor. He'll be first on the list. Somewhere for him and Heather to set up home at last.'

Trevor Vinney, a pale, resentful young man who worked, without enthusiasm, as a mechanic at a Winchester garage, had a small dark girlfriend and a smaller darker baby. The girlfriend spent a good deal of the day sitting in the village bus shelter, with the baby beside her in a pushchair, smoking cigarettes she rolled herself and staring at passing traffic with an angry longing.

175

'Your new neighbours, dear,' Mrs Betts said to Liza. She raised her eyebrows almost to her richly tinted hairline.

Liza said, 'But that's so quick. I mean, we only heard about it two months ago—'

Mrs Betts leaned forward.

'Quite frankly, Mrs Logan, it isn't all as it should be. Something's been going on.'

Sharon stopped dusting. She put her hands on her hips and waited. Mrs Betts lowered her voice.

'I intend to find out. My friend—'

'You'll find nothing on Mr Prior,' Sharon said clearly. 'He's straight, is Mr Prior. Dad worked for him since he came and he said he was a right bugger but he was straight.'

Mrs Betts adjusted the cuffs of her cardigan.

'Don't use bad language in the shop, please, Sharon.'

Sharon glared. Then she turned and went to the far end of the shop where blue packets of aspirin and yellow bottles of disinfectant and scarlet boxes of sticking plaster comprised what Mrs Betts called 'my first-aid corner'.

'I can say what I like to her,' Mrs Betts confided to Liza. 'I pay her the basic industrial wage and I mind her terrible manners for her. She won't leave. Oh no. I'd have to sack her. Where else would she find a job which meant she knew all the gossip in the village before anyone else?'

Liza glanced down the shop.

'Trevor Vinney—'

'Precisely. There really is no time to be lost. Do you think Dr Logan might come round to our point of view now that reality is staring him in the face?'

'I don't know,' Liza said. 'I'll try.'

She was suddenly oppressed by fatigue and dull despair. This day had promised so much and had failed in everything. The granting of planning permission for the field was merely the last dreary straw.

'May I have five pounds' worth of first-class stamps?'

'Mrs Logan,' Mrs Betts said. 'I really have no wish whatsover to intrude upon your and Dr Logan's personal grief, but there is no time to be lost. Letters, you know, appeals to our MP. Now, Mrs Logan, *now*.'

Liza looked up at her as she slid the stamps over the counter. Her powdered face was smiling, but absolutely implacable. No wonder Mr Betts had run away. Rumour said he had run a long way away, too, to Australia, and not for another woman at that. He had simply fled.

In the kitchen, Sally was giving tea to the children. She had made them sandwiches, whose crusts she had not cut off, and poured out mugs of milk. On the way from the garage, Liza could see through the kitchen window that they were eating and drinking with perfect docility. When she entered, however, Imogen immediately shouted, 'Not milk! Not milk! Juith! Juith!' and Mikey squirmed off his chair and said he didn't want to eat his crusts.

'How can you stand them?' Liza said to Sally.

Sally said, with truth, that they didn't do this to her. She got up, retrieved Mikey, took Imogen's mug away from her and put a teapot down in front of Liza.

'Mr Prior's got his permission.'

'Thank you, Sally. Yes. I heard. In the post office.' She poured out tea and then, cradling the mug in her hands, looked out of the kitchen window into the dark and doomed field beyond.

'Seems a shame,' Sally said.

'I know.'

'Mrs Jago's been in. Left you a letter. She said—'

Mikey put a crust between his teeth and then blew it to the far side of the table. Imogen immediately did the same.

'I can't stand it,' Liza said.

Sally reached over and took both the children's plates away.

'Fine. End of tea. No biscuits.'

'Bithcuit!' Imogen wailed.

Sally scraped the sandwich remains into Nelson's supper dish.

'Too late.'

'No! No!'

'Yes,' Sally said. 'Perhaps you'll remember next time.'

'I'm hungry,' Mikey said.

'I expect you are.'

Liza said, 'Sally, I'd propose to you if I wasn't already married.'

'It's always easier if the kids aren't yours.'

Liza thought of Bradley Hall. Immediately, she wished she had not. She looked at the dresser drawer where her letter and card lay hidden. Did Blaise . . .

'Bithcuit,' Imogen whined, leaning against her.

'No. You were silly with your sandwich. Remember?'

'Pleath. Pleath bithcuit—'

Sally stooped to pick her up.

'Come on, madam. And you, Mikey.'

'Whaffor?'

'I'll give you what for. Just come.'

'Sally. Thank you so much—'

'Mrs Jago said would you ring her—'

'Yes. Yes, of course. It'll be about the field.'

'Can't imagine anything worse,' Sally said, shuddering, 'than having all those Vinneys and Durfields next door.'

She opened the kitchen door and an icy blast from the hall bounced in.

'Cold,' Imogen said at once. 'It'th cold.'

'How would you know?' Sally said, bearing her away. 'How would you know inside all that podge?'

178

When the door was closed, Liza opened Diana's letter:

Too awful that Richard should get his wretched permission. And simply *whizzed* through – we had to wait nine months for permission to change the garage roof from flat to hipped. Can you ring me? Love, D.

Liza dialled. She imagined the telephone ringing out in Diana's large, warm kitchen where cooking took second place to feeding the dogs. It rang and rang. Liza counted to twenty rings and then she put the receiver down.

Cutting through the lanes from the main road to Basingstoke, Diana Jago passed an unremarkable car unremarkably parked in a gateway. This was a common occurrence. Travelling salesmen, particularly, criss-crossing England on their private network of routes and shortcuts, were often to be found parked in gateways, either eating sandwiches and gazing glassily at the field beyond, or asleep against their head rests with their mouths open. It was only when Diana was twenty yards past this car that she realized that the man in it had been neither eating nor sleeping. He had been staring in front of him in a most unnatural way. He was also Archie Logan.

Diana's kindness, which was genuine, was not of a sensitive, delicate kind. The moment the message about Archie sitting staring in a closed car had travelled from her eyes to her brain, she braked, put her car into reverse and shot back to the gateway. Then she got out into the fierce grey air, and knocked on the window six inches from Archie's face. He wound it down. His expression was quite without surprise.

'What are you doing? Are you all right?'

'I was thinking.'

'So I saw. But you don't look the thing at all. You look frightful. Are you ill?'

'No,' Archie said.

Diana thought for a moment.

'Wind the window up,' she said.

Obediently, he wound it. She came quickly round the car and opened the passenger door.

'Now, look,' she said, getting in. 'It's like a fridge in here. Whatever's the matter won't be helped by freezing. Not even grief. Start the engine at least and we'll get the huffer huffing—'

Archie shook his head.

'No. No.'

Diana took his hand.

'Archie—'

He looked away from her, out of the car window, but he did not remove his hand.

'Archie, dear. Would it help to talk?'

There was a silence.

After a while, without turning his head, Archie said, 'I'm so angry.'

'Yes,' Diana said. 'So should I be in your place. A perfectly wonderful life like your father's cut off quite needlessly while all kinds of utterly useless, intolerable people go on and on—'

'No,' said Archie. 'Not that.'

He turned his head to her.

'Not that. Not his dying. About how he died.'

'But I thought – I thought it was a coronary.'

'It was.'

Archie took his hand away and put it, with his other one, on the steering wheel.

Staring straight ahead out of the windscreen, he said, 'She did it. She caused it. They were in bed, they—'

'Archie!' Diana said. 'Stop it! Stop it at once—'

'I wasn't there!' he shouted, turning to her. 'Don't you see? I wasn't with him and if I'd been with him

180

when he died, I'd have understood. As a doctor, as a man, there's something that I won't ever know now, that I would have known. Death is so important, so significant, perhaps it is even the key to life, it inspires awe and peace all at once. I know all that. Intellectually, I know all that. But I don't know it in my heart and soul, I don't feel it. If I'd been with my father, I would have felt it, I would have known for ever more what that stupendous, suspended time is like when everything is suddenly clear, comprehensible. That moment of death, that extraordinary, precious moment after death—'

He stopped.

Diana said gently, 'But you couldn't be there. You were his son, not his wife. It isn't reasonable to think you should have been there. And if he did die while they – while they—' She paused while endless impossibly improper terms thronged unusably through her brain. 'Well, what could be better? What better last moment could there be for any man?'

'He wasn't that sort of man,' Archie said. 'He wasn't impulsive, he was orderly. He liked preparedness. He was made to be different, he was changed. It killed him—'

'But he probably liked it. People do. He was released, perhaps. I mean . . .' Diana said, floundering. 'I often think that when I break my neck hunting, as I'm bound to do because I'm such a perfect fool, Simon'll marry someone quite different and he'll become different and probably quite happy. Not too happy, mind you, or I'll haunt him. But it isn't necessarily miserable, making a change. I mean, your father probably felt thirty-five again.'

'She didn't even tell me first,' Archie said.

'Who? What? I thought Marina rang Liza at once—'

'Liza was not my father's son. What right had Marina to tell anyone before she told me? She didn't even try to tell me. She didn't even ask Liza where I was. She just left a message. Hah!' Archie lifted his hands and pressed his palms to his temples. 'It might have been school-run arrangements. Dear Archie, your step-mother rang to say your father's dead.'

'But it wasn't like that. Liza came straight down to the surgery, she came to find you—'

Archie dropped his hands.

'I'm not blaming Liza.'

'It seems to me,' Diana said, 'that you are determined to blame somebody.'

'Only myself.'

'Well, it doesn't sound like that.'

'No,' he said, glancing at her. 'No, it doesn't, does it? Home you go, Mrs Jago. Enough humouring of imposs-ible men for one afternoon.'

'You aren't impossible. It's just this damned grief. So unpredictable.'

'It's more,' Archie said. 'More than grief. That's what's so damnable, really.'

Diana put her hand on the door.

'Will you be all right? Are you safe to drive?'

'Perfectly. I shall go straight back to the health centre and be a good little doctor.'

'I'm not patronizing you, you know—'

He leaned across and briefly kissed her cheek.

'I know. You are a kind woman, an excellent friend and a knockout on a horse.'

She got out of the car and closed the door carefully. Archie watched her climb into her own car and start it. She waved to him briefly, put the car into gear, pulled out of the gateway and drove off, her hand involuntar-ily on her cheek where he had kissed her.

'More thtory,' Imogen said.

She lay under her flower-patterned duvet with her hair brushed and her thumb poised for plugging in.

'No,' Liza said. 'You've had your story. Why do you always ask me things you know I must refuse so that I

182

am forced to say no all the time?' She leaned forward and kissed Imogen's bath-scented cheek. 'You make me into a nag and it isn't fair because I'm not.'

'Thall I love you?' Imogen said unfairly, putting her arms round Liza's neck.

'I'd rather be loved than exploited,' Liza said, thinking not only of Imogen.

'Kith, kith, kith,' said Imogen, rubbing her face against Liza's and then, after a minimal pause, 'More thtory.'

'You're outrageous. No. No more story. I'm going to read to Mikey and then I'm going to telephone Mrs Jago. Let go.'

Imogen released her arms and put her thumb in. Then she turned on her side and closed her eyes and shut Liza out of her life.

'Sleep well, darling.'

Imogen said nothing.

Mikey was sitting up in bed with his dinosaur book. He had brushed neither his hair nor his teeth, and, despite his bath, still smelled of grey wool and school and socks. He gnashed his teeth at Liza.

'I'm a pterodactyl.'

'Must you be?'

'This is my big jaw. And my wing stuck to my finger.'

'I'd like to read *The Lion, The Witch and The Wardrobe*.'

Mikey flung himself back on his pillow.

'That's a girls' book.'

'It most certainly is not.'

'There are no guns in it.'

'Nor are there,' Liza said quickly, 'in dinosaur books.'

Mikey sat up again.

'But there are teeth.'

'They didn't all have teeth. Some of them had beaks.'

Mikey seized his book and began to riffle urgently through it.

'No, no, listen—'

'Mikey,' Liza said. 'I spent all today with children. I've had enough of children. I don't know why I bother to argue with you, really I don't. If you won't let me read something civilized, I'm not reading at all.'

'You read to Imogen,' Mikey said sternly. 'You read her *Thomas Goes to the Doctor* and you said you would never ever read her that again and you did.'

'But there's nothing to read in your dinosaur book. It's all pictures, and very bad pictures at that.'

'You hold the book,' Mikey said, consolidating victory, 'and I will talk to you about the pictures.'

'They win all the time,' Liza said on the telephone to Diana Jago. 'They argue on and on and then they win.'

'Don't argue back—'

'I know. I get caught up before I know where I am.'

'It's the penalty of having clever children. Ours were so dense it was no problem to outwit them. Liza, I wanted to talk to you about this field.'

'Yes. It's awful. I'd no idea it was happening so fast.'

'I want to twist your arm,' Diana said. 'Simon thinks you'd have a great effect if you went to see the Chief Planning Officer in person, as a representative of the family most affected.'

'It's too late! He's got planning permission—'

'Outline. The developer has yet to consolidate it. If he gets it, then we can't appeal. We have got to make sure he doesn't.'

'Why me?' Liza said, shutting her eyes.

'Because you are pretty and appealing.'

'Thanks a million!'

'Will you?'

I'm too tired, Liza wanted to say. I'm too worn down with Archie and the children and Andrew dying. I'm too disappointed in today, I'm full of frustration . . .

'All right.'

'Excellent,' Diana said. 'The Chief Weasel is called Derek Mullins. Quick as you can. Richard's talking to a developer already, the man who built those nasty little objects on the King's Stoke crossroads. And Liza—'

'Yes,' she said, leaning against the kitchen wall.

'Don't be too hard on Archie.'

'What?'

'He's taken quite a knock—'

'Don't you start,' Liza cried, springing upright. 'Don't you start telling me how precious and special his grief is and how there was never a father and son like those two. I don't want to hear another word. All that distinguished their relationship, if you ask me, was that Andrew spoiled Archie rotten!'

'I didn't so much touch a raw nerve,' Diana said later to Simon over supper, 'as tread heavily on one. She simply flew at me—'

'What is this?' Simon said, prodding at his plate.

'Liver.'

'Are you sure?'

'Yup.'

'Will she go and see Mullins?'

'Reluctantly. Things aren't good there.'

'They'll be worse if she doesn't go and see Mullins.'

'I'm not given,' Diana said, 'to feeling sorry for people. I don't care for it much and I loathe people for being sorry for me. But I am sorry for the Logans. Aren't you?'

Simon put his fork down.

'Tell you something. If I have to eat this liver, I'll be very sorry for myself indeed.'

'Suit yourself,' Diana said. 'I don't care and the dogs'll be thrilled.' She looked at her plate. 'Do you know, I think you're right. It does look pretty filthy. Shall I make a cheese sandwich?'

Archie came in just before nine and Liza, with a faint air of martyrdom, gave him supper. He thought, as he

185

ate it, that however delicious it was – which it was – it was soured by the resentful dutifulness with which it was seasoned, and that he would very much have preferred to have opened his own tin of soup, which came without much flavour, admittedly, but also without emotional strings.

While he ate his goulash – Liza had not, even on the first day of the new term, forgotten the sour cream – she sat the other side of the kitchen table and flicked through the newspaper. She had a mug of camomile tea. Archie had a glass of wine; Liza had declined one. Archie could not tell her about his encounter with Diana Jago and Liza could not describe her disappointing day nor her powerful desire not to go and see the Chief Planning Officer. Neither of them could mention Marina and speculate about Andrew's will because Archie had said he could face nothing of the kind just now and Liza had declared she could not face Archie's attitude. So he ate and she rustled and each struggled to endure the misery of their several solitudes. The telephone rang as Archie was finishing and a woman from Lower Stoke said her husband had just broken the fish tank while cleaning it out and had cut his hands and was pouring blood like a river. Archie gave her instructions and said he'd be right over.

'Why can't people ever, ever manage to stay in one piece for a single hour?' Liza said, looking up from the paper.

'The surprising thing,' Archie said, 'is that so many of them do. All their blessed lives.'

Then he kissed Liza's hair and went out into the black darkness. She put his plate and glass into the dishwasher, let Nelson out, laid breakfast, retrieved Nelson, toured the ground floor shutting and locking and switching off, and then went upstairs to run herself a bath.

Archie was away for almost an hour. Liza heard his car, and then a familiar sequence of doors and

186

footsteps and then he appeared in their bedroom doorway and looked at her.

'Was it serious?' she said, glad of something she could ask him.

'Yes,' he said. 'Yes. He's caught a vein. He's gone into Winchester to be stitched.' He paused. 'I'm just going to write a letter.'

'A letter?'

Archie never wrote letters.

'Yes. A letter. I won't be long.'

'To Thomas?'

'No,' Archie said. 'Not to Thomas. To Marina.'

Liza turned towards him, delighted.

'Oh!' she cried. 'Oh, Archie! I'm so glad!'

Chapter Twelve

The flat in Victoria was not an agreeable place to be. Sir Andrew had bought it out of a mild nostalgia for the tall red sandstone houses of his Glasgow youth, because it was on the first floor of such a building. But he had had little aesthetic eye for his surroundings, and, since the building was heavy with competent Edwardian stonework and joinery, he had been satisfied, untroubled by the gaunt height of the rooms and windows. He had observed the solidity with pleasure and was impervious to the atmosphere.

The atmosphere added to Marina's suffering. The flat faced west, so that the only sunlight was the tired low light of late-winter afternoons, which came filtering through gauze curtains with difficulty and fell unenthusiastically upon the surfaces of the heavy, alien furniture that had belonged to her long-dead, never-known parents-in-law. There were almost no pictures, merely a handful of dim sepia drawings of buildings and a mountainous landscape or two, purple with heather. The books were numerous and entirely factual except, Marina discovered, for one Alistair MacLean novel, a paperback, lurking embarrassedly at the end of a shelf of august political biography. She took it out, before Morley's *Life of Gladstone* crushed it utterly, and thought how it added to her sudden isolation to realize that this man, whom she had loved so much, clearly never read fiction. If she hadn't known that, what else had she not known?

She had too much time to speculate about such things; too much time while she simply waited. It was unlike her to wait, unlike her not to act and begin to push life, however wretched it might be, forward again. But she could not act. She attempted to do all kinds of things to force herself to act, like making inventories of all Andrew's possessions, or having an estate agent round to value the flat or even, on one particularly bad day, to buy herself an air ticket back to New York which was clearly, she told herself, what she must do. But she could not bear, in the end, to do any of those things. She could not bear to do anything that seemed to separate her from Andrew. She could tell herself, a thousand times a day, that he was dead and gone, gone for ever, but she simply could not bring herself to perform a deed that proved the reality of that insupportable fact.

She understood, she thought, why Archie was so stone silent. He had not been in touch since the funeral and she guessed that he, too, was in the cold-turkey state of suffering before grief becomes assimilable. Sometimes she talked to Liza on the telephone, but she didn't like to do that too often until she had recovered something of her self-possession. Her pride, as well as her heart, was tormented by grief. So, while she waited for herself, she also waited for Archie. The flat would be his, so would the contents, so would all Sir Andrew's money, and the Scottish cottage she had never seen; she had no doubts as to all that happening, eventually, when she could come to life a little again. In the meantime, all she could manage to do was wait. I'm just waiting, she told herself, over and over again, I'm just waiting for something to happen.

At Bradley Hall School, influenza arrived with the first snow. It was unsatisfactory snow, thin and wet and disobliging about being moulded, but the flu was much more wholehearted. The classrooms thinned out dramatically; Dan Hampole took to his bed with a bottle of whisky, a kettle and a brown paper bag of lemons, and then Mrs West, usually dauntless in the face of child-spread infections, telephoned to say she could not even raise her head from the pillow.

'I'll do extra,' Liza said to June Hampole. 'Sally won't mind coming in more often for a while. I'll take some of the English classes.'

The garnet pin still lay in the glove compartment of the car, and Blaise O'Hanlon had as yet been no more than polite and friendly.

'I'd like to be here more,' Liza said truthfully. 'I'd like to help. It's sad at home just now.'

June Hampole said it would be a godsend, just for a week or two.

'Fine,' Archie said that night. 'Do. We're all better busy, just now.'

More snow fell, snow with greater purpose. The garden at Beeches House disappeared under its uniform white blanket and Imogen became imperious to be out in it for hours at a time, mesmerized by her own tracks and, even more, by the faint arrow-headed ones sketched out by birds. Sally came every day without complaint, and Archie and Liza left, often at the same time in the morning, their car tyres creaking up the hard-packed lane. The house grew tidy and a little impersonal in Liza's long absences so that when she returned to it after dark on the short winter days it felt pleasurably unfamiliar, as if the domestic responsibility was no longer all, heavily, hers. Just now, that suited her. Her romantic imagination, thirsty for relief from Archie and his father's death, was quite taken up in persuading Blaise O'Hanlon that he need not obey her stern instructions to behave himself to the letter. In such a frame of mind, it was a relief to leave so much domestic administration to Sally.

It was Sally who took the call from Pinemount. She had put Imogen and Mikey to bed and was coming downstairs with her arms efficiently full of the next morning's dirty laundry, when the telephone rang. A pleasant man's voice asked to speak to Dr or Mrs

Logan and, when Sally said neither of them were back yet, the man said his name was George Barnes, from Pinemount, and that he would ring later. Sally wrote the message down and left it where she usually left messages, and cleared up the kitchen until Liza, bright eyed from the cold and a most enigmatic and exciting encounter, came in from school.

Liza did not look at the messages. Recently she had felt reluctant to, as if they represented in some measure the ordinary shackles of life that part of her at least had managed to shed. She felt a strong disinclination to discover, each evening, that the garage could not service her car the day she wanted; that Chrissie Jenkins had put her on the new Sunday School rota for the third Sunday of each month until the summer and that Mikey's school runs would be disrupted for six weeks because of parental skiing holidays.

Her inclination instead, that evening, was to go upstairs and look at herself in the mirror in the bathroom where the light was bright and truthful. She wanted to see if she looked different, now that Blaise had kissed her. Or, to be absolutely accurate, now that she had kissed Blaise. She had, at last, after many of the most delicate manoeuvrings, found Blaise alone in his classroom after school, and had attempted to return the pin to him. He had said no. He had been very flustered.

'No,' he said. 'No. Really. It was for you. You must have it.'

She put the box down on his desk. His evident confusion excited her and made her feel both strong and controlling.

'I can't take it. It was absolutely sweet of you, but it's out of the question.'

His face darkened. He looked away from her, at the poster of the Battle of the Boyne where the ragged Irish troops had the faces of gypsy angels.

'Blaise—'

'You don't understand—'

'Oh, but I do,' Liza said. 'I do. Look. I'll show you that I do.'

And then she had put her arms around his neck, and kissed him.

'There,' said Liza, smiling. 'There.'

And she had walked out of the room and the school and left him standing there with the little box lying before him. She had climbed into her car, and laughed, simply laughed out loud at the adventure she was having, at her power. Hadn't Blaise said she had power? And now, looking at herself in the bathroom mirror, she wanted to laugh again.

Downstairs, a door banged and Nelson barked, too late as always. There was a pause and Liza began, without hurry, to brush her hair. Archie came upstairs, holding the list of telephone messages.

'Did you see this?'

Liza watched him in the mirror. She waited for him to kiss her.

'No. What is it?'

'George Barnes rang from Pinemount. Why didn't you ring back?'

'Because I didn't see it.'

'But you were back before me.'

'Only just. I haven't done anything yet. I haven't even been in to see the children.'

Archie said, 'I'll ring. I'll ring now.'

'He's probably got flu, poor boy.'

'Do you want to ring, then?'

'No,' Liza said. 'No. You do it.'

She put down her hairbrush. A tiny shame nibbled at the corner of her pleasure.

'Thomas—'

'You go and kiss the little ones,' Archie said. 'I'll telephone.'

Imogen lay asleep on her back in a welter of stuffed animals and open books, illuminated by the dim glow

192

from her toadstool nightlight. She never woke at night except if her toadstool was switched off, when she would wake instantly and roar with rage. Liza piled the toys and books at the foot of the bed, and settled the quilt around Imogen's stout small body. Imogen opened her eyes.

'Hello, lady.'

Liza stooped to kiss her.

'Night night, darling. Go back to sleep.'

But Imogen had never left it. Mikey, on the other hand, lay full of ploys to keep Liza upstairs. He put an arm like a clamp about her neck.

'I hurt myself at school and I didn't cry.'

'Oh, Mikey. What kind of hurt?'

'My head. On the locker door. Can you write a note saying I musn't have school fish? Please, Please, please, please. Donovan doesn't have to have fish—'

'No. No, I couldn't.'

She began to disengage herself.

'I'm sick of Sally putting me to bed,' Mikey said. 'Why does she have to? It's so boring, always Sally. I'll never learn to read with Sally, only with you.'

'It's only for a little while—'

She stood up.

'Where's Daddy? I heard him. Don't go yet, don't go. If I have to have school fish, I'll be sick on the floor—'

Liza fled downstairs.

'I see,' Archie was saying into the telephone. 'Yes. Thank you so much. If you're sure—' He listened a little. 'We'll talk about it and I'll ring you back. Yes. All right then. Good night.'

'What?' Liza said at once.

Archie turned round and leaned on the back of a kitchen chair.

'Thomas has been having nightmares. He has walked in his sleep on two or three occasions. They don't seem at all worried. George Barnes said he simply thought we ought to know.'

'Nightmares!'

'About his grandfather,' Archie said. 'George Barnes wanted to know exactly what happened.'

'Like your insisting he saw the body and went to the funeral.'

'I told him Thomas had done both.'

'I bet you didn't tell him you—'

'Shut up,' Archie said. He took his hands away from the chair. 'I'm going down to Pinemount.'

'Why?'

'I want to see Thomas.'

'But George said they were coping, that there was no need—'

'Liza,' Archie said, 'I need to see Thomas.'

'You won't help, you can't, you're too emotional. You just want the drama of it; it's all a part of this great drama of yours you won't let go of—'

Archie lunged forward and seized her wrist.

'No.'

Her eyes were full of alarm.

'I thought it was going to get better,' she said. 'Since you wrote to Marina.'

He let her go.

'That has nothing to do with this. Will you come with me? I'll go tomorrow, I've a half-day.'

'I can't. I'm teaching.'

'Cut it.'

'No,' Liza said. 'I can't. And anyway, I don't think either of us should go.' She paused and then she said, 'It isn't fair. Trust the professionals. Your father always said so.'

'Please yourself,' Archie said. He looked at her. There was something in her he couldn't even recognize. 'I'll go, all the same. I'll go tomorrow.'

The New Forest struggled patchily through the snow with clumps and tufts of bush and bracken. It looked, Archie thought, driving through it, forlorn and shabby with its snow mantle disintegrating messily into smudged blots, a landscape very suited to his mood. It was a relief to have to concentrate upon driving, with the great lorries on their way to Bournemouth and Poole hurling up filthy plumes of slush that made it sometimes impossible to see. It was even more of a relief to have something to do that satisfied him; to have a proper mission.

He had supposed, after he had written to Marina, that he would feel better. He had supposed that it would release him. It had been a dreadful letter. He had written it after brooding on it for days, and then reread it the next morning, and still sent it. An excited horror filled him at the recollection of it, at the memory of the accusations with which he had crammed it. He had been sure that, if he exorcized himself of all the anger and bitter unhappiness he felt, then he would be free again to return to the Archie he had once been, the one he remembered as being both content and purposeful. The satisfaction of being a doctor would return, as would his delight and comprehension of Liza. His isolation would at last be over.

But it was not. The letter was sent and silence followed its sending. He became absolutely neurotic about the post arriving, wrenched apart by both longing for a reaction and dreading one. And in the midst of his divided feelings was a very strong consciousness that the letter had changed nothing, only added to his confusion and his sense of being paralysed. Rather than set him free, his bonds were even tighter. He, who had always supposed himself to be courageous, was terribly afraid.

The grey road, blurred with greyer slush, bore relentlessly on between the stretches of unremarkable Forest – what a poor thing William Rufus would think his Forest had dwindled to – and bungalows, and petrol stations with red plastic canopies and spinning signs advertising videos. How ugly, how temporary, what an utter, utter waste of being alive, of having chances. Why did people opt for the second rate? Was he doing that? Was he letting his life slide and drift into some decent, dreary stagnation?

The sign for Pinemount's village appeared trimly on the left-hand verge. Thomas. Archie braked sharply and turned down a lane into sudden countryside.

Thomas said he would like toasted tea cakes and a banana milk shake. The Wimborne tea shop was almost empty, furnished in immemorial tea-shop style of wheelback chairs and dim checked tablecloths and imitation horse brasses hanging on straps against walls of cream embossed paper. It smelled of dust and butter. Thomas, who looked perfectly normal, was mildly excited to be allowed out with his father for an hour and regarded the tea shop as the most appropriate place to be. He said Bristow's parents always gave Bristow tea here which was why he knew banana was the best kind of milk shake to have.

Archie said, 'Darling. What about these bad dreams?'

Thomas looked embarrassed.

'Who told you?'

'Mr Barnes.'

'Mr Barnes,' Thomas said. 'He's so interfering.'

'Not at all. He's kind. He was worried about you.'

Thomas took a bite.

'Once I woke up on the stairs.' His voice was awed. 'It was amazing.'

'Could you tell me about the dreams?'

'Not really.'

'Mr Barnes seemed to think they were about Grandpa.'

Thomas looked down.

'I don't know what they were about.'

'But you told Mr Barnes that they were about Grandpa.'

'I told Matron,' Thomas said, chewing. 'She kept asking and asking.'

'Darling Thomas. Do try and tell me. So I can help you. Do you think about Grandpa?'

'A bit.'

'Does it worry you?'

Thomas put down his tea cake. He said loudly, 'I don't like Mummy crying. Or you. Why do you?'

'We're very sad,' Archie said, too quickly. 'Because of Grandpa.'

Thomas looked at him.

'No.'

'Darling—'

Thomas said in the same loud flat voice, 'Rackenshaw's parents are divorced. So are Harris's. I don't want you to. I don't *want* it.'

Archie put his arms round Thomas.

'Darling Thomas, don't be an ass. What on earth put such a thing in your mind?'

Thomas was in tears. He put his damp and buttery face into Archie's shoulder.

'You might. You quarrel. And then Grandpa isn't here now.'

'You are in a muddle, aren't you?' Archie said, trying to keep his shaking voice light. 'Such a muddle. It sometimes happens, you know, when something awfully sad happens, like Grandpa dying, that people get a bit short-tempered, because of being so sad, and one of the deeply unfair things about life is that you get crossest with the people you love the most, that's all . . .'

Thomas pulled away and picked up his milk shake.

'I don't want to talk about it.'

'But if you don't talk about it, the bad dreams might go on.'

'No, they won't.'

'How can you be sure?'

'They just won't.'

197

'Thomas,' Archie said, 'are you making all this up?'

'No,' Thomas shouted, going scarlet.

'I have to ask you things, you see, to try and make it better.'

'I want to go back to Pinemount.'

Archie leaned forward.

'Is it better this term? Do you like it now?'

'I just want to go back,' Thomas said. He turned half away from Archie. 'Thank you for tea.'

Archie was close to tears.

'Darling Thomas. Listen just one moment. Mummy and I are not getting a divorce. Absolutely not. And, although Grandpa isn't here with us in body any more, we needn't be afraid of that. We must remember him and enjoy remembering him. He would want that, wouldn't he?'

'Mr Barnes said you can't see God but He's everywhere,' Thomas said, still turned away. 'But I don't believe him. If I wasn't here, there'd just be a space.' He got hurriedly off his chair. 'I'll miss prep, Daddy.'

Archie stood up.

'But you'll remember what I said. No need for worry. No need at all.'

Thomas glanced at him and then moved towards the door to the street.

When Archie had paid the bill, and joined him there, Thomas said, 'Why didn't Mummy come?'

June Hampole sat on the end of her brother's bed. He had made himself very comfortable, with an old ponyskin car rug, two of the kitchen cats and a portable wireless. June had rather thought he was sufficiently recovered to get up, but Dan said the convalescent period was the time when one had to be particular'y careful and that he was pleased to announce that the idea of two eggs baked with cream, sea salt, black pepper and unsalted butter had become increasingly preoccupying as the afternoon wore on.

'I'll try,' June Hampole said. She looked out of the window at the early black February evening and said, 'Oh, dear Dan, you were right and I simply don't know what to do.'

'Ah,' he said.

'It's Blaise and Liza Logan.'

'Now,' Dan said, settling back into his pillows. 'Now I am surprised. I thought that would be over. I thought Blaise returned to school looking like someone who has emerged thankfully from an obsession.'

'No,' June said. 'I saw them.'

'Did you pounce?'

'No—'

'Damn,' Dan said. 'Damn this flu. I'd have pounced. You'd better tell me.'

'I really don't want to. It's so pathetic, somehow, so banal. They were in the courtyard by her car, and they were kissing.'

'Where were you?'

'In the little sick room making sure that poor Edward Milligan who always has something the matter, and who, I am sure, is about to get flu, hadn't been forgotten up there. I looked out of the window. Not for anything particular, just because one does look out of windows. And there they were. Kissing. And—'

'And?'

'Oh, Dan,' June said. 'Liza Logan looked so much as if she were liking it.'

'Ha!' Dan said. 'Of course, Blaise is very personable.'

'Don't be frivolous, it's so unhelpful. What should I do?'

'On reflection, nothing.'

'Nothing! But last term you were advising me to have a word with Liza—'

'That was last term,' Dan said. 'I think the situation was different then. I think the balance has shifted. Do you know anything about Blaise's Christmas holidays?'

June picked up one of the cats and tried to settle it on her knee.

'No. Only that it was fun, he said. I've really hardly seen him, what with the new term, and flu.' The cat strained itself out of her grasp and returned to its ponyskin hollow. 'It's so silly, but I really feel I want to cry. She's such a dear, such a good, reliable teacher, so popular. That bloody boy, Dan, that blasted, bloody boy!'

Dan leaned out of his nest and took his sister's hand.

'Don't cry, Juney. It's not worth it. Really it isn't. Don't think about it and don't do anything. It'll be over in a minute, no bones broken. And now what about my eggs? Butter in first—'

The kitchen was dark and cold, and when June switched on the light there was a lot of scuttling. The kitchen cats, who had followed her down, began to wail for supper, leaping on to every surface she approached in order to be able to nag her more effectively. She couldn't think, getting out eggs and butter and the little coddling dish she knew Dan would want, why she should feel so upset. But she did. She almost felt betrayed and as if she had been made a fool of, although there was no logic to that, she knew. She got down on her hands and knees to light the reluctant oven while the cats screamed and pushed their hard greedy heads at her hands. If only Liza had not looked so eager – no, not exactly eager, more persistent. Every line of her body, even inside a winter coat, had looked tenacious, and her hands had been behind Blaise's head in a most decided way. The oven spluttered, belched out a blast of raw gas, and produced a small grudging row of blue flames. If Liza is humiliated, June thought, if Liza humiliates herself, I shall feel it so keenly. And what other outcome, with that charming, feckless boy, can there possibly be?

Sally Carter, giving Imogen lunch in the kitchen after a

morning of nursery school, saw the van draw up in the field gateway a hundred yards down the lane. She left Imogen picking up single peas with her fingers, and went to stand by the sink so that she could see properly. There were three men, wearing the sludge-coloured outdoor jackets you got so sick of in winter, and two of them went round to the back of the van and opened it and took out bundles of stakes made of raw, yellow new wood. The third man had a plan which he unfolded into the wind, and stood studying it while its edges flapped like sails. When the other two joined him, he doubled the plan up into a manageable size and began to point towards Beeches House. Then all three of them began to cross the field. The surveyors have come, Sally thought. The appeal's failed. Mr Prior's found a developer.

'Finished,' Imogen said. She leaned back in her chair and closed her eyes in triumph.

Sally took a carton of yoghurt out of the refrigerator. It was the last one. In fact, the fridge was almost empty. Mrs Logan didn't seem to be concentrating.

'No,' said Imogen.

'It's all there is.'

They looked at each other. Imogen said conspiratorially, 'Raithinth—'

'I don't see why you shouldn't,' Sally said.

She took a jar of raisins out of a cupboard and put a handful of them on a saucer. Imogen sighed with pleasure. The telephone rang.

'Is Dr Logan there, please?'

'I'm afraid not,' Sally said. 'He's out doing calls just now.'

'I know. I just rang the surgery. I hoped he might have called in at home.'

The caller sounded American. Sally said, 'Is that Lady Logan?'

'Yes,' Marina said. 'I'm so sorry. I should have said so at once.'

201

'Is it urgent?' Sally said, slightly hoping for a little drama in a long afternoon alone with Imogen.

'In a way,' Marina said. Her voice was hesitant. 'Don't worry. I'll try the surgery a little later. Is Mrs Logan there?'

'No,' Sally said. 'She's teaching full time just now.'

'Oh. Oh, I didn't know. And Imogen. Is Imogen there?'

Sally carried Imogen to the telephone.

'I've got raithinth,' Imogen said. 'Heapth of raith-inth.'

'Darling,' Marina said. Her voice shook.

'Thally gave them to me.'

The line went dead. Imogen gave the receiver back to Sally.

'Gone,' she said.

In London, Marina sat by her telephone and wept. The urge to speak to Archie had been so violent, and not being able to gratify it, and then her disappoint-ment and simultaneous relief, in addition to the unexpected poignancy of hearing Imogen, were all too much. She could hear herself crying, great tearing, deafening sobs; could the people in the next flat hear her, even through these redoubtable walls? She had tried to make something happen, and it had refused her, and now, for these terrible moments at least, everything was worse than ever.

She had been going to say to Archie that she understood. She had been going to try to refrain from telling him that his letter had caused her several days and nights of anguish, and only tell him instead that he must attempt to teach himself to see that they were on the same side, that their pain and loss were in many ways the same, that they might even help each other. She had vowed to think about this for a week or so, and maybe write it to Archie in a very carefully judged letter, but the urge to speak to him, to tell him in her own voice, to hear him, had come upon her with such strength that she had seized the telephone idiotically, all at once, in the middle of a working day. And she had had the impression, when she had rung the health centre, that Archie had actually been there and had refused to take her call. On my own, Marina thought, loathing her self-pity. That's all that's come out of this. On my own again.

Chapter Thirteen

When Archie went back to the hospital later in the day, the curtains were pulled round old Mrs Mossop's bed. In the morning, in response to a call from the hospital, he had taken Sharon Vinney in to see her mother, who was in a coma and lay, fathoms down in herself, like a tiny beaked primeval bird.

Sharon had cried and cried. The features of her coarse handsome face became quite blurred with crying. She sat shaking with tears by the hospital bed, begging Archie not to leave her alone there.

'But you might prefer to be alone,' Archie said. 'It might do you more good. So that you can talk to her privately.'

Sharon shook her head. Her stiffly bleached hair hardly stirred.

'It's too late. It's too late for that.'

'It isn't too late for you,' Archie said.

'I can't stay here. Honest I can't. I need a cigarette—'

Archie stooped over the bed. Granny Mossop's breathing was so shallow it hardly stirred the impersonal white folds of her hospital nightgown. Why, in God's name, was she not granted the dignity of her own? He looked at Sharon.

'Why isn't she in her own nightgown?'

Sharon fled. Following, Archie caught up with her in the car-park. She was drawing furiously on a cigarette.

'I don't want to hear anything from you,' Sharon said. 'As a doctor you're stuck in the Dark Ages. All talk, you are. All talk and no tablets.' She glared at him with reddened eyes. 'Talk to Mum! She's dead, isn't she, as far as I can see. She's gone.'

'No,' Archie said. 'But she will probably die today.'

Sharon began to weep again.

'No thanks to you!'

Archie drove her home in silence. She snuffled intermittently and blew her nose on crumpled paper tissues.

When he dropped her in front of her cottage, Archie said, 'Would you like to go back this evening? Because I'll take you, if Cyril's busy.'

Sharon struggled out of the car and stood for a moment looking across the lane at the unfriendly winter fields.

'What's the use?' she said. 'What's the bloody use?'

Archie went back alone. He took evening surgery, and then he paid two home visits and then he drove to Winchester. The geriatric ward, dim except for one or two pools of light over patients' beds, was quite quiet. Archie parted the curtains by old Mrs Mossop's bed and went in.

She looked much as she had that morning. He felt no urge at all to examine her, merely a wish to sit down by the side of the bed and hold her hand. He slid a forefinger up the inside of her wrist. Her pulse was barely perceptible. He rested his elbows on his knees and enclosed her hand in his.

He sat there for a long time, in the gentle quiet. A nurse put her head in at one moment, and tried to catch his eye, but he did not see her. He did not think much, he merely let his mind bob and drift at will in the queer, sweet peace of being alone with the last minutes of Granny Mossop's life. And, when the end came and she died with no commotion, he did not stir for some moments. He did not want to. He wanted simply to go on sitting there, in that strange suspended time that had no measure, and breathe in the momentousness of her little, silent ceasing to be.

He did not let go of her hand. In the feel of it lay all the significance and simplicity of that moment, all comprehension of this end of life which seemed at once quite familiar and yet huge with awe. He did not want to let go. He wanted this curious time that was no time to go on and on until he could be sure what it was he had learned, until he could articulate it as well as feel. There was no hurry to let go. There was nothing else to do. This time was the only thing that mattered and it was quite outside human things, worldly things. Archie bent his head until his forehead rested on his hands that held Granny Mossop's hand. Here was the still centre of everything that turned and whirled.

The curtain rings rattled faintly on their rails. Slowly, Archie raised his head. The night sister was looking in on him.

'He's a one-off,' she said to a staff nurse later over a cup of tea. 'You'd have thought she was his own mother. Wonder what he did it for?'

'I have something to tell you,' Archie said.

Liza was marking comprehension exercises on the kitchen table. She wore a new polo-necked jersey and she had tied her hair back, as Clare did, with a black velvet ribbon. It made her look less sweet, more sophisticated. She put the forefinger of her left hand on the line of an exercise book to mark her place, and waited.

Archie pulled out a kitchen chair opposite Liza and sat down. Some early forced daffodils stood in a blue-and-white jug between them and Archie pushed them aside so that he could see her.

'Two things, actually.' He paused. 'Granny Mossop died. An hour ago. She was quite unconscious before she died.'

Liza said, 'Oh, I'm sorry. I'm so sorry.'

'Yes.'

'Does Sharon know?'

'Yes. I think she is still determined that her mother's cancer was my fault.'

206

'But you know, don't you, Archie, that that's just a cover-up for her own guilt.'

'I don't know what I know,' Archie said in a voice of peculiar gentleness. 'I just know I was glad to be there, glad to be with her, when she died.'

'You were there!'

'Yes. I've just come from the hospital.'

Liza put her hand across the table.

'There can't be many doctors like you.'

'It was chance. Chance that I was there. A lucky, lucky chance.'

'How Sharon will abuse you for doing what she failed to do!'

'I don't mind,' Archie said. 'I don't mind any more.'

Liza pushed away the open exercise book.

'And what was the other thing? The second thing?'

'Marina,' Archie said.

'Marina!'

'I wrote her a terrible letter.'

'But I thought—'

'I know. I let you think it. But it was not a letter of sympathy, it was one of blind rage. I accused her of killing my father with her demands and depriving me of understanding his death.'

'Oh, Archie,' Liza said.

'Yes.'

She put her hands over her face.

'How could you—'

'I could easily. Then. But not now.'

She took her hands away and looked at him.

'What are you going to do about it? Poor Marina, it's unthinkable—'

'I – I must speak to her. She tried to telephone and I wouldn't take the call.'

'You must go and see her,' Liza said with energy. 'You must go up to London at once and see her. And—' She shut her eyes. 'Archie. What can you say?'

'I shall have to hope,' Archie said, 'that I'll know when I get there.'

Liza got up and went to fiddle with things on the dresser: two oranges in the fruit bowl; a ragged pile of opened, unanswered letters; a pair of sunglasses with one lens missing that Imogen liked to wear, her face turned to the ceiling so that they wouldn't fall off.

'You scare me,' Liza said. 'You really do. Your reaction to some things seems so unhinged, you're so obsessive, so relentless.' She looked round at him, swinging the sunglasses from one hand. 'It doesn't seem to make sense, the way you behave. One minute you're being really imaginative and sweet with Granny Mossop; the next you're writing horrible letters to poor Marina. And Thomas. What did you say to Thomas? I wish I'd stopped you going. I don't trust you, Archie. I can't. You make it impossible for me to trust you. Suppose everybody felt they could just let go, like you do? How do you think we all feel, living with someone so unpredictable, so immature?'

Archie, gazing at the hard yellow of the infant daffodils, said nothing.

'I don't know what I feel any more,' Liza said. 'I really don't. I'm worn out by you.'

Archie raised his face.

'Is it really all my fault? All of it?'

'I don't want a row,' Liza said.

'So I may not defend myself?'

She came back to the table and began to rearrange the books on it.

'I really must finish these. And it's late.'

She held her breath. It was such a risk she was taking, such a test of her power. Archie pushed his chair back and stood up. She waited for him to lunge at her, seize her wrist, grab her shoulders, even kiss her. But he did not. He simply stood for a moment looking quite impenetrable and not at her, and then he went out of the kitchen and she heard his steps along the polished boards of the hall, and then up the stairs to bed.

Archie reached London in the early afternoon. It was a sudden, soft, fair day, a false herald of spring, and his overcoat, a doughty tweed affair acquired ten years before in Inveraray, felt a cumbersome nuisance. He took it off and slung it round his shoulders and decided, in order to postpone his arrival in Victoria, to walk from Waterloo, across the river. Marina did not, after all, know that he was coming. He had told Liza that he had telephoned, because she had asked him, but he hadn't. He did not know why he hadn't, he had just felt unable to. It might well be that Marina would be out, and he did not know what he would do then. He did not know, in fact, what he was going to do at all except go there, and see her. And, for some reason he could not fathom, the prospect of seeing her filled him with all kinds of feelings, but not with dread. It did not cross his mind that she might refuse to see him.

It had not crossed Marina's mind, either, that he might come. She had resolved that her next move was to be some sinking of pride and then to speak to Liza; no, not speak to her, ask her. Ask her advice as to what she should do next, about Archie. She would dearly have liked to ask what she should do next about the rest of her life, too, but her pride, so carefully nurtured over more than half a century, drew the line at some things, and showing herself too vulnerable and helpless before Liza was one of them. She was, in fact, sitting by the window in the quiet dead time of mid-afternoon, making a list of things she might say to Liza, and trying out ways of saying them, when her intercom down to the building's front door rang imperiously. Going to answer it, and supposing it to be the young man from the estate agency who had said he might be round on Thursday but more likely Friday, she discovered that it was Archie.

He did not take the lift. She stood on the landing by her front door and watched his head come up the stairs, steadily round and round the lift shaft. He was wearing a big coat, like a cloak, with the collar turned up around his neck, and his hair, Marina thought, had grown longer and looked very thick. As he came up the last flight, she took a pair of large spectacles framed in pale tortoiseshell out of her jacket pocket, and put them on. He stopped two steps below her.

'I've never seen you in glasses.'

'I only wear them,' Marina said, 'when I want to see particularly well.'

She led the way back into the flat, into the sitting room where Mikey had hidden in the sofa cushions and declined to look at his dead grandfather.

Archie pulled his coat off his shoulders and said, 'I've no business to ask you to help me, but I've no idea how to begin.'

'I wish I smoked,' Marina said. 'It's so useful for such moments as these. Les mauvais quarts d'heure are one thing, les mauvais moments quite another and almost worse. Why did you come at such an impossible time of day? What can I offer you at three in the afternoon? Too late for lunch, too early for a Martini.'

'Is it?'

'Is that what you want? A Martini?'

'No,' Archie said. 'No. I don't want anything.'

'In that case,' said Marina, sitting down at one end of the sofa and turning her spectacles on him, 'why have you come?'

Archie put his coat down on an armchair and crossed to sit the other end of the sofa.

'You know why.'

'I'd like you to explain, however.'

He looked at her. He spread his hands.

'It's so odd,' Marina said. 'I've been so sorry for you, so desperately sorry, even to the point of feeling I should apologize to you for marrying your father, for

210

being there when Andrew died, for making – yes, goddammit – for making Andrew so happy. But now you are here I don't feel abject at all. Nor contrite. I feel very strong and pretty determined. So you tell me, Archie Logan, all that's been going on and see if you can't make a better fist of it than you have done up to now.'

Archie put his head back into the cushions. He felt weirdly at ease.

'Liza thinks – at least I think she thinks – that I am having a very tiresome, extreme form of male menopause.'

'And?'

'And I expect she is right.'

'That's a cop-out,' Marina said. She smiled. She had not smiled for days. Archie turned his head sideways to look at her.

'Shall I tell you how I feel?'

'I think you'd better,' Marina said. 'I think it will relieve both our minds.'

Archie said, 'I despise people who do this.'

Marina waited.

'I don't know much about Dante,' Archie said. 'Except for that lovely picture, and one other thing. It was something to do with being banished from Florence for trying to rule with justice and finding himself wandering alone in the countryside, in a dark wood, without companions or possessions or a map. I seem to remember that that was a metaphor for how he felt inside, as if he had lost the centre line, after fighting for it, and was completely at sea. Didn't know where he was going or what he was looking for. Just felt a great tearing yearning for what he had lost and also for something more, something that would illumine the rest of life and give it vitality.'

He stopped.

After a while Marina said, 'There is an interesting theory about such crises. They are thought to affect creative people particularly and I would class you as creative. The theory is that at this halfway point in life a crisis does occur, a crisis such as Dante had, and what it represents is the first confrontation with death, now that half one's life may be presumed to be over. And that prospect of death paralyses the victim – he sees death as a kind of helplessness. Sometimes it paralyses him almost literally. Look at poor Rossini.' She looked sideways at Archie. 'Do you buy my theory?'

'Oh yes,' he said. 'I buy it. But I think it is only part of the trouble.' He looked about him. 'Poor Marina. What a horrible room this is.'

'I've had too much time to think that. Also to think how incongruously redolent of Andrew it is.'

'Sell it,' Archie said. 'Just sell it.'

'I began. But I feel it's yours.'

He turned his head again.

Marina said, 'I know he left it to me. I know that. But I don't need it, I don't want it. I can't recognize him here.'

Archie gazed at her. Then he turned his head away from her, very slowly, and said in a voice thick with tears, 'I was with a brave old patient when she died three nights ago. I was there all the time, and afterwards. I've been at plenty of deaths but I've never understood a death before, not like that, not suddenly knowing death. I can't remember it now, but I knew then and I'll know for ever that I knew. That's one reason I've come. I thought I could only know such a thing with my father. I thought you had deprived me of that. That's why I wrote – one of the reasons I wrote.'

'I know,' Marina said. 'You made yourself perfectly plain.'

He whipped his head round and leaned sideways to seize her wrist.

'I'm so sorry. Oh, my God, Marina, I'm so sorry.'

'Dammit,' Marina said. 'Dammit. Do *not* make me cry.'

'Please cry—'

She bent forward over his hand.

'I didn't know one could be in such pain as this. I didn't know what it was like to miss someone so much. I'm just ripped to pieces, Archie, and I can't stand it and can't stand your seeing it.'

She took her hand away from his and fished in a pocket for a handkerchief and blew her nose fiercely.

'I like it,' Archie said.

She shook her head.

'We weren't talking about me. We were talking about you. You said Dante's dark wood was part of the trouble. What was the rest?'

He leaned forward and put his elbows on his knees and stared down at the carpet.

Then he said without looking at her, 'I want you.'

He raised his head and stared across the room at a formidable Edwardian chiffonier, its fretted doors lined with leaf-green silk.

'I was jealous of my father. I still am. And, now that he is not here, and like you I am shaken to the core with missing him, I want you more than ever.'

There was a little pause, and then Marina said, 'Now, you look here. Just you look at me. I'm almost old enough to be your mother, I'm a granny in specs.'

He turned his head and looked at her over his shoulder. She had not moved from her sofa corner.

'Marina,' he said.

He stood up and stooped over her, taking her hands and pulling her to her feet. Then he took off her spectacles and laid them on a nearby lamp table.

'Archie—'

'Shhh,' he said.

He put his arms around her and held her hard against him and kissed her hair and her neck. Then, like someone at the top of a helter-skelter, Archie took

213

his steadying hands away from the sides and let himself go.

'I want you,' Archie said to Marina, and bent to kiss her mouth.

He caught the last train from Waterloo to Winchester. It was sleepy and seedy, full of tired yawning people with unbrushed hair, and the aisles and tables were strewn with used paper cups and discarded evening papers. It seemed to Archie a glorious train. It appeared to have a reality, an energy quite disproportionate to its appearance and purpose. He found a seat in an empty quartet of four and threw himself into it, pressing his face to the dark glass to see his extraordinary, illuminated countenance reflected there.

It had been so hard to leave her. He had hardly managed it, probably would not have done if she had not ordered a taxi and locked herself in the bathroom. He had stood in the passage outside the locked door, dressing slowly, and laughing, calling out to her, perfectly idiotic with happiness and fulfilment. She had come out at the end when the taxi came, in a white towelling robe with her hair on her shoulders, and he had seized her.

'I can't go, I can't, not now, not after this—'

But he had gone, because she had made him go, walking down the stairs as he had come up them, wrapped in his big coat, except that going down he looked up at her, all the way, and she leaned on the banisters and looked down, all the time, for the very last glimpse of him. In the taxi he had wanted to laugh. Dark, bright streets went by, Parliament Square, Big Ben, the oily glitter of the river, the way he had walked only that afternoon, before he had made his discovery.

This discovery, he thought lying back in the train, was what he had been seeking, this revelation of quite another dimension to himself, almost as if he had only been alive in part before. Marina had not wanted him to be serious, too intense. She had tried to tease him.

'But you're a mere boy, that's all that's the matter with you. Experience is all. Take it from me. From one who knows.'

Oh, and she did, she did. Archie closed his eyes, but, even with them closed, his head seemed to be brilliant with light.

Liza woke when he came in.

'It's after midnight.'

'I know. I'm so sorry. I should have telephoned.'

He sat down to unlace his shoes.

'How did it go?' Liza said. 'Was it all right? Did you take her out to supper?'

'We had supper, yes.'

He stood up and began to pull off his tie.

'But it was all right?'

'Yes. Yes, it was fine. I'll tell you in the morning.'

'Did she understand? Has she forgiven you?'

'Oh yes,' he said, throwing his shirt down on the floor. 'She's forgiven me.'

Liza wriggled down into bed again.

'You don't deserve it.'

'I know.'

'Thank God that's over, then,' Liza said, half muffled by her pillows.

'And you? Did you have a good day?'

'Oh yes,' she said. She sounded as if she were smiling. I'm a swine, Archie thought, I'm an utter, bloody swine.

'I'm just going to have a shower,' he said.

'Leave it. Leave it until the morning.'

'No. No, I can't do that. You go back to sleep.'

Mikey's speedboats still lay cluttered round the bath plug. Archie stepped in among them, and turned on the shower, hurtling cold needles, deliberately too cold. He wanted to sing and to weep. Whatever he had

215

done, whatever came now, he had never felt so absolutely alive before.

In the morning, Liza did not seem much interested in the details. She wanted to know how Marina had looked and if she had reprimanded Archie, but she did not want to know how he had explained himself. Archie told her that he thought Marina had been wearing trousers and a pale jersey and, as far as he could recall, a checked jacket, but he wasn't sure.

'And ear-rings?' Mikey said, eating Coco-Pops.

Archie couldn't remember. He did remember about the spectacles, but they now seemed to him so intimate that he didn't mention them. Liza asked several times if Marina had been angry with him.

'No,' he said, 'not angry. Just firm and a bit crisp.'

'Did she mention your letter?'

'No. I did. I said sorry.'

'So I should hope,' Liza said. 'No, Mikey. Those are already covered with sugar.'

She pushed the sugar bowl away across the table.

'Is this full-time teaching going on much longer?' Archie said. He shamed himself, but he could not help planning.

Liza said, 'One more week.' And, because she did not want her face to betray anything, leant across and said, 'Don't *do* that,' to Imogen who was voluptuously licking honey and butter off a strip of toast. Then she summoned up a shred of defiance and said, 'Why? It doesn't affect you, does it?'

'Of course not.'

They looked at each other, seeing nothing.

'Not nithe,' said Imogen, putting down her bald toast.

'Whose fault is that? You eat it, anyway.'

Liza got up and began to assemble her school bag and car keys.

'Hurry up, Mikey. My run today.'

'Can I sit in the front?'

216

'No. You can't sit in the front until you are twelve, as well you know. Where's Sally? It's almost ten past. Imogen, eat that toast.'

Archie picked it up and held it in front of her.

'Come on, now. A bite for your nose. And one for your ears—'

His well-being felt to him as if it were gleaming on his skin, like a healthy dog's coat.

'Not ear'th.'

'Neck, then.'

'No. *Bottom*,' said Imogen and shrieked with rapture.

'OK,' said Archie, laughing too, longing to laugh. 'A bite for your bottom.'

Liza said, 'Oh, Archie, for heaven's sake don't encourage her.'

'It's only a game. Isn't it, Imo? A silly toast game.'

Liza looked out of the window. Sally, on her bicycle, was coming down the lane, her scarlet muffler a splash of colour against the tired late-winter landscape.

'There's Sally. Now, Mikey, up to brush your teeth.'

'And one for your knee and one for your left big toe and look, it's gone.'

Archie leaned sideways and kissed Imogen's packed cheek.

'Honestly,' Liza said. 'You do seem happy.'

'You don't sound very thrilled—'

Liza took a dark-blue jacket off a hook on the door and struggled into it.

'Of course I am. If it lasts. I suppose your conscience is clear, that's why.'

'No,' Archie said. 'No. My conscience is not clear at all.'

Liza shouted through the doorway.

'Come on, Mikey! Come on—' She turned on Archie. 'Look, you've said sorry to Marina; that's over, so please, please can we not have a big deal about that, too?'

'Certainly,' Archie said.

Sally opened the door and came in. It struck her that, in some indefinable way, the atmosphere was not only better than usual, but exhilarating, like the first autumn morning of frost.

Before he went down to the surgery, Archie took Imogen and Nelson out into the field where the yellow wooden stakes now stood everywhere in the rough grass. He had not seen Richard Prior for several weeks, and Mrs Betts's impotent fury at the prospect of defeat had caused him to buy his stamps at any post office he passed, rather than endure her tirades at Stoke Stratton. The last time he had been in, she had dropped his change into his palm so that she need not contaminate herself by touching a traitor, and he had felt a dull rage at her stupidity and obstinacy. Now he felt gentler. In fact, watching Imogen weave in and out of the line of stakes that represented the bigger house's front wall, Archie was sorry he had been rude to Mrs Betts, and even sorrier that he had opposed Liza, had belittled her objections. It was too late, for any practical purpose, to be sorry, with the stakes so menacingly there, and the developer's board up loudly by the gate, but it wasn't too late to say sorry to Liza for more intangible things. And yet, he thought, caught breathless by a sudden wild leaping of his heart, if he started saying sorry to Liza now, where in heaven's name would it all end?

Diana Jago, on her handsome hunter, hailed him from the gateway. Imogen and Nelson began to race across, squealing and barking. The horse displayed admirable indifference.

'Sorry,' Archie called, running up. 'So sorry—'

'It's excellent training,' Diana said. 'I reckon if a horse is Imogen-proof, it's bombproof. Hey, Imo?'

Imogen climbed up two bars of the gate and pushed her face through, blowing at the horse. Diana looked down at Archie.

'You look better.'

'Do I?'

'I've been worried stiff about you. Frightful bore. I hate worrying. And the lovely Liza looks less peaky.' She waved her crop at the field. 'I think you are unspeakable to back this. Really I do.'

'I wish I hadn't upset Liza.'

'Good,' Diana said. 'Excellent. Marriage is a pain in the neck but it ought at least to give you someone to hang in there with. I say,' she leaned down a little. 'The tom-toms tell me not a Vinney was there when poor old Granny died. But you were. Lynne Tyler said you went specially—'

'No, no. Chance—'

'Don't believe you.'

She smiled down at him with affection.

'You've got a rare old daddy, Imogen.'

Archie looked down.

'Bottom,' Imogen said.

She got off the gate.

'Bottom toast!' she shouted, and ran away shrilling across the field.

Chapter Fourteen

'Look,' Stuart Campbell said, leaning on his desk, 'look, I know you have been through a deeply distressing time, but I'm afraid I must gently point out to you that life must go on.'

Archie, standing just inside the door with his hands in his pockets, said nothing.

'It's six weeks since your father died. I wouldn't presume to put a time limit on grief, nor to dictate anyone's personal reaction, but I'm afraid there is a general feeling in the practice that you are beginning to exploit everyone's sympathy.' He pushed a piece of paper with Archie's large hand on it across the desk. 'I got your note. You say you can't attend the practice meeting because of a patient's funeral. Archie, you haven't attended the last two meetings and, although I applaud your human conscientiousness in wishing to go to Mrs Mossop's funeral, I cannot help, at the same time, feeling that you have your priorities wrong.' He looked at Archie weightily and said, 'Our duty, I should not have to remind you, is to the living, not to the dead. Indeed, and this is something you may have forgotten in the last six weeks: if we allow the dead to preoccupy us too much, we cannot help but penalize the living.'

Archie said, 'I know.'

'Well, then.'

'It's a particular funeral. My reasons are very private and in some way tied up with my father's death. I am aware everyone's been carrying me recently and it won't go on.'

Stuart Campbell sighed. He rolled a pencil across Archie's note.

'Can't your wife go?'

'No,' Archie said. 'She's working.'

She had also refused to go. He had asked her, the day before, but she had refused even to consider it. 'But Bradley Hall is utter chaos,' Archie had said. 'You're always complaining about it, how the timetable is only made to be ignored. Why can't you change with someone?' Liza had shaken her head. 'Because I can't and I don't want to.'

Stuart got up and went to the window and stood there, gazing out and chinking the change in his pocket.

'Archie, I admire you. You know that. You've been the perfect makeweight in this practice, a standing reminder of our human commitment. But I seem to spend too much time defending you just now, making allowances.' He turned round. 'We are the premier practice in this area now, I hardly need remind you. We get a lot of applicants. We can't carry anyone for too long.'

'Six weeks?' Archie said, with some show of spirit.

'But it isn't six weeks, is it, Archie? It's longer. Much longer. Isn't it? When did you—'

He stopped. Then he said, 'I think you had better come to the meeting.'

Stoke Stratton church was surprisingly full, not just with its own villagers, but with people from the neighbouring villages who had been to school with Granny Mossop or had helped her look after the land girls when Stoke Stratton House – now so expensively Jagoed – had been requisitioned in the war. Richard and Susan Prior, whose habits over such things were meticulous, occupied the second pew. Archie, coming in a little late, elected to join them.

'Good man,' Susan said.

The coffin was as small as a child's. It stood on an iron trestle and was almost obliterated by an immense cross

221

of yellow and white chrysanthemums tied with purple ribbons with which Sharon Vinney had attempted to assuage her complex and miserable feelings. She sat in the front pew opposite the Priors, in a new black-and-white jacket and skirt, attended by Cyril and her straggling brood of children and hangers-on, all dressed with extreme care, and almost all in tears. The chancel step overflowed with their flowers, extravagant, inappropriate bouquets, stiffly wired and beribboned, which would later be piled in the hearse and driven away to the crematorium with the tiny coffin. There was not a tribute among them, Archie thought, that Granny Mossop would have spared her contempt.

Even Chrissie Jenkins had come. Granny Mossop had been, after all, as she explained noisily to everyone, their oldest parishioner. She sat in front of the Priors, a dark coat open over her nurse's uniform to make the greater commitments of her life visible to everyone. She turned to smile at Archie, a conspiratorial smile that conveyed her consciousness of the obligation that busy professionals like themselves had to perform those little personal services in life that make all the difference. Archie, who found her a woman of singular unattractiveness, would normally have returned her smile with no more than a nod; but today, with his whole being overflowing with gratitude for being alive, he smiled back. In a moment, on his knees with his eyes closed against the riot of spray carnations and hothouse purple iris, he could, after all, think about Marina.

Colin Jenkins stepped forward. His face bore the marks of inner conflict. An ardent supporter of the new democratic services, with a deep distrust of the English of Cranmer's prayer book, he was forced today, at Granny Mossop's wish, to speak over her coffin the language of archaic and unjustified privilege. He could not even be sure she had not left such a wish just to spite him.

' "I am the resurrection and the life," ' Colin Jenkins said without enthusiasm, ' "saith the Lord. He that believeth in me, though he were dead, yet shall he live; and whosoever liveth and believeth in me shall never die." '

Archie hid his face in his hands. How could it be that such life, such intensity of life, should come out of death? And did he care how it had come? No, that did not matter at all. All that mattered was that it had come. And it had.

In the junior cloakrooms at Bradley Hall, Blaise and Liza were doing after-school duty. Once every departing child had been paired off with the relevant coat, bag, and toy brought to show Mrs Simpson who ran the kindergarten class, the duty consisted of a dilatory clearance of the detritus of boots and shoes left stranded on the concrete floor. The cloakrooms, made out of Bradley Hall's onetime coal and wood stores, were lit by bluish-mauve neon strips and provided as glamorous a setting for an assignation as a public lavatory. Blaise went along the aisles between the rows of pegs screwed into frames of red-varnished pitch-pine, kicking the shoes into lockers with dull fury.

'Next week,' Liza said from the adjacent aisle where she was painstakingly trying to find mates for stray boots, 'next week, I go back to part time.'

'Jesus,' Blaise said, kicking. 'Jesus, Jesus.'

'It's probably just as well,' Liza said provocatively.

'For what?'

'You know. You know perfectly well.'

Blaise put his hands on a pitch-pine bar and swung his head and shoulders through the dangling shoebags at Liza.

'I'm sick of all this. I've had enough. I'm going mad, raving mad.'

'But we've seen each other every day, I've even—'

'Kisses,' Blaise said derisively. 'Rotten little kisses. Cock-teasing kisses.'

Liza stood up, still holding a gumboot.

'I'm exhausted,' Blaise said. 'You exhaust me. It's all games, isn't it? Little girly games.'

Liza began to tremble slightly. The blue shadows thrown down by the light made Blaise's face skull-like in its intensity.

'No.'

'Look,' Blaise said. 'I'm sick of being played with. It's a particularly horrible sort of tease, what you're doing. Last full day, you say to me all smug and prissy: No more treats. Had that. Back to hubby now.'

'Shut up,' Liza said.

Blaise took his hands off the beam and vanished from sight.

'Go home,' his voice said. 'Just go home to hubby and the kiddiwinks and bloody well leave me be.'

Liza put down the gumboot and went round to the adjoining aisle. Blaise glared at her.

Liza said, 'You started all this. Remember? Never leaving me alone, letters and phone calls and badger, badger, badger. Now you can't get what you want—'

'What do I want?'

There was a small highly charged silence. Later, looking back, Liza recognized that silence as the last moment of her fantasy, the final seconds of the extravagant illusion with which she had fed herself for so many months.

She said, proudly, fatally, 'You want me to go to bed with you.'

And Blaise, suddenly exchanging petulance for vengeance, said, 'Not any more.'

She looked at him. He looked back, his chin slightly raised.

'What?'

'You blew that,' Blaise said fretfully. 'Weeks ago. Stringing me along. Games, games, all the time—'

'But just now, you said—'

'Oh, that's habit. I got in a muddle. I got so confused and exhausted I couldn't remember where I'd got to. And anyway, you seemed to expect it.' His voice grew accusing. 'You've been expecting it all term, haven't you? Talk about the boot being on the other foot! Well, you're too late.'

Liza felt for the top of the lockers and sat down on them. Shoebags bumped round her, redolent of rubber and old sock.

'Just now,' she said, 'just now, you said being so near and yet so far was driving you mad—'

'I didn't mean it,' Blaise said. 'I didn't mean that. I mean having you darting me pregnant glances, lying in wait for me—'

Liza put her hands over her ears.

'But you kissed me! You said—'

'Of course I kissed you. You kissed me. I could hardly spit you out, could I?'

Liza looked up at him. His face was black against the bluish light.

'You're loathsome,' she said. Her voice shook hopelessly. 'And you're mad.'

Blaise said, 'Anyway, there's a girl in Dublin—'

'Coward.'

'I met her at Christmas. She's my age.'

'Go away!' Liza screamed. 'Go on, get out, go away—'

The door at the far end of the cloakroom opened and let in an oblong of yellow light.

June Hampole called, 'Who's there? Who's shouting?'

They emerged sheepishly into the brighter light.

'Oh, Liza,' June Hampole said. 'Oh dear.' She looked at them both. 'How sordid.'

'Not any more,' Blaise said angrily. 'Nothing any more. Nothing.' He tried to push past June into the lit passage beyond. She put up an arm and stopped him.

'I think we'd better talk,' June said. 'Don't you?' She

looked at Liza and sighed. 'Please come to my study, both of you.' She turned and began to walk back towards the school hall, Blaise following. He did not even glance at Liza. There was nothing for her to do but bring up the rear.

'I couldn't go home,' Liza said. Her face was blotched with crying. 'I simply couldn't face it.'

'No,' Clare said. 'No. Of course not.'

'I've made such a fool of myself—'

'No,' Clare said kindly. 'You allowed someone else to make a fool of you.'

'No!' Liza shouted.

There were empty coffee mugs on Clare's kitchen table and a pink sea of used paper handkerchiefs.

'I'll never get over it.'

'Of course you will.'

'I can't believe I could have let it get that far. I can't believe I was so stupid. How can I face anyone after this?'

'No-one knows,' Clare said. 'Do they?'

'I wish I hadn't come,' Liza cried, seizing another handkerchief. 'I wish I hadn't told you!'

Clare, magnanimous in rare moral superiority, merely said, 'I shan't tell anyone, and I'm sure June Hampole won't.'

'I shouldn't have come out! I simply didn't think, I was so churned up. I should have stayed inside, shouldn't I?'

'Blaise would have split on you.'

Liza looked at her sister.

'Can you believe how he's behaved?'

Clare thought, as she always thought, of Robin.

'Oh yes. Easily.'

'Months and months of besieging me, a year or more, never letting up! And he came round here! Didn't he? He came round and declared undying love, didn't he, Clare, didn't he—'

226

Clare got up and took the kettle over to the sink to fill it.

'I don't want any more coffee. Haven't you got any brandy?'

'I've got sherry,' Clare said repressively.

'Sherry, then. Clare—'

'Yes?' Clare said, putting down the kettle and opening a cupboard where her still-intact sets of wedding present glasses stood in shining rows.

'Please, Clare. Don't tell Archie. He mustn't know. Not ever. Please, please, don't tell Archie.'

Clare put two small glasses engraved with partridges on the table.

'Of course I won't.' She put a bottle of sherry beside the glasses. 'He may just know already, mind you.'

'Did you tell him? Have you? What did you say, what—'

'I haven't said anything,' Clare said. 'To anyone.'

She filled the partridge glasses and pushed one towards Liza.

Liza said angrily, 'You fancy Archie, don't you?'

Clare said nothing.

'Sorry,' Liza said.

'As a matter of fact,' Clare said, 'I'm going out to dinner tomorrow night.' She paused. 'To Chewton Glen.'

Liza gazed at her.

'A solicitor in Old Jewry,' Clare said. 'I've known him by sight for ages.'

Liza swallowed her sherry.

'I ought to go.' She looked into her empty glass. 'Clare. I'm so sorry. I don't think I've ever behaved worse in my life.'

Clare touched her arm.

'It isn't all your fault.'

'It is,' Liza said, getting up and peering under the table for her bag. 'It is. And, even if it wasn't, I couldn't have handled it worse.'

She straightened up, clutching her bag.

'I hope you have a lovely dinner. With your solicitor.'

Clare thought of him.

'Well, the food'll be all right, anyway.'

Liza leaned forward and kissed her cheek.

'Bye. And thank you—'

'Drive carefully,' Clare said. 'And ring me. If you want anything.'

Thomas stood in the call box. It was a new one, made entirely of toughened glass, and he was afraid that each passing car might contain a master from Pinemount on his way to the Goat and Compasses for his evening drink. They all went there, every night, and got pie-eyed. Bristow said their breaths afterwards were like methylated spirits and that his parents would take him away if they knew that the whole staff got pie-eyed every single night at the Goat and Compasses.

The call box was, of course, out of bounds. You could make calls home from school, if you got a signed chit from your div. master and Matron timed you, standing by the telephone in the sick-room passage, listening to absolutely every word. If every member of the staff craved drink at the Goat and Compasses obsessively, so Matron craved information. She didn't like a single thing to happen she didn't know about. Rackenshaw timed her to see how long she could last before asking where the pretty photo of his mother was, and she had managed two days. Rackenshaw told her he'd put it in the dustbin, but it was under his mattress all the time. Rackenshaw took it out at night and looked at it under the bedclothes with his torch which he kept hidden in his sponge bag.

Thomas didn't want Matron to know anything any more. She had been horribly kind to him when his grandfather died and Bristow had said that was mostly because his grandfather had been famous. Thomas didn't want anybody to be kind. He didn't want anybody to know that he was scared of going to sleep, because of the dreams. He had devised all kinds of minor tortures for himself to stay awake, the most successful of which was quite simple and merely involved sitting up in bed in the dark dormitory, cold and alone and determined. He nearly always fell asleep in the end, but could now goad himself awake again before sleep tipped him over the last edge down into the black pit where the mad dreams waited for him, dreams where everything was grotesquely large or small, and imbued with panic.

Thomas had three ten-pence pieces. He had quite a lot more money, saved from the holidays, hidden in little amounts in various places in his locker and his tuck box and his desk in the div. room. They were given twenty pence each Sunday for church collection – it went on the bill, Bristow said – and Thomas had, luckily, been given his as two ten-pence pieces the last three Sundays, so he had put one in the church collection, and saved the other. He put one in the telephone now, and dialled Beeches House. It was cold in the telephone box and the plastic receiver was even colder against his ear.

'Hello,' Liza said. She didn't sound normal.

'Mummy—'

'Thomas! Thomas, darling, where are you—'

'At school,' Thomas said.

'Darling. Are you all right?'

'Sort of.'

'It's visiting Sunday, on Sunday. Not long—'

'Your voice sounds funny.'

'Does it?' Liza said. 'I expect I've got a cold. From school.'

'Are you crying?'

'Of course not,' Liza said, closing her red eyes.

'Where's Daddy? Can I speak to Daddy?'

'He's in London,' Liza said. 'He's helping Marina sort things out. Grandpa's things.'

'Has he gone for long?'

'No. No, I'm sure he hasn't.'

'Mummy,' Thomas said, dissolving. 'Mummy.'

'It's two days until Sunday. Only two. Don't cry, darling, please don't—'

In the dark call box, Thomas cried silently, opening his mouth as wide as he could to prevent sobs getting out. He pressed another coin into the machine.

'Darling?' Liza called anxiously. 'Thomas?'

'I sneezed,' Thomas said thickly. 'Why are you crying?'

'I'm not. I'm not, I promise you. I'm fine. Listen, Imogen's got a new game. She plugged all the little holes in the telephone with sunflower seeds. Isn't she awful?'

Thomas giggled weakly, obediently.

'And Mikey and that dreadful Sam he so dotes on scribbled all over each other's faces with magic marker and Sally scrubbed him and scrubbed him but he still looks all scribbly. I hope he'll be clean by Sunday. Thomas?'

'Yes,' Thomas said, pressing his tired wet face to the glass wall.

'Better now? A bit better?'

'Yes,' Thomas said dully.

'Listen, you think about your awful brother and sister. You tell Bristow. And only tonight and one more night, and we'll be down to see you. That's all.'

'Bye,' Thomas said.

He put the receiver back in its cradle and pushed open the door. It was raining softly, the kind of quiet insistent rain Thomas associated with Scotland. He would get back to school wet. Matron would notice. Grizzling drearily to himself, Thomas set off along the verge at a trot, back towards Pinemount.

They stood together in the corridor of the flat. Archie

230

leant his shoulders against the front door, his arms folded as if he were preventing Marina from getting out. She stood close to him. She wore her spectacles.

'I mean it,' Marina said.

He looked down at her. He was quite unable to look anywhere else.

'The last time,' she said. 'I should not have allowed it again.'

'Ah,' he said. His voice was lazy with satisfaction. 'So you wish I had not come. You wish we had not made love.'

'I can't wish that,' Marina said.

'Tell me.'

'Stop it,' she said. 'Don't seduce me. Don't bully.'

He unfolded his arms and reached out for her. She stepped neatly back, out of his range.

'Archie. I mean what I said. You—'

'I'm listening.'

'I adore sex with you.'

'Again.'

'But you are not mine to have. Sex with you isn't for me.' She looked up at him. 'I'm not a marriage wrecker. Maybe I'm not even for marriage, maybe I'm too realistic. I'm certainly too realistic to destroy a family.'

'So what becomes of me?'

'You're a grown man. You decide. And go catch your train. You should have left hours ago, you'll miss it—'

'Do you suppose,' Archie said, not listening, 'do you suppose that I am likely to give you up the moment I find you? Do you really think, after all that battling through the fog, I'm going to go back into it? Are you? Do you want to feel as you did a week ago?'

'Never again,' Marina said.

He took his shoulders away from the door and stood upright.

'I'm not a marriage wrecker either.'

'But you cannot have both—'

'I can,' Archie said. 'I have.'

She looked up at him, through her spectacles.

'But I won't let you. Don't for a moment mistake what I want. But I've lived long enough not to believe in melodrama any longer. Nor in the staying power of deception. Truth always works its way to the surface somehow. Wives have a nose for truth.'

Archie stepped forward and put his arms around her.

'Go catch your train.'

'In a minute.'

He took off her spectacles and put them in his jacket pocket.

'I don't believe you can stop any more than I can.'

He kissed her.

He said, laughing a little, 'I know just how women feel.'

She stiffened.

'How can you know such a thing?'

'You see?' Archie said, delightedly holding her away from him. 'You see? Instant outrage. Women have the monopoly on feelings, don't they? Women are the ones whose lives are limited by frustration, burdened by society's refusal to let them fulfil themselves, women are the ones trapped by stereotype. Right? That's it, isn't it? I'm not allowed inside that sacred personal life, am I, because I'm a man. I've got my work, I'm the breadwinner, that must satisfy me. But I've got it, whether you like it or not. I've broken into the circle where emotional life colours everything, conditions everything.' He pressed Marina against him. 'Everything is better because of you. Everything. I'm richer, stronger. I found you. I discovered myself. If this is what women have been battling for all these years, I'm with them, all the way.'

'How you do talk,' Marina said.

He laughed.

'I do, don't I? I can, now. That's another thing, isn't it, talking? Women think men can't talk, won't talk. Reticence is some sort of male plot to frustrate them of their emotional dues. What about men—'

'Archie,' Marina said. 'Beloved, beautiful Archie. Go home. Go *home*.'

She could hear him laughing, all the way down the stairwell, and when he reached the street door she heard him yell out, wild and exultant, 'Marina!' Archie shouted, 'Marina!' and his voice came spiralling back up to her. 'Marina!'

Chapter Fifteen

Dan Hampole said gently, 'There was no need for this, you know.'

He held Liza's letter out to her. They were standing in June's study, the three of them, and some pale, uncertain spring sunlight was falling through the tall windows and lying pointedly on all the dust.

Liza blushed.

'My dear,' Dan said. 'What harm came of it? What harm to the school?'

'Much more harm,' June said, fidgeting with her cardigan buttons, 'much more harm if you were to resign. Blaise will go at the end of the summer, anyway. It was all planned.'

Liza looked down. She had been compelled to write that letter. It was the only expiation she could think of, the only source of even the faintest consolation. If she had felt lonely before, all those months, she had felt doubly so, all weekend. Everything in her, accustomed over long years, had cried out to confide in Archie, to be comforted by Archie. Her secret weighed upon her like an albatross. Writing the letter had, briefly, lightened that burden. She, who had for so long jealously cherished her private fantasy, now longed for frankness. Values that had temporarily seemed an imposition on her freedom had acquired a sudden, fierce poignancy. Thomas, on Sunday, had at intervals appeared too vulnerable to be borne.

'Can't he leave?' she had begged Archie. 'Can't he leave now, and come home?'

'We'll talk about it,' Archie said. They were in the

car, in the discouraging Sunday-evening dark, driving home. Mikey and Imogen, subdued by the day, were quiet on the back seat. 'We'll talk. Really. When we're alone.'

Liza said now, 'I don't know what happened. I wish I could explain. I seemed – to get disorientated, somehow, blown off course—'

'It's over,' June said. She hated confessions. 'Don't tell me,' she would say to transgressing children. 'I don't want to know. All I want to know is that you are sorry.' She looked at Liza. 'Closed chapter. Really. All forgotten.'

Liza shook her head.

'Not that.'

Dan took her arm.

'Come on,' he said. 'No more tears.'

He led her out through the hall and on to the terrace where three William Kent urns sprouted bleached stalks from last summer like wispy hair.

'In my experience,' Dan said, 'normal people don't do daft things quite arbitrarily. I do, of course, all the time, but then I am not normal, by normal standards.' He took her arm. 'You are normal.'

'I know,' Liza said in despair.

'Don't you despise it.'

'It's so dull,' Liza said, 'being orthodox.'

'My dear, without the status quo, the whole contraption would fall apart at the centre.'

'It's easy for you to say that!' Liza cried. 'You can disregard it, you don't feel it's up to you to push it along. I'm tied to it. I was brought up to it. People like me can't have adventure, don't dare. We don't feel consumed by the huge things, only by the little ones, petty ones, mean ones—'

'What a dear you are,' Dan Hampole said, patting her hand.

'It isn't enough.'

She looked away from him. The great stone slabs of

the terrace were cracked here and there, and furred with aubretia and weeds.

'I love my husband, you see,' Liza said.

'I don't doubt it.'

'You haven't met him—'

'I know of him. Everyone round here knows of him.'

Liza said sadly, 'He knows how to live, you see.' She remembered a phrase of Archie's. 'Big bites. Life in big bites.'

Dan Hampole gave her hand another pat and let it go.

'I shouldn't tell him, all the same.'

'Oh, I won't, I couldn't—'

'It's one of the few things I've learned, keeping mum.' He looked at Liza. 'Don't say a word and don't give young O'Hanlon an inch.'

Liza gazed at him.

'You had your reasons,' Dan said. 'Nothing's for nothing with good girls like you.'

She drove home slowly in the quiet, sad afternoon. Good girl, Dan Hampole had said, a good girl like you. But her kind of goodness had no virtue in it, she thought; it was merely an absence of badness. Really good people, blazingly good people, were often impossible to live with, fascinating, relentless in their advancement of good. Look at St Francis. I'm not good, Liza thought unhappily, I'm just decent. Marina contradicted me when I said England was full of girls like me, but she didn't really know; her judgements are made with her own vision of style and strength. I look different to her because I'm English, that's all. I'm not different; I'm just a fool.

She stopped the car in the village. Diana Jago was standing by the letter box, tearing stamps off a long strip and sticking them on to a pile of letters with a thump of her fist. She wore tight blue jeans and riding boots and a quilted waistcoat and a silk headscarf.

'You Logans,' Diana said. 'Completely gone to earth. Thought you'd emigrated. Where have you been?'

'Working,' Liza said. She got out of the car and leaned against it.

'You look worn out,' Diana said.

'Thanks so much—'

Diana pushed the last letter into the box.

'There we go. The last of the final demands. Simon appears perfectly able to run a bank and totally, utterly incapable of making anything but a hash of his domestic finances.'

'I thought bankers like Simon had their secretaries do that.'

'I don't let his secretary do anything outside the office. I've learned the hard way. Come back for a cup of tea.'

'I shouldn't—'

'Ring from my house. Just half an hour.'

'Oh, Diana,' Liza said. Tears rose and spilled. 'I was going to buy a ball of string, would you believe, and freezer bags—'

'Don't cry,' Diana said. 'You'll start me off and Ma Betts will see. Don't, Liza. Come on, get in my car. You can't drive if you're blubbing. We'll pick your car up later.'

'We keep crying,' Liza said, bundled up on Diana's front seat. 'All of us. Archie, me, Thomas. It's frightful. At least when Imogen cries, it's only temper.'

Diana swung her car off the road and down the lane towards the river.

'You're so kind.'

'Nonsense.'

'Diana,' Liza said, 'have you ever made a really awful fool of yourself?'

'Yup,' Diana said. She turned the car into her smoothly gravelled drive and stopped it by the white front door guarded by two stone lions bearing shields.

'And?'

237

'And nothing. It's just something you have to live with.'

Liza followed Diana across the hall, hushed by its depth of carpet, and into the kitchen. It was stencilled in blue on yellow, with complicated, unsuitable urban curtains, and on the table lay a sprawling pile of tack.

'Always clean it in here, in the winter,' Diana said. 'Much warmer.' She reached for a roll of paper towel, spun off several feet of it and threw it at Liza. 'Now blow your nose.' The sound of the Jago Labradors, penned in their outdoor kennel, came penetratingly through the closed windows. Diana banged on the nearest one. 'Shut up! Bloody dogs. Sit over there, it's the only comfortable chair. Chuck the cat off.'

Liza lifted an enormous square tabby off a cushion in a Windsor armchair and sat down, settling the cat on her knee.

'These deaths knock you for six, you know,' Diana said, getting a catering-sized box of extra-strong tea bags out of a cupboard. 'I wouldn't be surprised if it's worse for Archie precisely because he thought he was so used to it, and could cope.'

'It got full of complications,' Liza said. 'Complications and crossed wires.' She turned her face away from Diana and looked at the yellow wall beside her where a circle of blue-and-white Spanish pottery plates hung like a childish clock. 'I didn't see,' Liza said. 'I was so busy with myself. I've always been so used to him being in charge, of himself as well as us. I never thought to look. I was fed up with him. I got carried away by something else.'

Diana put tea bags and boiling water into thick mugs painted with crude lemons. After a few seconds, she fished the tea bags out with a spoon and flicked them approximately in the direction of the sink. One fell short, on to the floor. Diana took no notice. She carried the mugs over to Liza and then went across to the refrigerator and got out a bottle of milk.

'Milk?'

'Please.'

'Look,' Diana said, sloshing it into the mugs, 'I think Archie feels pretty much the same as you.'

Liza turned her head back quickly.

'Does he?'

'I think he'd agree with you about crossed wires. I know he's having second thoughts about Richard's repulsive plan. Here. Drink that nasty brew. If we were in your kitchen, it'd be Lapsang Suchong and a homemade cake—'

'Don't you believe it. Diana—'

'Yes.'

'Diana, d'you really think Archie feels as I do?'

'I think he feels,' Diana said, remembering Archie's glowing face in the field a week before, 'I think he feels that you haven't been communicating particularly well recently, and he'd like to put that right.'

Liza said, leaning forward, 'There's Thomas, you see. We have to do something about Thomas. He looks awful, so strained. But while it was all tied up in Archie's mind with Andrew and Andrew's wishes, it seemed hopeless even to talk about it. Perhaps now—'

'As Nanny used to say, grasp the nettle.'

'Yes,' Liza said. She was smiling. 'Of course.'

She reached across the table and put her mug down.

'Come on, cat.'

She stood up.

'Go for it,' Diana said.

Archie was standing in the kitchen, propped against the dresser and reading the local paper. He was humming. Something about him made Liza a little doubtful as to how she should begin. She got carrots and onions out of the cupboard and put them on a wooden board on the draining board and began to chop. She chopped the carrots into tiny dice and the onion into wafery rings.

Then, without turning round, she said uncertainly, 'Archie—'

'Yes.'

She looked at her reflection in the night-black glass of the window above the sink. She couldn't see her expression, only her outline, and beyond that, against the lines of plates and jugs on the dresser, Archie, ankles crossed, reading the paper.

'Archie, I want to say sorry.'

He didn't look up.

'What for?'

She battled to keep her voice steady.

'For the way I've behaved. About Andrew. About extra working. About us.'

He looked up. She could see his face, tiny and clear, in the black window.

'That's all right,' he said easily.

'No.'

She turned round. He looked absolutely unperturbed.

'I feel awful about it,' Liza said. Her chest was bursting with the desire to be free of her shame. 'I'm so sorry. I've been horrible.'

He didn't move. He said, smiling, 'No, you haven't. It's been a bit rocky for everyone. I've been a pain, too.'

She bent her head. It was as impossible to stop tears as it was to stop breathing. Perhaps she shouldn't stop them, perhaps they would, as they invariably did, bring him over, bring him to her, make him put his arms round her, hold her.

'Archie,' Liza sobbed.

'Don't cry,' he said kindly, from across the room.

She put her hands up to her eyes. They smelled of onion. They made the tears worse.

'I've refused to listen,' Liza said. 'I've refused to talk. I've belittled you.'

Archie put the paper down.

'Look,' he said. 'It doesn't matter. I said so. A lot of

240

the things you said have been quite justified. I'm sorry, too.'

He was still smiling, a kind, impersonal smile.

Liza said, desperate to reach him, 'And there's Thomas—'

'I know.'

'You said we could talk, when we're alone.'

'Do you really think this is the moment, with you in tears?'

'Archie!' Liza cried. She ran across the kitchen and flung her arms about him, pressing herself against his side. Against her hip, in his jacket pocket, something snapped sharply.

'Oh, God,' Liza said. 'What's that?'

'It doesn't matter—'

She dropped her arms and put one hand into his pocket. She brought out half a pair of pale tortoiseshell spectacles, broken cleanly across the bridge.

'Dior,' Liza said. 'Christian Dior.' She did not look up at Archie. 'Marina's glasses.'

Neither of them moved. Liza gazed down at the broken spectacles.

'Why?' said Liza, sick with a sudden new fear. 'Why should Marina's glasses be in your pocket?'

He lay awake, long after she had exhausted herself into sleep. It wasn't a good sleep, he could tell, because she gasped and drew shuddering little breaths and every so often her feet moved convulsively, or her arms. He had made love to her. She had wanted him to, begged him to, but it had not been a success for either of them and it had left her weeping worse than ever, beside herself with weeping.

It was both strange and horrible. Strange because she had not uttered one angry word, and horrible because she had seemed alien to him, pitiable, but not significant, not central. He had tried not to be rough with her, but then had been afraid that, if he were not rough, if he did not goad himself on with a spur of violence, he would not be able to climax and he did not know how he would deal with her, if that happened. As it was, he had dealt with her very badly. He had hurt her, all over. There was not an inch of her body and mind he had not hurt. He could hardly comprehend the damage he had done.

He stared into the darkness. There was no wind, only the faint far sound of owls and across that, cutting sharply now and then, the imperious scream of a vixen wanting a mate. It must have been three o'clock. Perhaps even later. They had talked until almost one, on and on, round and round.

'I don't understand,' Liza said over and over again. 'I don't understand about sex. Not like that. Not when you've known it with love, for making children. Didn't you think of me?'

He had not, while he was with Marina. Before Marina, he had thought of her so much, but then he had been almost a different person then, another man.

'Don't work it out,' he'd said. 'Don't even try. There isn't logic, there isn't a pattern. The changes are like the shifting shapes desert sand gets blown into by the wind. I wasn't deliberate. I'm not now. You weren't.'

'But Marina. Why Marina?'

'Oh, Liza,' Archie said, shaking his head. 'You know why Marina. You know that yourself.'

There had been a long, long silence then, which she had broken by saying flatly, 'You see, I thought she was mine.'

Then she turned on him.

'Is that why? Is that why you chose her? Because she loved me?'

'No,' he said truthfully. 'It never crossed my mind.'

A double betrayal, Liza had said, repeating it again and again, a double betrayal. Both of you. I can't believe it, I can't believe this has happened, but it has, hasn't it, it has.

'Could I have stopped it? If I'd been looking—'

'I don't know.'

'Will you stop it now? Will you? Did you mean to go on, if I hadn't broken her glasses?'

'Yes,' he said.

'You meant to keep it secret.'

'I meant not to tell you.'

'But now? What now?'

'I don't know,' he said.

'But why can't you stop? Why, why—'

'Because,' he said, 'I am afraid to.'

I am afraid, he thought now. I am afraid of doing without this, now I have found it. He rolled on to his side, away from Liza, clenching his fists between his thighs. It was a different kind of fear to any he had known before, involving neither heart nor muscle, but more the possible death of the spirit, the loss of light. What had Liza said to him, all those months ago? 'It's me that's changed.' She did seem to have changed. She had been sharper with him, more impatient, superior. And then tonight none of those things; just abject, pitiful, childlike.

The door opened six inches. A head came round it three feet from the floor.

'My toadthtool'th gone out—'

Archie raised himself on one elbow.

'Imo—'

'It went ping,' Imogen hissed, coming in further.

'Shhh. You'll wake Mummy.'

He slid out of bed and pushed Imogen out of the room.

'Where are your pyjamath?' Imogen demanded. She looked at his nakedness with reproof.

'I'll get a new bulb. Get back into bed.'

He padded down to the kitchen. The vegetables still lay forlornly on the chopping board, the newspaper on the table. Three twenty-five, the clock said inexorably. He found a miniature bulb in the cupboard – Liza did

243

not forget things, run out of things – and carried it upstairs to Imogen. She was not in bed. She stood beside him until the toadstool glowed again in the dark room, and then she climbed in and lay there looking up at him with Liza's face framed in Liza's red curls.

'Put your pyjamath on,' Imogen said, and turned on her side, plugging in her thumb.

Liza woke in the dawn. There was no natural light, but a yellow glow came in dully from the landing. Someone had not shut the door. Swimming wretchedly to the unwelcome surface, Liza cast a glance at Archie. He was asleep, turned away from her, and for some reason he had put on his only pair of pyjamas, pyjamas they had bought once while staying in a country hotel in Scotland where the lavatory was half a league down public passages from their bedroom. Why on earth had he put them on? Liza could only suppose, pulling her aching body out of bed, that he had put them on to make himself yet more separate from her.

Everything ached, inside and out. She found her dressing gown and the espadrilles she used as slippers and went out on to the landing. A small metal aeroplane lay against a skirting board and over the banisters hung Mikey's school tie, needing mending, spewing a pale woolly tongue of lining out of its split sheath. She picked it up and put it in her dressing-gown pocket and went slowly downstairs, her espadrilles slapping roughly against her heels.

In the kitchen, Nelson stirred in his basket out of token politeness. She filled the kettle and put it on, scraped the cut vegetables into the rubbish bin – oh, my God, she thought in despair, isn't it just typical of me that I should think, even on a morning like this, that I ought to use the bloody things for making stock? – folded up the newspaper and put it, with all the other newspapers whose life was not yet exhausted, in a square willow basket. The half of Marina's spectacles lay under the newspaper. Liza picked it up and ran a finger over the tiny golden CD on the earpiece. Then she carried it across the room and dropped it through the swing lid of the rubbish bin, on to the carrots and the onions. Last night – she stopped. She would not, at this fatal low-ebb hour before life began again, allow herself to think of last night.

But what else was there to think of? Last night stood there, mammoth, immovable, blocking her path to any other thought. What was to be gained by refusing to confront not only the fact that Archie had been to bed with Marina, and that he had wanted it and she had allowed it, but also that Marina had real power, the power of her personality and her sexuality which could make such a difference to Archie? And when those facts had been confronted, Liza thought, spooning China tea into a pot and adding boiling water from the kettle, then she had to go on, resolutely, and face the additional fact that Marina's power did exist and that the power Blaise O'Hanlon had tried to persuade her she had did not. Marina, schooled by her interesting, unsatisfactory upbringing and her peculiar, unhelpful life, had made something of herself. She did not, as Liza did, see herself always comparatively, and mostly at a disadvantage.

She looked down at the teapot. Heavens, what is the matter with me? Why do I go on making tea in teapots with loose tea when my whole world is falling apart? Why am I such a slave to ritual, to the show of things? Why don't I go and find the brandy or break the glass cases of Archie's stuffed fish or, like the girl jilted by a major newspaper editor, hack the crotch out of all his trousers? Because I'm normal, as Dan said; because I'm designed not to rock boats and, when I try, when I have a dash at it and try, I make a complete and utter mess of it and a fool of myself into the bargain. And I end up whining like my sister Clare.

I want to die, Liza thought, staring out of the window at the dull silver line of new morning that lay along the distant hedge of the doomed field. I just want to die. I don't want to bear this, I don't want to live through bearing this. And I don't even yet know what I have to bear, what Archie will do. What had he said last night? 'Domestic dramas,' he had said at one moment with distaste. 'These domestic dramas—' She felt quite impotent with angry misery, remembering that. That was what life was, that was what afflicted everyone. How typical of Archie to believe that his life could be lived on a more thrilling level, for higher stakes, how typical of his exaggerated, greedy appetites for things. And yet, and yet, he knew how to lift his eyes from the ground, he wasn't afraid to push forward, he wasn't alarmed by mad people or bad people or sick and revolting people. Had he turned that vast tenderness of his upon Marina? Had he? Oh, the vicious pain of it, if he had.

The sky was now metallic-grey, and life outside the window, in the hedges and the beech trees, was beginning to clear its throat. Liza found her sewing basket, and took Mikey's tie out of her pocket and began, with small, precise stitches, to confine the lining inside the tube again. M. A. Logan, said the name tape on the tie, in red capitals. Michael Andrew Logan. And Thomas was Thomas Andrew Archibald Logan. Liza's father's name was Brian. It had not occurred to either Liza or Archie to christen either of the boys Brian. They were Logan boys; Liza had felt it to be so, wished it to be so. She wanted Andrew back with a sudden hopeless fierceness, she wanted his sweet affection for her, his Scottish uprightness, his sense of order. If he had not died, none of this would have happened. Or would it? Was something stirring deep in Archie long before Andrew had even married Marina? And, at the same time, had she begun to want something more, to spread her wings, to seem different to herself, and to Archie?

She got up, rolling the tie round her hand and returning it to her pocket. Never had the prospect of a day seemed more distasteful to her, more alarming. She had no idea as to how she should behave, no inclination to adopt one kind of attitude rather than another. Feet thumped overhead. She glanced at the clock. Ten to seven; the alarm had gone off, Archie was going to shave. Slowly, slowly, Liza began to open cupboards and drawers and lay the table for breakfast, bowls and spoons and mugs and plates, boxes of cereal, jars of honey and yeast spread. Nelson got out of his basket and shook himself vehemently, slapping his ears against his head like leather sails. A voice came down through the ceiling, a muffled, steady voice. Archie had turned on the weather forecast, in the bathroom, as he always did, so that he should afterwards hear the news. Then there were thumps and a squeal and quick feet tore along the landing. She must go up, before Mikey put on yesterday's socks again, and give him his mended tie. On it went, on and on. Was that what she and Archie had wanted in their several ways, just to get off the treadmill for a while? Oh, shut up, Liza told herself angrily, shut up, shut up, excuses, excuses.

She went out of the kitchen. The quick feet raced back along the landing.

'Mikey!' Liza shouted. 'Mikey! I hope you're dressing—'

A grey wool foot appeared between the banister bars.

'I've lost my tie.'

'No,' she said. 'No. I've got it here. I mended it.'

The foot disappeared.

'Drat you,' Mikey said. 'Drat you. I didn't want it mended.'

Chapter Sixteen

It seemed to Thomas a perfectly possible plan. Even if it wasn't, he was going to try it, because it had become necessary. You could, it seemed, signal and signal and the right people took no notice, while the wrong ones noticed every detail and made an embarrassing fuss and so drove you to hide the signals. Matron was a wrong person, the number-one wrong person, and Mr Barnes wasn't much better. Kindness, Thomas had decided, was an awful thing to be saddled with. It made you look like a baby and then, on top of that, you had to say thank you for it.

He had gathered all his money together from all his hidey-holes and hidden it under Blue Rabbit's skin, pushing the coins in through a split in his side seam. There was nearly six pounds. This seemed to him a significant amount and quite enough to get him to London by bus. He had considered the train, but it was very expensive, and there would probably be a difficulty at the ticket office over selling a ticket to someone who, though tall for his age, was definitely only a boy on his own. The national buses, on the other hand, with their red, white and blue livery, ran from Poole and Bournemouth to London for only a few pounds. Thomas had seen them, on his journeys to school, and the fares were painted on the back, in scarlet letters. Return, it said, four pounds fifty. Thomas only needed to go one way and in any case was only a child, so perhaps it would only cost him a pound. He had to get to Bournemouth, of course, but he thought he could do that, on local buses, one into Wimborne, another down to Bournemouth. If he did that at a carefully chosen time of day, when the buses were full of state-school children going home, he thought he could just mix in, not be noticed. And when he got to London – and this moment shone in his mind like a little, bright lantern – he would telephone Marina. And then, in some way which she would achieve, it would all be over.

'Grown-up people,' Marina had said to Thomas without the faintest trace of condescension, 'make the mistake of thinking that life for the very young is amusing. It isn't.'

For Thomas, that moment at his grandfather's wedding lunch had been a revelation. It was not simply that Marina had known and understood the great perils of Thomas's life, but that her understanding and her manner had abruptly inspired him with absolute trust. He knew she knew and that she would tell no-one. She had not laboured her point, she had gone on at once to mock the pretension of the hotel and, in so doing, had sealed her and Thomas's little secret nugget of sympathy. She had said her own childhood had been either exciting or alarming. Thomas felt that in his, the two sensations overlapped so often that he hardly knew which was which. The dreams of recent weeks appeared to him as the perfectly natural result of fear and thrill, and thus, even if dreaded, not to be wondered at. He would be able to describe them to Marina and she would not try to belittle them with disgusting baby comfort. 'Don't worry,' people had said – Matron, Mr Barnes, even Archie. 'Don't worry,' as if Thomas could be seduced out of his troubles with a kiss and a sweetie, like Imogen. Marina wouldn't do that. She would, instead, Thomas was sure of it, help him to attack the monster instead of pretending it wasn't there.

The certainty of this, of her ability to help him, made the business of getting to her relatively unalarming. The best moment for getting out of school was after afternoon games, with the showers and changing rooms full of confusion and yelling, and half the masters guzzling tea in the staff room. The hoard of money was prised out of Blue Rabbit and hidden at the back of his football-boot locker, ready to be transferred, at the last minute, to his shorts pocket, just before he initiated his plan. Then, he would embark on a deception to give him time to slip away while everyone else surged avidly in to tea. Thomas planned to complain of a painful foot, and be sent up to see Matron, and then do a quick U-turn in the locker-room corridor, skid out through the courtyard door and have a good half hour's start before anyone noticed he was not in prep.

'I can't see anything,' said John Thorne, who had taken football that afternoon. He was holding Thomas's foot.

'I know,' Thomas said. 'It feels deep inside. Sort of squashed. I expect it happened when I fell over.'

'Did you fall over?'

'Yes,' Thomas said. 'Trying to get the ball from Rigby. Ow,' he added, as John Thorne turned his foot.

'But you weren't anywhere near Rigby.'

'I meant Bennet,' Thomas said.

'Stand up.' John Thorne said. 'Now up on your toes.'

'Ouch,' Thomas said. 'Ow. That really hurts.'

'You'd better see Matron.'

'Yes, sir.'

'Be quick.'

'Mr Thorne—'

Thomas had planned this.

'Yes.'

'Would you keep a bun for me? In tea—'

'All right,' John Thorne said. He thought Logan looked rotten. 'It'll make you hurry.'

In seconds Thomas, his money clutched hard against his thigh, was through the courtyard and into the laurustinus hedge that bordered Pinemount's drive. He looked back fleetingly. Nobody. It was a great temptation to run easily on the drive, but he dared not risk it. He must stay inside the hedge, stumbling a bit, scaring himself with snapping twigs, until he reached the gate, and could dodge out into the lane and then behind the left-hand field hedge. It seemed to take a long time, blundering down the hedge, and so intent was he upon it that he did not for a while hear the even, running adult feet coming down the drive behind him.

'Logan,' John Thorne called. 'Logan, stop running.'

He stopped at once.

'What is all this? Where are you going?'

Thomas began to shake terribly.

'To my grandmother. In London—'

John Thorne, who was young and kind and clumsy, came off the drive into the hedge and put his hand on Thomas.

'Sorry, Logan. No go. Sorry.'

Tears began to pour down Thomas's face. He put an arm up, across his eyes.

'Please, please—'

'I heard your money chinking,' John Thorne said, 'when I told you to stand up. That's how I knew. Look. Don't be afraid. I'll come with you to Mr Barnes. Don't be afraid.'

Thomas looked up at him through a sliding screen of tears. Afraid? Why should he be afraid of Mr Barnes? Why did no-one ever see what the really frightening things were?

'Sir,' Thomas said obediently.

John Thorne took his arm. He would have liked to put his own arm round Thomas's shoulders but was doubtful about walking back to school in such an embrace.

'Come on, old boy. Come on. We'll get you sorted out.'

'I don't want that,' Thomas said. 'I don't want it. I just want to see my grandmother.'

'We'll tell Mr Barnes that. Shall we?'

'Yes,' Thomas said dully. He remembered suddenly, 'Not my mother and father. Not them. My grandmother.' His voice was urgent. 'It must be her!'

The sick-room door opened.

'Thomas,' said George Barnes, who never called boys by their Christian names. 'Thomas, here they are.'

He looked up. Matron had put him to bed, for some reason, but he wouldn't lie down, he simply sat there in his pyjamas and looked without seeing much at Rackenshaw's newest *Dungeons and Dragons* magazine, kindly lent as a restorative.

'Darling,' Liza said.

Thomas saw she had been crying again.

George Barnes said, 'I'll leave you together—'

The door closed with elaborate softness.

Archie came over and sat on the edge of the bed and looked at Thomas. Thomas looked down at the dragons.

'Can you tell us? Can you tell us why you tried to run away?'

'Why didn't you ring? Why didn't you, darling? I'd have come and collected you at once, you know I would—'

'You wouldn't,' Thomas said. 'You didn't.'

Liza was fumbling for a handkerchief. Archie took out his and handed it to her.

'We can take you home now,' Archie said. He longed to hold Thomas but every vibe of Thomas's held him off. 'For ever, if you like.'

Desolation filled Thomas.

'Not come back to Pinemount?'

'Not if it gives you nightmares. Not if you need to be at home.'

Thomas said clearly, 'I need Marina.'

Nobody said anything. Sensing a powerful advantage, Thomas said rudely, 'I can't talk to you.'

'Darling—'

'I'm not a baby!' Thomas shouted. He was so angry with them. Why were they so blind and stupid and unable to see? How could they have all their horrible secrets and be all upset and not tell him the truth about why they were upset and then pretend they didn't know what they'd done? He turned round and lay down with his face in the pillow.

'Come on,' Archie said gently. 'Come on, darling. We are going home now.'

'We needn't talk about it at all. We needn't talk about anything you don't want to.'

Fatigue was stealing upon Thomas, the opiating fatigue of emotion, too much fear. He sighed and stirred a little. Archie bent over him and lifted his long, thin, reluctant body out of the bedclothes.

'Come on, old boy. Give us a bit of a hand—'

They took off his pyjamas and dressed him like a doll, vest and pants and socks and shirt and shorts – silent shorts; where was his money – and jersey?

'Where is my money?'

'Here,' Archie said. 'Mr Barnes gave it to me.'

'It's mine!'

'Take it, then.'

Elaborately, maddeningly, Thomas counted his money and put it in his pocket. They might be able to lift him bodily out of bed, but they couldn't lift his mind out and dress it and take it tamely home. Liza wanted to hug him, so he let her, but it only made her cry again.

They went down the main staircase together, Archie and Liza holding Thomas as if he was an invalid. He resented this but could not summon up one ounce of physical resistance. Mr Barnes came up, and then Mrs Barnes appeared and so did Matron, and there was a lot of bustling about and officiousness and then he was put on to the back seat of the car where they made a nest for him with cushions and rugs. The car smelled familiar and Archie's black doctor's case was on the floor behind the front seat. Thomas lay down. Liza bent over him, tucking the rug round, murmuring. He heard them both get in and the click of the seat belts and then the engine started and made the car throb underneath him. He put his hand into his pocket and held the money. Then he slept.

They drove in silence. There was, if they spoke, only one subject and if they even dipped a toe in that ocean they would be at once sucked in and whirled about in cataracts and waterspouts. Liza knew Archie had telephoned Marina to say — she had to believe this — that they would never see each other alone again, but she also knew he had not wanted, in any way, to make such a call. He had been reluctant to elaborate the reasons for this to Liza — 'Don't ask me, don't keep asking me for answers you then say you can't bear to hear' — but she knew what they were. He was not simply averse to looking at life ahead without Marina, he was also afraid to.

'But you can't mean it! You must be exaggerating. How can you be that deep in, in two evenings?'

'Don't ask me,' Archie said, meaning it literally.

'But I must and you must tell me; you owe it to me to tell me—'

He had looked away from her.

'If something comes to you as a revelation, a discovery, at the end of a long journey, it can happen in seconds, you can recognize it in an instant.'

'Rubbish!' Liza had shouted angrily. 'Absolute rubbish. What value has anything so selfish beside twelve years of marriage and three children?'

'It is quite separate.'

It was the separateness that gave Liza such pain, a complicated, many-headed pain, because for so many months, separateness was exactly what she had craved and now it was the last thing she wanted. But had she —

oh, these wearisome analyses, she thought, leaning her head back in the dark car – had she instinctively sought comfort from Blaise's admiration because Archie had withdrawn himself in some way that her subconscious self had recognized and reacted to? Was she in part responsible for Archie's turning to – no, headlong rushing at was more accurate – Marina, because she had been self-absorbed and had allowed herself to believe the enchantments Blaise had spun about her? Did Thomas's troubles all stem from his sensitive unhappy perceptions of tension between them . . .

'Don't,' Archie said abruptly.

'Don't what?'

'Don't keep looking for something to blame. Or someone.'

'There must be some kind of explanation, some reason. Life isn't so arbitrary—'

'People are.'

Liza thought of Dan Hampole. Without the people who trudged along shoring up the status quo, he'd said, the whole contraption would fall apart at the centre.

She said cautiously, 'Unhappy people?'

He sighed. He said, 'Oh yes.'

She waited, staring fixedly at the red tail-lights of the car in front.

'It's those who are unhappy who break the rules,' Archie said. His voice was very quiet and she had to lean sideways to hear him. 'And it's those rule-breakers who test the rules to see if they still hold good, and who push out the boundaries. Without them there would be fewer new horizons.'

He waited for her to accuse him of making excuses, of trying to glamorize something hackneyed and squalid, but she didn't. She didn't say anything. They drove for a long way again in silence and on the back seat Thomas turned in his sleep and snuffled slightly.

Poor Thomas. Poor troubled, muddled Thomas, already beginning to make the fatal human mistake of taking himself too seriously. When George Barnes had rung and described, in soothing, measured tones, Thomas's abortive attempt to run away, Archie had waited then, as well, for Liza to accuse him of involving the innocent in his seedy trails, of creating confusion and upheaval in blameless lives of order and regularity. But she had not done that then, either. She had been very frightened for Thomas, and about him, but she hadn't turned on Archie.

He glanced at her. Her face was turned away from him, towards the blank black banks of the Winchester bypass.

'How is Liza?' Marina had said on the telephone.

'Shattered.'

'Of course.'

Archie had been about to say that there was something withdrawn in her, too, something unexpected and private, but Marina forestalled him.

'I shall come down and see her, of course.'

His heart had leapt.

'You will?'

'Of course.'

'Then I shall see you.'

'Archie—'

'Can you imagine how I am to go on, how—'

'Stop that!' Marina commanded, from London.

'Don't you feel it? Doesn't it mean anything to you?'

She had put the receiver down, cut him off. She had left him as she had left him several times before, desperate for more, for revelations and displays of dependence she would not give.

'Are you in bed with me,' he had demanded, 'because you are missing my father?'

She had looked at him without expression.

'That is none of your business,' she said.

She had said that to him, too, when he had asked

256

what she would say to Liza. He longed for her to come down to Stoke Stratton, longed for it fiercely, and dreaded it, too. What a bond women had. What power. And yet, looking quickly again at Liza, he knew he had power now, too, power over her as he had had when they first met and he had borne her away to Scotland. The difference now was that he was not sure he wanted it any more and he was very sure he did not know how to use it.

He swung the car up Beeches Lane, flicking up the headlamp beams. They caught, at once, the huge gleaming developer's board by the field gate. It was painted cream, with a wreath of daisies and poppies and ears of corn around the border, and, in the left-hand corner, a fatuous tabby cat lifted a paw towards the lettering. 'Home At Last', it ran. 'Beeches Lawn, a luxury four-bedroomed house of distinction'. And underneath, in smaller letters, 'Beeches Close. Starter homes of character'. Beyond the board, in the field, an immense pile of bricks loomed like a factory, and straw from their packing blew about in the dark air and scratched against the windscreen.

'Richard's putting those on the open market,' Liza said.

'What?'

'I heard in the post office. He's offered them at twenty-five thousand with mortgage help to anyone under thirty-five born in the Strattons. There's only been one taker. The rest are muttering about the money.'

'Prefer to sulk in rented cottages—'

'Yes,' Liza said.

Archie said awkwardly, 'I'm sorry about that, all that—'

She wanted to laugh.

'That!'

'Yes,' he said.

'Oh, Archie. As if any of that mattered now!'

From the back seat, Thomas rose, instinctively wakened by the approach of home. He was unable to prevent feeling pleased.

'I'm hungry,' Thomas said.

Clare was not impulsive. Or rather, she was afflicted by impulsive feelings which she was afraid to implement in case she could not carry off the consequences. But, emboldened by her dinner at Chewton Glen – her solicitor, though hardly prepossessing to look at, had turned out to be a good companion and more than easy with the wine list – and a further invitation to a point-to-point at Hackwood Park, Clare thought she would simply drive out to Stoke Stratton, without telephoning first.

Liza had not telephoned since she had sobbed all over Clare's kitchen. That episode had left Clare feeling quite indulgent and, at the same time, less dissatisfied with her own life, a state of affairs rather assisted by the solicitor. Being early March, the evenings were growing lighter, and, if she left her office dead on five, she could be in Stoke Stratton before half-past, while the children were still up and could prevent her visit looking, in any way, too tremendously enquiring. She was fond of the children in a bleak, half-hearted way, but she believed them to be spoiled, particularly Imogen, and was too apt to see them as part of the list of assets that Liza possessed and she did not.

She arrived, as she had estimated, at twenty-five past five. Archie's car was gone, but Liza's was parked in the drive with the tailgate up and a box of groceries inside, waiting to be carried into the house. Clare made a quick mental check of what the box contained – packs of white lavatory paper (Archie, Clare knew, had taught Liza to despise pink or blue, or, worst of all, peach), tins of dog food, cereals, an immense bottle of liquid detergent of a size no single person ever aspired to, rafts of fruit yoghurts, loaves, nets of oranges –

before picking it up and carrying it round to the kitchen door.

'Yoohoo,' Clare said, pushing the door open with her knee. 'Delivery man!'

Liza was standing at the kitchen table, laying sausages for the children's supper on a baking sheet. She had not taken off her jacket since coming in from school, and looked tired and drawn.

'Oh!' she said. 'Clare. Oh, how nice of you—'

'I met it sitting there, on my way in.'

She put the box down on the table and kissed her sister.

'I went to Sainsbury's,' Liza said. 'I forgot that box.'

The door from the hall was pushed open and Thomas, in a Batman sweatshirt, came in with half a model aeroplane.

'Thomas!'

'Hello,' Thomas said indifferently.

'You're back early. It isn't the end of term, is it?'

'He wasn't well,' Liza said, opening the oven door and banging the baking sheet inside. 'Were you?'

Clare and Thomas kissed without fervour.

'You look fine now.'

'Mikey's hidden the glue—'

'He's a lot better. Aren't you, darling?'

'Will you make him find it?'

'Thomas, not now. Clare's just come.'

'Please, please—'

'Five minutes,' Liza said. 'Five mintues' peace.'

'Mum—'

'Thomas,' Liza said, raising her voice, 'go away or I'll never help you find your glue.'

The door banged behind him sulkily.

'What was the matter?' Clare said.

'Tea?' Liza said, unbuttoning her jacket. 'Coffee? Whisky?'

'Tea would be lovely.'

'I'm going to have whisky,' Liza said.

'But you never drink whisky.'

'I do now.'

Clare said, 'Liza, what's going on?'

Liza said nothing. She took off her jacket and hung it behind the door and put tumblers on the table and a half-full whisky bottle.

'I almost never drink this,' Clare said.

'Nor me. But this is no moment for almost never anything.'

'Liza—' Clare said pleadingly.

Liza looked mutinous. She poured whisky into the tumblers and then ran water into a green jug embossed with vine leaves (Clare remembered Archie bringing that jug home, from a junk shop somewhere) and put it on the table.

Then she put her hands to her face and said, 'Archie's been to bed with Marina and Thomas tried to run away from school.'

Clare sat there. She stared at the whisky in the glasses.

Liza said, 'I'm OK, though,' and burst into tears.

Clare went round the table and put her arms around her sister. Liza, who was always rounded and pleasantly resilient to touch, felt bony and awkward.

'Marina,' Liza sobbed. 'I can't bear that it's Marina.'

'Is it over?'

'I think so. But he doesn't want it to be.'

Clare took one arm away and used it to pour water into the whisky glasses.

'Here,' she said to Liza.

'I didn't mean to tell you,' Liza said, blowing her nose. 'I don't want anyone to know, not anyone. Certainly nobody here; not the village.'

'But they needn't.'

Liza took the tumbler and gulped.

'Oh, Clare—'

'Poor Liza. Poor little you.'

'Oh no,' Liza said, looking at Clare. 'Oh, not that. You know that's not true.'

'Have you told him, told Archie about you and Blaise?'

'Heavens, no—'

'Don't you think you should?'

Liza sat down on a kitchen chair and said, spacing the words as if she were spitting them out, 'I could not bear him to know.'

'But he has told you—'

'No. I found out. I put my arms round him and bust her glasses. They were in his pocket, after—'

'So then he told you?'

'Yes.'

'Everything.'

'Oh yes.'

Clare thought about Marina. She remembered saying to Liza, of Marina, 'You and I will never be that sexy. We never have been.' They had been stunned by Marina; they'd got frightfully over-excited about her and pretended they were at school, high on a crush on a prefect. And Archie had been so rude that day, sulky and prickly with hardly veiled insults. Archie. Clare grew hot thinking about him. Faithful, strong-minded, protective Archie, in bed with his stepmother, his widowed stepmother. It was the stuff of Sophocles, not the stuff of a doctor in Stoke Stratton, a country doctor.

She said in a voice choked with bewilderment, 'Will you part?'

'I – I don't think so.' Liza took a swallow and pulled a faint face. 'I don't know. I don't know if he can go back or come back or whatever it is.'

'But the children—' Clare lowered her voice. 'Is that what was the matter with Thomas?'

'Partly. And partly Andrew dying and partly, would you believe it, being convinced that, if he saw Marina, everything would be all right.' Liza raised her tired face to Clare's. 'To be honest, I don't really know what's the matter with Thomas. I only know parts of it.

261

He's very angry with us. But he's slept better the last two nights. And he's eating. Archie—' She bit her lip. 'Archie told him yesterday that relationships were two-way traffic systems and he wasn't too young to realize that. Rich, really, coming from him.'

'But what have you had to complain of, up to now?'

Liza sighed.

'How do you mend trust?'

'Aren't you breaking it, too, keeping your secret?'

'I'm ashamed,' Liza said.

Clare stood up.

'That's something else altogether.'

'What a mess,' Liza said, draining her glass. 'What a mess.'

The door opened. Thomas had added a baseball cap adorned with a golden bat to his ensemble. He hissed at his mother.

'Glue. Glue. Glue.'

'Coming.'

A muffled roaring came through the open door.

'That's Imogen,' Thomas said. 'We zipped her into a sleeping bag. She wanted it, till she was zipped up and then she didn't.'

Liza moved towards the door.

'At least with Imogen around we can't see ourselves as tragic—' She paused in the doorway. 'One day,' she said, looking back at Clare, 'one day we'll have a whole conversation which doesn't even mention us. I promise.'

Clare backed her car out of the drive and turned it away from Winchester. The solicitor had said he would telephone between six-thirty and seven, but she was confident enough to think it quite a good thing if she were not there, as well as being certain he would try later. She drove through Stoke Stratton, past the post office outside which Mrs Betts was talking to the postwoman, a stout, highly made-up woman in a bursting dark-blue uniform, who shared many of Mrs Betts's aims and prejudices. As Clare drove by, Mrs Betts peered in the fading light to see who it was. It was a severe temptation to wind down the window and call helpfully, 'Dr Logan's sister-in-law!'

'Dr Logan's sister-in-law,' Mrs Betts informed the postwoman.

The health centre car-park was full, it being the middle of surgery. Clare parked on the edge and went into the cheerful, heartless waiting room where people sat with the despondency induced by waiting.

'I wonder if I could see Dr Logan? I'm not a patient, I'm his sister-in-law.'

Her voice carried clearly round the room. The receptionist said that, if she would care to wait, Dr Logan might be free after all his patients.

'Could you tell him? Could you tell him I'm here?'

The receptionist looked as if this was a well-nigh intolerable request.

'After the next patient.'

'I may see him?'

The receptionist looked affronted.

'Oh no. Certainly not. After the next patient, I will tell him you are here.'

Clare drifted over to a chair beneath a threatening plant with fibrous stems and hideous shining dark leaves, fingered like crude hands. Magazines on yachts and country life and children's board books entitled *Miffy Goes Skating* and *Watch Me Jump!* lay in a ragged heap on the table in front of her. Beside her, a neat old man dabbed forlornly at a streaming eye and opposite, an obese young mother, her tyres of flesh pushing against fancy pink knitting, placidly fed a vast baby out of a bag of onion-flavoured crisps. Their smell hung in the air, fried and synthetic.

It was a long wait. Clare read *Watch Me Jump!* which seemed to encourage the kind of exhibitionism Imogen favoured, and then a long, earnest article on the few remaining untouched Saxon meadows of England. The old man disappeared obediently towards Dr Campbell's disembodied voice over the intercom, and then Archie, unseen, asked tiredly for Tracy Durfield. The great pink-knitted girl crushed the crisp bag into the carpet tiles with her foot and, heaving the baby into her arms, shambled towards the door to the surgeries. Clare picked up *Miffy Goes Skating*. Miffy turned out idiotically to be a rabbit.

It was almost an hour before Archie came to the glass doors, and pushed one open and said, 'Clare.'

She stood up. He looked no better than Liza.

'How good of you—'

'Why?'

'It's good of you to come,' Archie said. 'Whatever for. It's good to see you.'

He led the way into his surgery and offered her a chair by a pinboard which bore riotous drawings by Mikey and Imogen among height and weight charts and exhortations to avoid animal fats but cleave unto olive oil. He then sat down in his own chair and leaned his elbows on his knees.

'I suppose you've been with Liza?'

'Yes. But she didn't ask me to come. She doesn't know I'm here.'

'Ah,' Archie said. He looked at her. 'So have you come to say to me what I would expect, in these circumstances, a loyal sister to say?'

'I hope I'm loyal,' Clare said. 'I don't know. But I think I'm right.'

She paused. Archie waited, polite and weary.

'I've got something to tell you,' Clare said.

When Clare had gone, Archie sat at his desk for a long time and drew on his scrap pad a huge stylized sun with rays like sword blades. He gave the sun heavy-lidded eyes and a sleepy, lazy smile. He wrote 'Liza' beside it, several times. Clare had said Liza was too ashamed to speak to him of her non-affair with the young Irishman at Bradley Hall. What do you mean, Archie said, what is there to be ashamed of? And Clare had stumblingly said something about loyalty and Archie had perceived that Liza had humiliated herself, because the affair was never consummated, had come to nothing, had been no more than a brief colliding of two separate fantasies.

'You won't be angry with her, will you?' Clare had said.

'Oh no,' he said. 'No. I wouldn't dream of it.'

He felt no anger. He felt nothing but a dim pity, a mild incredulity that Liza could have been so willing to be deluded. He thought he might have met the man once, on a Sunday morning, when he had come to Beeches House looking for Liza, and he had seemed like a delightful undergraduate, eager and charming, polite; not a threat, not someone of substance.

Archie got up to lock his surgery door. Then he went back to his drawing of the sun and looked at it and felt a stab of pain for Liza, pain about her, pain on her behalf. Then he reached for the telephone and dialled Marina.

'I knew it would be you. I told you not to call—'

'Marina,' Archie said, leaning against the clean grey wall of his surgery. 'I am desperate to see you.'

She said nothing. He could not even hear her breathing.

'Just once. Just once more. I must know, I must fully understand, I must get something of you so deep in me that, even if we never see each other again, I will have that, I will never lose the richness you have given me; the gate will never swing shut again—'

He paused. There was another silence and then she said, 'My dear, you mistake me. You mistake the gate.'

'Never in this world—'

'I may have woken you up,' Marina said more

strongly, 'but I am not the answer. You have to be your own answer.'

'Do I mean nothing to you?' Archie said stupidly.

'Holy shit,' Marina shouted furiously. 'What kind of garbage question is that?'

Archie straightened up.

'Quite right. Sorry. I'm consumed by wanting to see you, be with you.'

'It wouldn't help. There's nothing that will help either of us right now. When you can face that, you'll have taken the first step through your gate.'

'Aren't you afraid?' Archie said. 'Aren't you afraid of the future?'

'I'm appalled at it. But I'm not afraid. Maybe I'd prefer fear to horror. What a choice!' She paused and then she said, 'I'm going to see Liza.'

'Why?'

'Unfinished business. Something I want to give her.'

'Of course,' Archie said, closing his eyes. 'I regret saying why—'

'Why do you Logans have to be such decent men? It's a killer to—'

'To what?'

'I was unwisely going to say self-control.'

Archie began to laugh. His eyes were filling with tears.

'We would rather be ruined than changed,' Marina said.

'What?'

'I'm quoting. W. H. Auden: "We would rather be ruined than changed, / We would rather die in our dread / Than climb the cross of the moment / And let our illusions die".'

Archie said, 'But you aren't my illusion.'

'No, my dear, I am not. I am your cross of the moment.'

'Marina—'

'You pay heed to Mr Auden, Archie,' Marina said.

'There's no glamour to being ruined. Only a man would be romantic enough to think there was.'

'I don't want to change.'

'There you go,' her voice suddenly sharpened. 'And now I'm going, Archie. I'm going back to America.'

He gripped the telephone.

'When, when—'

'In a week.'

He turned his face and pressed his forehead to the wall. Then, without another word, he took the telephone receiver away from his ear and replaced it quietly on the handset. Almost at once, someone began knocking on his surgery door.

'Dr Logan? Dr Logan? Mrs Durfield is on the telephone. Could you—?'

Chapter Seventeen

'Exposed!' proclaimed the banner in Stoke Stratton post office. Beneath it, pasted to a sheet of blossom-pink card was a cutting from the local paper. Richard Prior, claimed the cutting, had swindled his village. Those starter cottages he had declared he would insist upon building, and for which he had gained initial planning permission, had proved a smoke screen. They were being advertised as three-bedroomed cottage homes now, with country kitchens, and integral garages, priced at three times the amount he had promised to pin them to. 'Nobody wanted them,' Farmer Prior contends. But who has he asked? Not a single villager in Stoke Stratton. 'It's a plot,' a long-standing resident, Cyril Vinney, told the *Chronicle*. 'It's a dirty trick.'

Cyril Vinney, Marina thought, standing outside the post office, wrapping her coat hard round herself against the wind. Cyril Vinney, dirty tricks, swindles, this dreadful little shop, all part of English village life, all far more part of it now than Anne Hathaway or Gilbert White. She had stopped there because she was early and her visit was enough of a burden to inflict upon Liza without being early, too. She had gone into the post office, and Mrs Betts, spying her cashmere coat, had instantly evolved a new and repulsive manner, at once familiar and egregious.

'Lady Logan. What a very unseasonal day. How can I help you?'

'I'd like some candy for the children,' Marina said.

Mrs Betts began to put jars on the counter, folksy imitation old-fashioned jars containing humbugs and toffee and aniseed balls.

'I'm afraid the children have no aesthetic taste,' Marina said. 'They like garbage.'

Mrs Betts gave a little laugh. Charm bracelets shaking deprecatingly, she pointed out packets of snakes and spiders made of scented jelly and a jar of brilliant balls marked 'House of Horror Gobstoppers'.

'Perfect,' Marina said.

'Staying long?' Mrs Betts said.

'No,' Marina said. 'Only a flying visit.'

'Another time, then,' Mrs Betts suggested. 'The village is charming in spring. The daffodils, you know.'

It seemed the moment to seal her own fate.

'This spring,' Marina said, 'I shall be looking at American daffodils.'

Mrs Betts rolled her eyes with mock rapture at the heady, impossible notion of foreign travel.

'A spring holiday—'

'No,' Marina said. 'Home.'

Carefully sealing up the paper bags of sweets, Mrs Betts pushed her luck.

'Oh, Lady Logan, how I understand. When Mr Betts was taken, I felt I could not endure Southampton a moment longer—'

Marina snapped two pound coins down on the counter.

'Is that sufficient?'

Mrs Betts was, momentarily, thrown. She gave Marina her change in silence and then hurried to open the street door. It was only when she was outside that Marina observed the banner. 'Exposed!' Horrible word, cruel, suggestive of defenceless things abandoned, precious things laid bare, secrets branded with slurs of squalor and shame. She was still holding the paper bags. What disgusting things she had bought! Their sweet, clamorous, offensive smell rose even in the cold air. There was a little bin close by. Above it, another of Mrs Betts's hand-lettered signs read 'In here

please. And help us to win the Michelmersh Cup!'
Marina dropped the paper bags into the bin and
moved away to her car. With luck, Mrs Betts would
find them later.

Liza waited in the hall.

'Will you stay and see her?' she said to Archie. 'Do
you want to?'

'No,' he said. 'I won't.'

'Perhaps you should—'

'For whose sake? Yours?'

'No.'

'Then not,' Archie said.

He was kind to her, kind and polite. He had told her,
the night before, with the same gentle courtesy, that
Clare had been to see him and had relayed to him the
story of Blaise O'Hanlon's infatuation with Liza. She
had waited in longing and dread for a reaction. There
was none. It didn't matter, he had said, don't worry,
poor Liza, stupid overexcited boy. He had sounded as
if the whole affair, which had cost her so dear, had
really very little importance, and scarcely any significance for him. It had been the most gigantic anti-
climax, and had left her seething with frustration.

'I can't touch you,' she had cried out to him, 'can I? I
can't, I can't—'

'Wait,' he said. 'Wait.'

'How long? How long have I got to wait? I've been
waiting months, years.'

He said, 'There's so much to confront, you see.'

And then he wouldn't speak again. Asking him if he
meant to see Marina when she came was a way of
forcing him to speak, goading him, trying to get
through. And yet again, he was elusive. I'd stay for
your sake if you want it, he said. How could that help?
How could it possibly help to be in the same room as
Marina and Archie and imagine . . .

She had sent Thomas down to the gate. Imogen was

not yet back from nursery school. It was a relief to ask Thomas to do something that he would actually do just now, because ever since he had come back from Pinemount he had been naughty, rude and disobedient, not at all the biddable, sensitive Thomas she was used to.

'You can't make me,' he'd said to Archie when requested to stop drumming on the table at breakfast with a couple of spoons, 'can you?'

'I'm not sufficiently interested to try,' Archie said.

Thomas drummed louder. Archie got up and went out into the garden and Liza saw him standing by the hedge looking at the poor field, the poor about-to-be desecrated field. Thomas drummed on, his eyes on Liza. After a few moments, she went out, too, and upstairs, and sat on the edge of their unmade bed and stared at the mark on the blue-and-white wallpaper where Mikey had once thrown a toy tractor. In the kitchen, Thomas put the spoons down, and snivelled.

Now, he swung on the gate. Liza could see him, swinging, as was strictly forbidden, on the end away from the hinge. At least his presence would ease seeing Marina. She had almost died, hearing Marina on the telephone calmly saying that she wanted to come down, that she wanted to see her, Liza. 'Yes,' she had said blankly. 'Yes. Thursday. No, I don't teach that day. Yes.' And it was arranged, settled, and here she was, jagged with nerves in the hall, waiting, as she and Archie had once waited for Andrew and Marina to come.

Marina drove Sir Andrew's Rover. She stopped it in the gateway and Thomas flung himself off the gate and into the passenger seat. They paused there a moment, and Liza, peering through the narrow windows beside the front door, could see that they were talking, talking with animation. Then Marina brought the car up the drive and stopped it and climbed out. She wore a camel-hair coat and her hair was loose. She waited for

271

Thomas and then she came up to the house, and he opened the door for her and she walked in and said, 'My dear Liza.'

Liza stared.

'It is so generous of you to let me come.'

'You made me,' Liza said.

Marina took off her coat and draped it over the newel post of the banisters.

'I had to.'

'Thomas,' Liza said. 'Will you go and fetch the bottle of wine from the fridge, and two glasses and a corkscrew?'

She went ahead of Marina into the sitting room.

'I don't know why you've come,' Liza said. 'You can't do anything for my peace of mind and I'm not much interested in yours.'

She sat down on the sofa. Marina went across to the window and looked out, and then she came back and sat beside Liza.

'But I hope I *can* do something for you.'

Thomas came in, carrying the bottle and glasses on a tray. Suddenly he was not an asset but a hindrance.

Marina said, before Liza could invent a ploy, 'Thomas, you may go and play in Grandpa's car as long as you absolutely promise not to touch the brake.'

'He isn't allowed—' Liza began, nettled at a more inventive authority than her own.

'Today he is. For fifteen minutes.'

Thomas, glowing, ready to lie on the drive for fifteen minutes if she asked him to, went dancing out, slamming the front door behind him.

'Look,' Marina said. Her voice was not at all steady. 'I'm not going to apologize. What I did – we did – is too complex for that. Apology isn't adequate, doesn't cover enough. And I'm not going to make excuses. It's all too deep, too complicated, too enormous.'

Liza wound the spiral of the corkscrew down into the cork of the wine bottle and pulled.

'I'm not interested,' she said again.

She poured the wine. It was white and cold, unsuitable for the day, appropriate to her feelings.

'No.'

'How could you do such a thing to me?'

'I don't know,' Marina said. 'I do not know.'

'And I suppose you think you'll feel better by saying you wish you never had?'

Marina stared at her.

'Liza, we shouldn't get started on all that.'

'You mean, please can we evade confronting what you've done?'

'Liza—'

'I'm so angry,' Liza said. 'I'm boiling with anger. It's such a relief to be angry.'

She held out a glass of wine. Marina took it by the stem.

'Have you tried being angry with Archie?'

'That is no business of yours.'

'Quite right,' Marina said more briskly, sitting up, tasting her wine. 'It is not. Archie is no business of mine in any way. I never thought to take anything that wasn't mine, never thought even to want it. Pain and grief can scramble your rational mind—'

'Oh, I know,' Liza said. 'I know. Don't expect sympathy from me. I'm a woman, remember? So are you. We had a bond. Did you think of that, as you climbed into bed with Archie, did you think of me?'

Marina took a swallow of wine. Liza's anger, so righteous, so justified, gave her such strength, but even in that strength she could not be expected to see where wings might briefly take you, forbidden great healing wings.

'No,' Marina said.

'I think you had better go back to London. I don't want you here, in my house, on my sofa.'

'I'm going back to America. I'm going at the weekend.' She stood up and put her unfinished wine glass on the mantelpiece among Liza's jugs. 'I'm leaving everything, the flat, my share of Andrew's money, everything. I've seen my solicitor. It's all in order. It's all yours. I've left it to you.'

'Suppose I don't want it?'

'You may give it to the children.'

She looked down at Liza.

'I've left Archie something, too.'

Liza looked away.

'I saw Maurice Crawford. They want to make the new series of *Meeting Medicine*, quite soon, this summer. They want Archie to take Andrew's place.'

Liza said woodenly, 'I'll tell him.'

The door opened. Thomas said, delighted, 'I turned on everything.'

'And then off again?'

'And on and off and on and then off—'

'Then please go and open the gate for me, like a kind boy.'

Liza burst into tears.

'I don't want you to go. I don't want you to go like this. Why did this awful mess have to happen?'

'Don't ask,' Marina said, putting her arms round Liza. 'Don't ask. I guess we'll never know.'

'But what about me and Archie? What will happen to us? What have you done to us?'

Marina dropped her arms.

'He loves you,' Marina said. 'He never stopped. What happened was no part of that.'

'Go away!' Liza cried. 'Go away!'

Marina went slowly out into the hall and took her coat off the banisters. She stood, holding it like a limp body.

'What you and Archie have,' she said to Liza across the space between them, 'won't be the same, certainly. But it won't be worse, either. It may well be better. Liza?'

'Yes—'

'Take the money. Take the flat. It's the best possible thing I can do for you. It has more value than financial, more value to you. It will help you, it will give you strength, a position of strength. My dear Liza, it will give you just the right, the healthy amount of independence. It will make you more of a partner with Archie, believe me.'

Then she put on her coat and walked slowly across the hall and out of the house.

Archie's journey home was impeded by an earthmover. Huge and ponderous and improbably painted the colour of egg yolk, it moved up the Stoke Stratton road with an air of majesty, its great hopper peering before it like a proboscis. Behind it, traffic could only crawl until it swung, almost with an air of triumph, into the field where it would soon begin to tear at the turf and expose the poor, raw entrails of the earth. As Archie turned into his own drive, he could see Thomas by the hedge, staring at the digger. Archie sounded his horn and Thomas came running.

'Did you see?'

'The digger? Yes, I did.'

'I don't want it,' Thomas said. 'I don't want it in our field. If there keep on being little new houses, it won't be country.'

'I know. I thought they would be a different kind of house.'

He got out of the car. Thomas looked pale and tired.

'Marina came.'

'Did she?'

'Mummy cried.'

Archie looked down at him.

'Stop her!' Thomas shouted. 'Stop all this horrible stuff!'

'Yes,' Archie said. He put his hand out to Thomas. 'Will you come in with me?'

Thomas said, on the edge of tears, 'Marina's going back to America—'

'Yes,' Archie said. 'She wants to. It's where she lived before Grandpa.'

'But I can't see her in America!'

'Why not? When you're older, you can fly to see her.'

'I don't expect you'll let me,' Thomas said, cheated of defiance.

'I expect we will. If Mummy agrees. Come on. Come in and find her with me.'

She was in the sitting room, sitting. Just sitting and staring. Archie went in and sat down next to her and Thomas stood in the doorway and glared at them.

'Liza,' Archie said.

He took her hand.

'I suppose you're waiting to hear what she looked like and what she said.'

'She said I could play with her car,' Thomas said loudly. Archie turned to him.

'Thomas, would you go and find Sally and the others? Just for a little while?'

'Why?' Thomas said. 'Why? Why does it always have to be bloody secrets?'

'It won't be. It will all stop. But I have to talk to Mummy.'

Thomas gave the sitting-room door a shattering slam and pounded down the hall. Then there was the second slam. Then there was a singing silence.

'Liza,' Archie said. 'I am so sorry.'

She turned to him. Her face was sore with tears.

'Don't start. Don't start that—'

'I want to stay married to you. I want us to go on.'

'But,' Liza whispered, 'you want her—'

'You're my wife,' Archie said. He took her hand.

Liza said, 'She's giving me the flat. And the money Andrew left her.'

'Then I suppose you can leave me if you want to.'

'I don't want to. But—'

'But?'

She looked down.

'I don't want you to stay because it's the decent thing. Or because of the children. I only want us to go on if we want to, us, you and me.'

'I do want that.'

'But you said you were afraid of losing a dimension you had found.'

'I am afraid.'

Liza stood up and put her hand on the mantelpiece where Marina's glass still stood. She touched it.

'I am afraid to live a little life,' Archie said, 'when I might live a much greater one.'

'That's how I feel,' Liza said. 'That's it exactly. That's how I feel all the time, trapped in littleness.' She turned away from him and hid her face.

'I was in an awful place,' Archie said, behind her. 'In my mind, and my feelings. It was all tangled up with my father and with you. I can't explain it, but Marina appeared to be the answer. She unlocked all the cages, turned the lights on, let me out. How valid that was, I don't know. I don't expect I'll ever know, but it was how it seemed. She was absolutely central to everything that was obsessing me. I thought she was the answer. I believed she understood. I still think that, that she understands, but the rest I can't be sure of.'

Liza did not take her hand off Marina's glass.

'I can't go back,' Archie said. 'That I am sure of. I don't think you can, either. We have to go on.'

Liza said, almost dreamily, 'Harness your dimensions to something else?'

'Oh, Liza.'

She half-turned.

'Marina has spoken to Maurice Crawford. They want you to take Andrew's place for the new series of *Meeting Medicine*. Could that fit your new dimension?'

'Never in this world,' Archie said.

He stood up, too, and came close to her.

277

'I'd hate it. I'd hate to try and do what he did.'

'Burned your fingers—'

'Don't.'

'Well, then,' she said. 'What are you going to do?'

He hesitated.

'I don't know. Literally. Today Stuart Campbell asked me to look for another practice. Take your time, he said. Nothing personal, old fellow. We need to alter the balance here a bit, expand, maybe look for people with hospital attachments, sure you understand, old boy, best for you probably in the long run if you're honest, quiet country practice, maybe, try Norfolk or the Dales, marvellous country for the children—'

She put her arms round him.

'You wouldn't think,' Archie said thickly, holding her, 'you wouldn't think I could mess that up, too, would you? You wouldn't think, looking at me, that I was such a superlative cocker-up of everything, would you? Give it to Archie Logan, if it's worth anything, give it to Archie and watch him make a complete balls of it, fuck it right up, people, jobs, relationships, you name it, he'll wreck it for you in a flash. No-one to touch him for it.'

'Oh,' Liza said with some spirit. 'Oh really. How you do exaggerate.'

'I always have—'

'I know,' she said. 'I know. It drives me mad.'

'You're smiling—'

'I'm not. I'm grimacing.'

The door opened abruptly.

'Yuk,' said Mikey at the top of his voice. 'Kissing.'

Chapter Eighteen

'I assure you,' Mrs Betts said, laying a hand upon her bosom, 'I assure you it's true. I heard it from Mrs Logan herself.'

Diana Jago declined to react. The post office was quite full, and its atmosphere had become highly attentive.

'As true as I am standing here,' Mrs Betts said, lifting her chins so that her voice might carry, 'Dr and Mrs Logan are being driven out by Mr Prior. His activities have made it impossible for them to continue at Beeches House. They are forced to sell it to the developer. I hope,' Mrs Betts said penetratingly, her eyes upon Trevor Vinney's girlfriend listlessly choosing sweets, 'I hope those who didn't have the courage or the decency to put in for those houses, having whined for them, now realize the consequences.'

The girlfriend took no notice. She hadn't hoped for a house; she had given up hoping for anything much when early, unwanted motherhood had made it very plain to her that hope of any kind was not for her.

'I think that's quite uncalled for,' Chrissie Jenkins said clearly. She held a card in a cellophane envelope with 'In Deepest Sympathy' printed in silver across a wreath of flowers. 'Dr and Mrs Logan are going on account of the children, for little Thomas. He has to have—' She paused. 'He has to have a special school.'

'Mrs Logan made no mention of that to me—'

'I expect she doesn't want it known.'

'So tell the whole post office—'

'They're going,' Sharon Vinney said, taking her not-daughter-in-law's sad little handful of cash, 'because

279

they've come into money. That's why. They can do better than Stoke Stratton now. Don't give them nuts to the baby.'

Diana Jago changed her mind about a reel of adhesive tape and a bottle of disinfectant and put them back on the shelves. She went out, past them all, and shut the shop door with emphasis.

'Poor Mrs Jago,' Mrs Betts said. 'I'm sorry for her, really I am. Always supposed herself such a friend of Mrs Logan's and has Mrs Logan confided her plans to her? Not a bit. You can understand her being upset, can't you?'

Diana drove her car at tremendous speed to Beeches House. It was the first day of the spring holidays and on the front lawn an assembly of stepladders and upturned chairs and blankets proclaimed that Thomas and Mikey were making a camp, the acceptable male version of playing houses. Sally Carter was on the grass behind the house hanging up washing while Imogen sat beside her in a plastic laundry basket and clipped pegs in a toothlike fringe down the front of her duffel coat.

'Is Mrs Logan in?'

'No,' Sally said, going on pegging. 'She's gone to Winchester.'

'To get a lorry,' Imogen said.

'A lorry?'

'For Thcotland.'

Diana crouched down beside the laundry basket.

'Why do you need a lorry for Scotland?'

'To put my bed in,' Imogen said. 'And the wheel-barrow and the thofa.'

Diana straightened up.

'Sally. What is going on?'

'They are going back to Scotland—'

'Back?'

'Dr Logan was born in Scotland.'

'Where the hell are they going?'

'Glasgow,' Sally said. She picked up a blue shirt of Archie's. 'I'm going, too. I'm going to look after the children and do a secretarial course.'

'The hell you are,' Diana said. 'The village is buzzing with rumours and here you all are calmly planning to go to Scotland—'

Imogen began to scramble out of the basket.

'Mummy'th come—'

Liza got out of the car. She saw Diana and waved, and then stooped back inside for an armful of brochures and a green folder.

'Look,' Diana said, running down to her. 'Look. I may not be exactly family, but I am a mate. Right? What is going on?'

'I was going to tell you,' Liza said. 'Really. When everything was settled—'

'What everything?'

'This house, where we'd go, Archie—'

'Archie?'

Liza looked at her with great directness.

'He's resigned.'

Diana stared.

'Resigned? From the practice? Whatever for?'

'We need a new start,' Liza said firmly.

Diana leaned forward.

'Look. Are you OK? You and him?'

Liza began to walk towards the house.

'Oh yes.'

'Liza—'

'Diana,' Liza said. 'I don't want talk. I don't want speculation. I don't want to be discussed as if we were a problem family.'

'You don't want to face facts,' Diana said.

Liza stopped walking.

'Oh, but I have.'

Her face was suddenly suffused with something Diana could not fathom.

'And now I'm going on. We're going on.'

'But are you all right?'

Liza nodded.

'We are going to live in Scotland. We're selling everything.'

'But Glasgow—'

Liza looked down.

'Yes.'

Diana whispered, 'What happened?'

'Everything.'

'Oh, Liza. Poor Liza. Poor Archie. What will Archie do?'

'I don't know. We don't know.'

'He'll still be a doctor, of course—'

'I don't know.' She looked straight at Diana. 'It doesn't matter. It doesn't seem to matter.'

'Because of money?'

'Only partly. Something else – something more – about living for living. I've got to learn—' She paused and then she said, 'It was me who said Scotland.'

'Good for you.'

'And I went to see the developer about selling this. I've given my notice in, at Bradley Hall.'

Diana leaned forward and kissed her cheek.

'Go for it,' Diana said. 'Just go for it. And this time, get it.'

Archie stood on the pale polished stone floor, a step above William Rufus. He had his back to the altar and before him the great vault of the nave rushed away towards the west window. At his feet, William Rufus lay modestly under his greenish pitch of lead, gleaming from the touch of millions of interested, speculating hands. Archie stood with his own hands behind his back and looked at the spires of wood and the arches of stone and remembered that other day when he had come in to William Rufus, bringing with him the shackles of his longing and his confusion.

282

They were still with him, but they no longer manacled him. He could still feel with real pain, feel all those past sensations; he could roll before his spiritual and sensual memories the death of his father, Marina's lovemaking, and the dying of Granny Mossop which now seemed to him no less than some kind of gift. He looked down at William Rufus. Nine hundred years dead and still remembered, if more for the manner of his dying than his living, as proof, if proof were needed, that the human heart possesses a muscle as elastic as it is enduring, as unpredictable in its behaviour as it is reliable in its need for reassurance.

'Pompous ass,' Archie said to himself.

He stepped down between the choir stalls and laid his hand briefly, with affection, on the tomb. Then he went quickly down the centre aisle and through the west door out into the sunlight of the Close. As he went up the steps, a stocky cleric came down them, an affable-looking man reading a letter. He glanced up and caught Archie's eyes. He looked vaguely familiar. Archie stopped walking.

'Hello!' the clergyman said heartily.

He held out his hand. Archie took it.

'Good to see you!'

'And you.'

'Haven't seen you for so long. How is everything?'

'Fine now,' Archie said. 'I think.'

'Good! Good!' He peered at Archie. 'And how's that boy of yours?'

'I think he'll be fine now, too—'

'Splendid bowler. Always thought that.'

'Sorry?' Archie said.

'Your boy. Splendid bowler.'

'He's only had one term of cricket—'

'One term?'

'He's nine,' Archie said. 'I think you've got the wrong chap—'

'Have I? Surely not. You're the musician, aren't you, the cellist, boy at the College, College boy—'

'I'm a doctor,' Archie said. 'I was a GP out in the Strattons.'

The clergyman slapped his forehead.

'Good Lord. Are you? Heavens! Frightfully sorry—'

They both began to laugh, backing away from one another.

'Yes. Never had a boy here, though of course one always hopes—'

'Of course, my word, yes, how stupid of me, how stupid—'

'Not at all, doesn't matter, really—'

Archie reached the top of the steps.

'Quite funny, really—'

'Absolutely!' the clergyman called. 'Absolutely! I just mixed you up with everybody else. Absurd!'

He vanished into the cathedral. Archie began to laugh. Mixed up. Mixed up with everybody else! The irony was perfect, perfect in every aspect.

He flung his arms up in appreciation towards the heavens and then, regarded with some apprehension by an elderly woman in a mushroom felt beret with a shopping basket on wheels, began to run, still laughing, over the shabby grass, back towards his car.

THE END

Other People's Children
Joanna Trollope

For eight-year-old Rufus, life has become complicated. His mother
and father, Josie and Tom, have divorced amicably enough, and are
set to pursue their separate paths. But other people have had to
become involved – like Matthew, who has just married Josie, and
Elizabeth, Tom's new friend. And even worse, there are the other
children – Matthew's three big resentful teenagers, who have been
conditioned by their own mother Nadine to hate Josie. Rufus is
supposed to regard them as his family now, although he doesn't see
why he should.

Most of the time Matthew's children live with Nadine, in a slum-like
cottage in the depths of the country. Nadine is determined that they
should hate their new life as much as she does. They come to their
father for weekends, and make it clear how much they loathe their
new stepmother. Rufus secretly prefers to be with his father in his
quiet house in Bath, and realises that he does not necessarily hate the
idea of a stepmother – not if she was like Elizabeth, sane and friendly
and welcoming. But where other people's children are concerned,
neat solutions seldom occur.

0 552 99788 9

BLACK SWAN

Next of Kin
Joanna Trollope

'HER FINE, GRIPPING AND UNFLINCHING NOVEL'
The Times

Two generations of Merediths farm the land running down to the
River Dean. Robin Meredith bought his dairy farm just before he
married Caro, his enigmatic Californian wife, while his father Harry
is an arable farmer on the adjoining farm, working the land, with the
help of his other son Joe, just as his father and grandfather had
before him. But now Caro has died, as much of a mystery to the
Meredith family as she was when she arrived twenty years ago,
leaving Robin and the rest of the family to cope with the loss.

With Caro gone, her adopted daughter Judy feels cut adrift, while for
Joe the despair at her death is far deeper than the family suspects.
And into the midst of this unhappy family comes Zoe, Judy's
London friend, an outsider with her strange townie appearance,
independent spirit and disturbing directness. Everyone
underestimates Zoe's power as a catalyst for change as the realities
behind the seeming idyll of a rural community become ever clearer.

'A RICHLY SATISFYING NOVEL, SOMETIMES DARK, BUT
COMPULSIVELY READABLE, AND IMAGINED WITH A WARMTH
THAT MAKES ITS DETERMINED REALISM ODDLY UPLIFTING'
Sunday Express

'A DEVASTATINGLY ACUTE PICTURE OF A HARSH RURAL
WORLD'
Sunday Times

'EXTRAORDINARILY POWERFUL'
Mail on Sunday

'CERTAINLY ONE OF HER BEST'
Daily Telegraph

0 552 99700 5

BLACK SWAN

The Men and the Girls
Joanna Trollope

'A DELIGHT. TROLLOPE IS NEVER LESS THAN GRACEFUL AND
SEARCHINGLY OBSERVANT'
Independent

'A RARE PLEASURE TO FIND CHARACTERS SO LIKEABLE THAT ONE
CARES WHAT BECOMES OF THEM'
Polly Feversham, *Evening Standard*

0 552 99492 8

A Spanish Lover
Joanna Trollope

'A HUGELY ENJOYABLE BOOK . . . FULL OF PERCEPTIVE
OBSERVATION AND IMBUED WITH A REFRESHING IRONY'
Miranda Seymour, *Sunday Times*

'WISE AND WARM, PROFOUNDLY SATISFYING AS WELL AS
ACUTELY QUERYING . . . A PERCEPTIVE CHRONICLER OF OUR
TIMES'
Clare Colvin, *Sunday Express*

0 552 99549 5

The Best of Friends
Joanna Trollope

'TRULY, I COULDN'T PUT IT DOWN. I'M TELLING YOU, TROLLOPE IS
A SIGNIFICANT CHRONICLER'
Val Hennessy, *Daily Mail*

'TROLLOPE HAS A KEEN EAR FOR THE YELPS OF DISTRESS, AS
LIVES ARE SLICED IN HALF BY SHABBY BETRAYAL . . . A BOOK
THAT IS AS ENJOYABLE AS IT IS THOUGHTFUL'
Penny Perrick, *The Times*

0 552 99643 2

BLACK SWAN

A SELECTED LIST OF FINE WRITING AVAILABLE FROM BLACK SWAN

THE PRICES SHOWN BELOW WERE CORRECT AT THE TIME OF GOING TO PRESS. HOWEVER TRANSWORLD PUBLISHERS RESERVE THE RIGHT TO SHOW NEW RETAIL PRICES ON COVERS WHICH MAY DIFFER FROM THOSE PREVIOUSLY ADVERTISED IN THE TEXT OR ELSEWHERE.

All Transworld titles are available by post from:

Bookpost, P.O. Box 29, Douglas, Isle of Man IM99 1BQ

Credit cards accepted. Please telephone 01624 836000, fax 01624 837033, Internet http://www.bookpost.co.uk or e-mail: bookshop@enterprise.net for details.

Free postage and packing in the UK. Overseas customers allow £1 per book (paperbacks) and £3 per book (hardbacks).